Aint No Love
in the Bean

Aint No Love
in the *Bean*

Part 1

Jaron and Shongi

authorHOUSE®

AuthorHouse™
1663 Liberty Drive
Bloomington, IN 47403
www.authorhouse.com
Phone: 1-800-839-8640

Published by AuthorHouse 01/06/2015

ISBN: 978-1-4969-5683-5 (sc)
ISBN: 978-1-4969-5682-8 (e)

Dedication

The first thing I'd like to do is praise God. Without God in my life watching over me, none of this would be possible, 'cause I know I wouldn't be alive today. The next two people that I'd like to show my gratitude towards --- are of course my mom and dad. I'm thankful for them and love my parents daily. Always love your parents no matter what. Sometimes they get on my nerves, but I still love them 'cause they could've easily aborted me, but they didn't and I'm so thankful. I know sometimes I may put my parents thru a lot of heartache and pain, but they still put up with all my bullshit. Especially my pops, always running up to the courts and jails to make sure I was good. Every time I got into trouble, my pops was right by my side! In fact, my pops is the realest dude I met! My pops never turned on me, (like some friends and family) he always was by my side, whether I was doing good or not. Stuck by my side during all my bids in jail....when nobody else was there, you were always by my side pops, love you! Also much love to my sister and brothers. All my nieces and nephews. Much love to all my family, from the O'Bannon's, Graves, and Montgomery's. I love all y'all even if I don't talk to y'all all the time.

Now I would like to say "Rest in Peace" to all my loved ones. I think about you all. "Teasia Montgomery", I miss you with all my heart. I know we might've had our fights, but I know deep down inside we had love for each other. You will always be a major part of my life. I will do my best to raise our son to be the best young man he can be and then raise him to a "King". I will never give up on our family. I still can't believe your gone, them cowards really had to take you away from me and the family. You didn't have to die like that in cold blood. The streets are messed up out here in the Bean. Ever since the night you died, Teasia, I stopped trusting and hanging with everybody. My friends are at an all time low. It's me and lil Jaron against the world. F.O.E. (Family Over Everything) for real Teasia. Even though you gone....I know you looking and can see what's going on. Just know I'ma make sure your name lives on. You will never be forgotten....I love you, Teasia Montgomery, may your soul rest in peace.

Shongi, damn bro, I still can't believe how you went out. Them dudes killed you on some coward shit. I would've never thought you would be gone. I never thought you or my Bm would go. Damn this shit is bothering me. But what makes me even more angry bro, is when these dudes try to smile in your face and act like shit is all good. You were right, bro, when you said, "Left, you can't trust these niggas as far as you can throw them..." Man you were so right. It seems like nobody has morals now bro. Just know one thing, Ima hold it down for lil "Armani" and make sure he good. Ima treat him like he my son. I know why God put us together and made us real friends; and for that I am thankful. And also thanks for being there for me during my entire bid; you made sure I went without. You and my friend "Twin", were the only friends that were ever there for me in my time of need. Everyone else shitted on me. The rest were family that looked out for me. So again thank you for everything bro. You will be truly missed by me. I love you little bro, Shongi, may your soul rest in peace.

Prologue

Jerome was sitting down in the blue chair inside his cell looking through the fiberglass window watching every car going by Nashua street jail. Every night he would sit there and stare out his cell window for hours at an time and reminisce. He was in his own world watching the females outside in front the jail skywriting to different inmates that were incarcerated; some of them were out there showing their breast and ass like it was legal to do in public. He could hear just about everyone on the unit banging on the windows going berserk from watching the different females giving them a little show outside the jail. Almost every Friday and Saturday, there would be a bevy of females outside the jail acting a fool. Most of them were so drunk and high they didn't care about the Sheriff's coming outside or pulling up and telling them to motivate. As long as it was warm outside every weekend, then that was all that mattered. They would be there faithfully putting on a show.

It's been two-years and three months since he was out there on the streets living the fast life. Now he was confined to a nine by twelve jail cell with a toilet and sink. He was being held without bail for a homicide. He got up out his seat and walked over to the dull steel mirror and stood there looking at himself, he could barely see his reflection in the scratched up mirror. Jerome looked at himself and shook his head in disbelief, he couldn't believe he was incarcerated on a murder charge. He knew it was a chance he might not ever be coming home again and that though alone made him sick to the stomach. It was nothing he could do but sit and wait it out like a trooper until it was time for him to go to trial. He knew the commonwealth didn't have a strong case against him without a witness, and that thought alone made him grin a little bit. His lawyer told him that they didn't have any witnesses and more than likely he would get acquitted at trial for murder. Now he just hoped that his name doesn't get implicated in what transpired with the key witness. The last thing he needed was another case miraculously popping up out of nowhere.

He walked over to his cell door and glanced over at the clock that wsa hanging on the wall by the C.O.'s bubble; it was 1:45 in the morning. He missed nights like these warm August nights out there on the streets shinning doing his thing. He missed pushing his Benz coupe through the city and having every female lusting after him like he was a big time celebrity. He missed walking up in the club with his comrades and shutting down the bar; him and his entourage buying bottle after bottle of the finest champagnes until the club closed. He missed bringing different females to the hotels and having one night stands. He missed going in the mall and spending thousands in the mall every other week on new attire. All those days that he lived it up to the fullest extent, were now fond vivid memories in the back of his mind that he constantly reminisced about.

He stood there looking at himself in the mirror with his shirt off and boxers on. He looked down at the tattoos of a man and woman tattooed on his right and left shoulders and started crying. Underneath the women's portrait said: R.i.p Mommy; and underneath the man's portrait said: R.i.p Daddy. *"I miss you mommy and daddy,"* he said to himself. He said a silent prayer for both his deceased parents and got in bed afterwards to try and sleep the pain away.

Chapter 1

"1992"

"Daddy! Daddy! Can I open one of my presents?" Jerome asked with a Kool-Aid smile on his face. "No Jerome, Christmas is tomorrow, you can open them in the morning," Troy stated. "Please daddy . . . ? Just one present that's all," Jerome whined, jumping up and down. Troy looked at his son and smiled when he saw how persistent he was being. "Ok—Just one present Jerome, grab one from under the tree and open it right here in front of me and mommy." "Thank you daddy!" Jerome reached under the tree and retrieved the biggest present with his name on it. He ripped open his present and smiled when he saw his Super Nintendo. Troy sat there on the Italian leather sofa watching his son get excited. "Mommy! Look what daddy bought me!" Jerome picked up the video game and showed his mother. "Baby I see it . . . . Daddy's gonna hook it up for you in your room so you could play your game," Karen said, with a smile.

Troy looked at her and shook his head no. "Karen, I'm not hookin' that game up for him 'til tomorrow morning, he's lucky I let him open it." Karen rolled her eyes at him and sucked her teeth. "Troy, go on and hook the game up for him so he could be quiet," she whispered, 'cause I wanna be nasty tonight baby." Troy looked at her and started smirking, "Aight . . . . C'mon Jerome so I can hook the game up for you."

Troy picked up the Super Nintendo off the floor and walked down the corridor to his son's room. Troy hooked up the video game system on the '19 inch Toshiba television. He put in Super Mario Bros and turned the game on for his son. "Thank you daddy . . . ." "You're welcome son." Jerome was mesmerized by the video game; his eyes never left the TV. Troy walked back into the living room and sat down on the loveseat.

"Baby you should see how happy that boy is—he love playing those video games . . . ." "Tell me about it, Troy that boy got more toys than Toys-R-Us; look at all those presents underneath the tree, he's not even gonna play with them all either," Karen exclaimed, shaking her head in disbelief. There were abundance of presents underneath the tree for Jerome. Troy spoiled his eight-year-old son rotten; anything he asked for he got. "It's all good baby 'cause every year it's gonna be like that, I'mma get my son whatever he wants. You wanna open one of your gifts early, too? I know you wanna baby don't front." Karen looked at him and started blushing. "Uh-huh, I can open anyone I grab under the tree, right?" "Yep, you can open anyone you want sweetie."

Karen got off the sofa, bent over in front of the tree, and grabbed a present from underneath the tree with her name on it. Karen tore the wrapping open hastily; she opened the black velvet box and smiled once she saw her five karat diamond bracelet glistening. "Baby it's beautiful! Thank you so much Troy . . . . I love you." "I love you too, lil mama." Karen walked over to him and kissed him slow and passionately. "Lemme help you with that baby," Troy said, helping her snap the bracelet. The clarity of the bracelet was exquisite.

It was nothing for Troy to drop a few thousand on his baby's mother; he was getting money in the streets of Boston. Troy was well liked respected in the city. He had been through a lot in his twenty-nine years he's been living; he escaped death numerous times beefing with different crews over drug blocks, and he beat a murder charge that could've had him doing life. Back in '83 Troy went to war with the New York boys over his block Zeigler street. Troy shot a few of them New York boys when they were beefing back in the days—and they shot him too, almost killing him. When he was coming up in the streets hustling in Roxbury he took it serious; you couldn't hustle on his block Zeigler street unless he said so. Troy and his comrades wouldn't let anyone get money on their block if they didn't know you, anyone that tried hustling on their block without their consent got dealt with; sometimes getting shot would be the repercussion.

But as Troy got older, he got wiser after catching cases on his block. After he beat a murder charge in '88 he had to fall back from hustling on the corner. Troy killed a stick-up kid who robbed him for his jewelry back in '85. After sitting for three and half years in Charles Street County Jail, Troy beat his case out of Suffolk Superior Courthouse.

Once he came home it was back to the basics; his Columbian connect blessed him with a package and he been strait since. All he did was plot and scheme on how he was going to orchestrate a crew together so he could prevail in the drug game while he was incarcerated. He vowed to never hustle on the block no more because it was too risky. He couldn't afford any more mistakes so he had to walk light and move right in the streets. Troy started getting money off his pager. He had Roxbury on lock. He had the streets sowed with cocaine in it. He had dudes hustling for him out Ruggles Street Projects, Mission Hill Projects, Lenox Street Projects, and on a few corners. While his workers were breaking packages down and serving fiends, Troy was selling weight to all his customers. His baby's mother and son didn't want for nothing.

"Baby it's gettin' late, it's nine-thirty go on and put Jerome in the bed so we can be nasty . . . ." Karen started caressing his dick slowly making him get an erection. Troy looked at her and smirked, "I'm bout to go put him in the bed now." "Hurry up 'cause my pussy is soooo wet right now and I need you . . . ." Troy got off the sofa and went to his son's room. Jerome was in a trance playing his video game, he didn't even notice his father walk in the room. "Bedtime lil man, turn the game off and get in the bed." "But dad—" "But nothin' boy, it's time to go to bed. Now go on and get in the bed before I tell Santa Claus not to bring you anything." Jerome turned off the video game and hopped in his bed. Troy tucked him under the blanket and kissed him on his forehead. "I love you, son." "I love you too, daddy." Troy walked out his son's room and went back into the living room.

Crook was sitting in his red late model Cadillac Deville smoking on some wet; embalm mixed with marijuana. He had his seat reclined listening to "Scarface" waiting for his comrade to come outside. "I needed money, so I robbed a liquor store, down on her knees big titties I kicked the hore, wanna go for bad I go for broke, pulled out my nine think it's a game she said nope . . . ." The wet had him high as a bird sitting in the car getting smoked out. Everything seemed like it was going in slow motion. All the cars that went passing by on Geneva Ave and pedestrians walking by. Even the music sounded like it was going in slow motion to Crook, the wet had his brains fried. He looked to his right and saw his comrade descending the stairs on the three family house. The tall, lanky man was dressed in all black attire. Crook hit the unlock button on the door and let him inside.

"What's the word Slim, you ready to go catch dis lick?" Slim gave him dap and then he reclined his seat. "I'm down for whatever, let's go get this come up and stop politicking." "My nigga . . . . that's why I fucks witcha lil daddy. You strapped right? 'Cause I only brung one burner wit me," Crook stated. Slim reached in his pocket and revealed a chrome .357 magnum snubnose and put it on his lap. "You just better hope this nigga have dem birds in the crib duke, I be damn if I run up in this nigga spot for nothin'." "Everything is all good dog, this nigga eatin' out here in the streets foreal, he gotta have some work in the crib and some dough," Crook proclaimed. "Here take this wet, I'm high as fuck . . . ." Slim took the blunt out his hand and started inhaling it slowly. Crook looked at his Cartier watch and started grinning. "Slim, it's 'bout that time, lets make it happen dog." Slim didn't even respond he just nodded his head yes.

Crook started the ignition and cracked the windows slightly so the smoke could get out the car, then he grabbed the strawberry air feeshner out the glove compartment and sprayed it throughout the car. After he finished spraying the air freshener he put the car in drive and drove up Geneva Ave heading towards Grove Hall. It was a quarter past ten o'clock on a Thursday night and everyone seemed like they were inside the house. The streets were vacant; only your regular hustlers selling on corners and stick-up kids were outside, even the streetwalkers were inside because it was so cold. Crook turned right on Blue Hill Ave and then he bared left on Warren street barely missing the red light.

It was complete silence in the car you could hardly hear the radio playing. Crook had the music down to a minimum while he was in deep thought. He glanced to his right and saw Slim flicking the last of the blunt out the window. Crook wasn't going to let his conscience stop him from doing what he had put together, even though he was wrong for what he was about to do to his right hand man. Crook didn't give a fuck about no one but himself; he would cross anyone if the price was right. But to make matters worse, he was about to bite the hand that fed him when he was down and out.

When Crook did his two-years mandatory in Deer Island for a drug distribution, his right hand man held him down while he was incarcerated; Crook didn't want for nothing. Every week he got money order from his right hand man; his commissary stayed full. He was getting a fifty-dollar bag from canteen every week. When he came home after doing his bid he got put on with some work. His right hand man made sure he wasn't broke. Crook got an apartment, car, money, and some clothes on the strength of his right hand man. The last nine months since Crook been home he been getting money; he accumulated more money selling drugs in the city than he ever did doing stick-ups. After everything his right hand man did for him, he was now about to lay him down for everything. Crook been plotting on his right hand man for the last three months. Crook was playing the game with no rules; he was playing for keeps.

Crook drove through the intersection of Mass Ave and Washington street bypassing Store 24 on his right and kept driving strait towards in town. He drove through the South End until he got to West Dedham street and then he turned off the ignition. The street was filled with all Brownstone apartment buildings. "Yo, that's the nigga crib down there on the right," Crook said, and pointed. "That's his blue BMW station wagon parked out front with the rims on it." Slim nodded his head to let him know he understood.

They both put on their black gloves and black skull caps. Crook pulled out his black nine millimeter berretta with the rubber grip and cocked it back putting one in the chamber. Then they exited the vehicle simultaneously and proceeded with caution down the street not trying to get seen by any pedestrians. Not too many people were outside on this cold December night. Just about every citizen was inside the house getting ready for Christmas. Crook started ascending the stairs on the apartment building and Slim followed behind him like a good henchmen. Once they got inside the corridor they ascended another flight of stairs to the second floor. They turned left down the corridor on the second floor and Crook stopped at apartment 11c.

They pulled out their pistols and put them on the side of their legs. Crook averted his eyes left and then right down the hallway making sure nobody saw what was about to transpire. "On the count of three I'm gonna kick dis door down and we gonna run up in there," Crook whispered. Slim looked him in his eyes and nodded his head. Slim didn't talk much whenever he was about to catch a lick. Slim been waiting for years to catch the right lick, and now was his time to come up. But little did he know he was never going to get his share of the profit.

———◆◈◆———

Troy was in the living room making love to his baby's mother on the sofa. He had his face between her legs sucking on her pussy slowly giving her clitoris all the undivided attention. Karen was on her way to ecstasy from the way he put his tongue down on her pussy making her legs tremble and eyes close. Troy was licking her pussy with pride enjoying the taste of her juices that were flowing out of her like a faucet.

"Uhhh . . . . ohhhh my god!!!" Karen climaxed and came all in his mouth and he licked it all up savoring the taste. "Make love to me baby . . . ." Karen cooed. Troy took his face out her pussy and inserted his hard swollen penis into her dripping wet vagina. "Mmmm, it feels so good daddy . . . . just like that, please don't stop . . . ." She moaned. Karen had her French manicured nails in his back while he was pumping in and out slowly hitting her with long deep death strokes.

Soon as Troy started to get his rhythm he hopped out of the pussy when he heard the door get kicked in making a loud boom. He heard footsteps running down the hallway getting closer and closer towards the living room. Troy tried getting up and going to his room where he kept his pistol at but it was no use; his room was at the other end of the corridor and he couldn't get there. When he saw who it was that coming to rob him he couldn't believe his eyes, he thought it was all a dream. Out of all the people in the streets who were sticking shit up, he would've never thought it would be his right hand man to come lay him down.

"Troy, you know what it is so don't make it no murder, where's the work at money?" Crook asked calmly. Slim had his pistol to the side of Karen's head ready to pull the trigger if he had too. Troy looked at both of them with rage in his eyes. "Dog it's like that Crook?! After everything I did for you! This is how you do me?! I knew it all along you was jealous of me, you fuckin' coward!" Crook walked up on him and hit him across the back of his head with the pistol. Troy winced in pain after getting hit across the head. He put his hand on the back of his head to try and stop the bleeding. Karen was laying there on the floor weeping praying they didn't get killed. "Tie both of them up Slim, that way this bitch don't try screaming." Slim passed Crook his pistol while he pulled out the duct tape from inside his jacket. Crook stood there with both guns aimed at Troy and his baby's mother while Slim duct taped their feet, mouth, and hands behind their back.

"Troy, I'm gonna ask you one more time, where the fuck is that work?! Slim, take that tape off his mouth," Crook demanded. Slim removed the duct tape from his mouth so he could speak. "Nigga fuck you . . . . I ain't givin' you shit!" "You ain't givin' me shit huh, we'll see 'bout that fuck nigga," Crook sniped, gritting his teeth. "Here Slim, take ya burner dog," Crook passed him the .357 magnum. "I'll be back in a minute Slim." Crook walked out of the living room and left Slim there watching them. Karen tried screaming when she saw Crook walk back into the living room with her son, but couldn't because her mouth was gagged. Troy broke down crying when he saw Crook holding his son with a pistol to his head.

"Troy, don't make me do ya fuckin' kid just to prove a point," Crook said, hoarsely. Jerome was standing there crying hysterically not knowing whether he was going to live or die. "Daddy . . . . help me please . . . ? I don't wanna die daddy!" Troy was laying there on the floor vexed praying his son didn't get killed over him. Troy knew he had to do something and something fast or him Crook you got that—I got five birds in my room, and I got hunnit and fifty thou in the safe." "You better not be lying either. Slim, watch his son and this bitch while I take this nigga to the safe." Crook untied his hands and legs so he could get up and walk. Crook grabbed him by the throat and shoved him down the hallway towards the bedroom.

Troy opened the safe up inside his closet and started taking all the money out. "Put that shit in bag," Crook demanded. Troy retrieved his son's book bag off the floor, dumped all the contents out, and started filling the bag up with stacks of money. "You been doing some serious stackin' I see," Crook said, with a grin. "Pass me that bag nice and slow, don't try nothin' stupid." Crook reached over with his left hand for the bag while he kept his right hand on the gun. Troy gave him the bag with no hesitation, he wasn't trying to get his family killed. Then Troy went inside his closet and took out a black duffle bag. "It's five bricks inside there," Troy said.

Crook looked inside the duffle bag and saw five white squares with duct tape around them. He put the money inside the duffle bag while he kept his pistol trained on Troy. Crook put the duffle bag over his shoulder and then made Troy walk back into the living room.

Crook tied Troy back up and made him lie face down on the floor next to his baby's mother. Jerome stood there watching his mother crying on the floor helplessly. Troy lied there on the floor praying to god that he lived through this ordeal, he didn't know what his fate was going to be. Crook walked over to Troy with a solemn look on his face and put the pistol to the back of his head. Troy knew he was going to die when he felt that cold steel upside his head, he said a silent prayer to himself. Crook pulled the trigger and Troy's brains got spattered all over the white carpet. Jerome was crying hysterically after witnessing his father get murdered. Karen was trying to wiggle her way out of the duct tape and get free, but to her dismay it was no use. Crook walked over to her helpless body and put one bullet in the back of her head killing her instantly.

"Crook, why the fuck you kill dem for?!" "I couldn't let that nigga live, he would've killed us both, Slim." "I ain't fuckin' wit you no more after this Crook! After we split everything up I'm doin' my own thing. C'mon let's get up outta here before popo come!" Slim concealed his pistol and put it on his waistline and started walking towards the door. Crook walked up behind him slowly and blew his brains out. The white walls were covered in so much blood afterwards it looked like someone painted the walls red.

Crook turned around and pointed his pistol at Jerome with his finger on the trigger. Jerome stood there crying looking him in his eyes never blinking once nor did he utter a word. Jerome glared at the dark-skinned man with hatred in his eyes. Jerome stared at his neck and saw the words M.O.B tattooed on his neck. Crook couldn't get himself to pull the trigger, so he let him live and left out the apartment. Jerome stood there looking at both his dead parents crying with his bottom lip trembling. Jerome couldn't move to call the police nor could he talk. He was shell shocked.

Chapter 2

Jerome stood there in his parents apartment shell-shocked not acknowledging what to do. For an eight-year-old to witness something so devastating, it almost ties aknot in your stomach.

"Daddy, daddy, please wake up! I won't pee my bed no more." Jerome felt the silencing chills run down his spine and heard no response. Now came the first biggest task of his young life, the entrance of his apartment was twelve feet away, but Slim's motionless body stood still in a pool of blood between him and the exit.

Jerome kissed his mother and father and promised he'd return hoping he could save their lives. He started walking on the tip of his toes to the door in silence. As he approached Slim's body, he became so stiff and remained silent, so silent you could hear his heart beating in his chest. As he got closer to the exit Slim grabbed his ankle and Jerome yelled in fear. "Awww! Help meeee!"

"Dios mio que paso Angel?" Gloria asked. "I don't know mama, I'm gonna go downstairs and see," Angel replied. Angel was a nineteen-year-old drug dealer who lived in the second floor apartment above the Jenkins with his forty-six-year-old mother, Gloria.

Jerome escaped Slim's less grip and found himself crying in the hallway. "Rome! What's wrong lil daddy? Why are you out here so late?" Angel asked. Jerome's face was so red that Angel knew something was unusual. Sobbing Jerome pointed to the door as Angel was hugging him in comfort. Angel departed from Jerome and told him to go upstairs to his mother. Jerome ran quickly up the stairs frightened. Angel entered Troy's apartment began observing the child's bloody footprints leading out the door. He pushed the door open and made it a squeaking noise. "Oh shit! What the fuck! Mama! Call 911!" Angel yelled. "Que paso Angel?" Gloria asked, while holding the helpless little boy whose ninja turtle pajamas were covered in blood. He shook his head in disbelief. "Troy e' Karen tha muerto!" Gloria called 911 and reported the incident. Ten minutes later the sirens could be heard from a block away wailing. Angel was standing on the front porch waiting for the cops to arrive. He started reminiscing about Troy his main connect. Troy has watched Angel grow up for the last six years and even fronted him a brick on consignment so he could make some money. Now his connect was gone and so was his wife. *"Damn! Troy who would do this!"* He said in his own thoughts . . . .

A Boston Police Patrolman arrived on the scene pronto. Angel informed him that there were three dead bodies inside the apartment. He immediately radioed dispatcher for Homicide and the paramedics. At that point the street was blocked off with yellow caution tape. News entourage were everywhere and neighbors were being nosy asking questions. The paramedics did not touch anything except cover the bodies until Homicide got to the scene. Captain Luff beckoned for uniformed patrolman to let the unmarked cruiser by who happened to be Roy Barros, the lead Homicide Detective in the case. Roy ducked under the bright yellow caution tape and flashed his badge to the Patrolman.

"What do we have here, Captain?" asked Detective Barros.

"We got an ugly one here—two victims, one possible suspect, one witness, three dead in total," Captain Luff replied.

"Any identification yet?" asked Detective Barros.

"Working on it," Captain Luff replied.

"I got it from here Captain."

Captain Luff walked away from the scene and left his best Homicide Detective alone so he could accumulate evidence. Roy Barros was in charge of the case so anything he wanted, he got. Detective Barros was a forty-eight-year-old Cape Verdean who been on the force for twenty-four years. He had fifty-one citations, and was a well respected cop who grew up in Dorchester, on Clarkson street. Roy Barros was a familiar with guys who ran the streets, and on certain nights you could catch him at Gigi's Bar on Bowdoin street having a few drinks. A lot of gangsters respected him for his vulnerable passes he'd give them.

As Detective Barros walked in the house he observed some of his partners and put on his gloves. His heart was felt soon as he seen a child's G.I. Joe action figure on the floor, he prayed he'd not find the body of a child. He walked over to the first body, Slim and he took out his notepad. Once he seen the black gloves on Slim's hands, he knew they had a dead suspect, who probably was with the killer and didn't comply with the according plans; second he moved on to Karen's body and had no motive, she was just an innocent bystander; third he moved to Troy's body and knelt down and pulled the sheet back, his heart was touched. He closed his eyes after he recognized a familiar face. Deep down inside he wanted to cry, but he controlled his emotions.

"You alright Roy?" Detective Sarah Thompson asked.

"Yeah," he sighed, "I knew this kid," Barros replied.

"How?" Sarah asked.

"I've arrested him three times, I've let him off the hook a couple of times, he hated me. In '73 five years after my Patrolman years, I became a Detective for the area C-11 Dorchester area," he continued, "My partner and I were doing a routine check looking for on going gang activity on Ridgewood street, we were in an unmarked car observing the area; then out of nowhere, two stick-up kids demanded us out of the car. One of them disarmed me and while the other guy was trying to disarm my partner, they ended up fighting over it and . . . ."

Sarah interrupted, "No!"

"Yes." Barros continued, "They shot my partner dead . . . ." Barros eyes started getting teary. "Guess who my partner was?" asked Barros.

"Who Roy?" asked Sarah.

"Moses Jenkins, Troy Jenkin's father. The man we stand upon now, is my deceased partners son, Troy."

"Sorry Roy . . . ." Sarah said with concern.

"Barros! You might wanna look at this," Captain Luff shouted.

As Roy walked into the master bedroom, he noticed footprints. There were boot prints all over the floor. He observed dirt prints on the pearl colored rug and found a safe wide open with nothing inside. He was very upset and determined to find this killer. Roy stood in the bedroom and took down more notes, and then asked . . . . "Who else has been in this room?"

"Nobody!" Captain Luff replied.

"Captain Luff, can I see you in private?" asked Barros. "Sure."

They left out the apartment and went outside on the side of the building. Detective Barros looked around making sure no other officers were around to hear what he was about to say . . . .

"Captain, I don't want no one on this case but me and Sarah. This case is personal to me. That was my partners son lying there dead on the floor; he was an alright kid, even though I've arrested him a few times."

Captain Luff sighed and said, "Alright, I understand where you are coming from Roy. Just make sure you get the perpetrator who did this shit! Or the Mayor is going to be all over my ass if we don't solve this Massacre case."

"Give me some time and I will find the motherfucker who did this. I don't care if it takes me the rest of my career," Detective Roy Barros said sternly.

"I'm pretty sure you will Roy, your one of the best I've seen in years . . . . just don't go around shooting motherfuckers for no reason, remember . . . . that mayor is gonna be all over my ass about this case. I'm going home to go get some rest, take your ass home and spend some time with your family. By the way, Merry Christmas, Roy."

"Same to you, Captain," Detective Barros replied.

Captain Luff walked off and got into his blue and white cruiser. Detective Roy Barros returned to the crime scene to finish jotting down notes. When he entered the living room, he saw a uniformed officer in there touching things and tampering with evidence, Detective Barros became furious.

"I've asked you nicely Burns not to interfere with this investigation that I am in charge of. Now would you please get the hell out of here."

"B-B-But I was just tryna help!" Patrolman Burns proclaimed.

Barros continued, "If you wanna help me do me this big favor, take ya big-fat-dunkin-donuts-eatin'-ass . . . . and get the fuck out of here! Show yourself the muthafuckin' exit to this apartment, and tell your men they can secure the yellow tapes. Oh, Burns, if they have a problem wit that—tell 'em I got a size nine boot big enough to fit in their ass, if they dare wish to fuck with me. I run this shit!" Detective Barros quipped. "Burns, no hard feelings, get me a coffee while ya at it."

After the commotion, Barros requested to see the witness and Sarah informed him that the little boy was upstairs with his neighbors who called the cops. Roy Barros took a fleet of stairs and went up to Gloria's apartment. Soon as he saw Jerome, he had a flashback of Troy who was ten when his own father Moses got killed. Jerome resembled his father very much but had no acknowledgement about his grandfather ever being his partner years prior. Roy Barros could already tell that Jerome was the son of Troy.

"Hey, lil man, you wanna tell me what you saw?" asked Barros.

Jerome stood there looking there like a zombie and all he kept thinking was 'Bung' 'Bung'. Both his parents getting killed then Slim grabbing him; over and over it replayed in his head. And he wouldn't say a word, he continued to remain silent and Gloria who babysat Jerome some times, was the closest comfort he had.

Detective Roy Barros was helpless at this point, he wasn't getting anywhere with his ex-partner's grandchild. He kind of understood, but he couldn't possibly imagine what was going through this kid's head. He departed from the scene at 5:57 a.m. On his way out the apartment he was clashed by news reporters, Boston Globe; Boston Herald; Fox 25 news; Channel 7 news, WB 56 news; they were all out there taking pictures of the three body bags coming outside the home. Detective Barros ordered witness protection to stand by the house until something was in position for little Jerome.

"Hi! My name is Maria Kent. We have live breaking news, which is being confirmed as "The Christmas Eve Massacre." Live in Boston, bringing you the latest in two minutes at six a.m., on Fox 25, stay tuned . . . ."

Chapter 3

Gina put her '50 television on mute as she heard footsteps in her apartment. She'd been up waiting all night for Crook to come home with his past excuses that he's known for giving. She heard in the living room opening their home safe and, she just waited patiently for him to try and sneak into their home master bedroom.

Gina was a bad bitch, 5'3, 135 pounds, light skinned, with a face comparable to Eva Mendez, they could pass as twins. Gina's ass was so fat, one day she was walking to Stash's Pizza on Blue Hill Avenue, a brother tried to spit game at her, and he crashed his Jeep Wrangler into a car that was stopped at a red light. She had that kind of effect on guys.

She wanted to confront Crook so bad, but she waited patiently for him to come in their bedroom. She continued to watch the morning news on Fox 25. Every morning she watched the news before she went to work at Upham's Corner Health Center, where she was a nurse assistant. She watched the news and continued to wait . . . .

"This is Maria Kent reporting LIVE! From the South End where police have confirmed this incident as the Christmas Eve Massacre, here where a mother and father were savagely murdered in a robbery gone wrong, one possible gunman was shot dead, and one eight year old was indeed in the home at the time of the murders, I have here with me Detective Barros from Homicide . . . ."

Crook walked in the bedroom and was so drunk, he didn't even notice Gina, who was still awake and pissed off that her man could not stay home on the night before Christmas with his family. Crook took off his chain and Boston Red Sox fitted cap, then he was startled by Gina.

"Nigga! Don't get comfortable, ya ass might be sleepin' on the couch again, so don't move until I finish my news!" Gina deamnded

"Fuck the news! Don't start this shit wit me again, Gina!" Crook replied.

Gina ignored him and continued watching the news.

"Detective Barros what happened here?" Maria asked.

"Well at this time I have three dead bodies, a very young witness, and one of the victims was very much known by the police including myself. Troy Jenkins 29', Karen Benson 28', and A.J "Slim" Parks 25' also known to the police for previous arrests."

"Any evidence at this time?" Asked Maria.

Crooks guilty conscience focused completely on the television as detective Barros answered . . . .

"Yes, as of right now the dead suspect, Mr. Parks was wearing Air Force 1 sneakers at the time of the murder. Inside the victims bedroom area there is a Timberland boot footprint approximately size 10 ½, which confirms there is a second suspect at large, because none of the bodies match the size," Stated Barros.

"Is the witness saying anything?" Maria continued.

"No! At least not yet, but I know one things for sure; I am going to get the sick fuck did this. No more questions!" Barros finished.

"This is Maria Kent reporting live from the South End for Fox 25 back to you Mike," Maria closed.

"I should have killed that lil' muthafucka," Crooks thought to himself.

"Where the fuck you been nigga?! I'm tired of you fucking aroud on me with those raggedy bitches!" Gina yelled.

"I wasn't with no bitches!" Crook replied.

"You lying nigga I told you Chris, and don't fuck with me!"

"Gina . . . . baby, I swear I was grindin' all night, then I stopped at Cataloni's and had a few drinks, no bitches I swear," Crook reasoned.

"Let me smell ya dick then," Gina requested.

"Damn! Every time I come home I feel like I'm getting booked at the police station with ya ass, want me to spread my cheeks, too? What the fuck!" Crook retorted.

"Pull ya pants down and shut up nigga!" Gina demanded.

Crook was mad as hell but he complied with Gina's demands because he knew he was innocent of her accusations, he took a deep breath and pulled his pants down as she observed and smelt his dick hoping she could find the smell of sex to support her accusations. Gina felt a little guilty for her over reaction and apologized.

"Sorry baby," she apologized.

"Damn I go through a hell of a search, and while you was down there harassing my manhood, you couldn't even give him a holiday greeting," Crook said, with a seductive smile on his face.

Gina got back on her knees and began stroking Crook's penis until he became fully hard and yearning for some of Gina's tight Trinidadian vagina. She licked his penis from the tip to his testicles and he enjoyed the facial expressions he was making. As Gina started stripping Crook of his clothes, she witnessed blood on his boots and began staring at him with a mad expression. Crook was so drunk that he didn't even notice the blood on his Timberland boots.

"Baby why you have blood all over your new Timberlands?" She asked.

At this point Crook was completely aware, no longer dazed, and startled by the question thinking of anything to say. Gina kept in mind the information that detective Barros released, her mind began racing with thoughts as she waited for Crook to answer.

"Shit got crazy in the hood today baby, this fool came up short with my paper, so me and 'Smooth' had to stomp that muthafucka out!" Crook lied through his teeth.

Foot steps could be heard coming down the hall ways as their daughter came running into their bedroom in excitement. They both threw on their bathrobes and Gina left the issue alone still unconvinced and curious.

"Mommy! Daddy! Mommy!" Mercedes yelled. "It's Christmas wake up."

Gina opened the bedroom door and kissed her young princess who was only seven years old. Mercedes was very excited, and then she jumped on Crook.

"Daddy can we open some gifts, pleeeeeaaaasssse?!" She begged.

"Of course you can baby there yours, just for you anything for my little princess." Crook replied.

Mercedes flew down the hallway to the Christmas tree, nearly knocking it down out of excitement. She tore all the presents up even some that weren't her own. She had got Barbie dolls, Barbie cars, and the last she opened a massive present that Crook though was from Gina and it came with a card. Gina had informed Crook that the huge package came when he wasn't home, so she waited for him to read the card that came along with the gift:

"To my main man and brother from another, I just thought for the holidays sake I would send my main man's princess a gift from the heart. Let's get rich or die tryin' homie. Merry Christmas! Much love, 'T'

"That's nice baby, who sent it?" Gina asked.

"My man from the bricks, you don't know him." He replied softly.

Troy's gift was a huge Barbie limited edition house worth two-hundred bucks. Crook's senses finally came to him as he took a blunt break in his bedroom. He sat on the toilet and rolled up, regretting everything he just did as he reminisced.

"Fuck Troy! How could I do you like that bro, when I was at Charles street jail, looked out for me, got me an attorney, made sure my commissary wasn't hurtin'. Damn . . . . what the fuck did I do this for? Troy you gotta forgive me," Crook prayed as tears rolled down his cheeks.

A couple of days after the murders, Troy and Karen's funeral were held at "The Love Tabernacle" on Kingsdale street in Dorchester. Many funerals were held there, even Troy's deceased father, Moses Jenkin's funeral was held there. Many friends came to pay their respects, and say goodbye. All of Karen's girls were in disbelief. Their girl did not look like the beauty goddess that she once was. They cried on their way past Karen's pearl white casket beside Troy's. All the hustlers, Gangsters, and O.G's in the city came to pay their respect to Troy. Troy had so much clout on the streets, that even enemies that had murder beef with each other, left problems at the door in respect for their deceased soldier.

Angel and Gloria did not allow Jerome to attend the funeral, because he was too young to see and understand. Crook also missed the funeral, he could not live with himself, and feared Jerome would probably recognize him. At the end of the ceremony, mourners stood outside the church wearing Troy and Karen's memorial pins, t-shirt, and jackets. The Boston Policemen led a convoy of cars through Blue Hill Avenue leading the way on motorcycles to Mount Hope Cemetery in Hyde Park. Troy and Karen were buried side by side, that same day.

Chapter 4

Gloria spent hours signing foster care parental custody sheets. On January 15, 1993 she became Jerome's legal guardian and Angel was his foster brother. Jerome was still not speaking, and he was hurt more than ever. Detective Barros had come by to see if Jerome had said anything, but he still said nothing. He even brought Jerome a belated Christmas present; a brand new Mongoose bicycle. The child had no fun. He was haunted and his heart turned cold at an early age. He relived that day almost every day of his young life and could not block out the nightmares.

Angel's customers became enraged and began dealing with other dealers. He started driving around the city trying to find a new connect. He met up with some of his peoples in the Cathedral projects, where his girlfriend lived and nobody could provide him with good quality drugs. Angel was angry, and he began noticing that his man Troy had the city on lock. Angel pulled his brand new '92 Honda Civic into the Sunoco gas station and got some gas. At the register, he ran into his boy Money Bags who was one of Troy's workers.

"What it do Angel?" Money Bags asked.

"I can't call it, it's a fuckin drought out dis bitch, ever since Troy passed I can't get no work out here," Angel replied.

"Hol' on, why haven't you hollered at Crook yet?"

"Oh yeah! He got bricks for sale?" Angel asked.

"Yeah! Man I jus copped a half of brick off him the other day," Money Bags informed him. "Here's his number cuz," Money Bags gave Angel the info.

"Good looks my nigga, I'ma get wit ya," Angel clasped hands with him and left.

Angel pulled off and headed down Dorchester Avenue, anxious to make that phone call. As he drove home he wondered, all of Troy's boys had called over to the house to see if Jerome was alright, but coincidently Crook was not one of them. He also tried to understand why Crook was not at Troy's funeral? Something was fishy.

When Angel got home he dialed Crooks number believing he had something to do with Tory's death. So he tested his beliefs as Crook answered the phone.

"Yo who's this?!" Crook answered.

"Angel, Troy's lil man that lives aboove him," Angel replied.

"What's good lil man, what can I do for you?"

"Before Troy got murked I gave him some gwop for three bricks, he tol' me he would have you give 'em to me."

"Yeah, I remember Tory tellin' me that, but I coulda swore he tol' me two of those things. Well . . . . all I got is two of dem things for you lil man."

"Damn! That's cool Crook, when can I get that?" Angel asked.

"Wednesday mornin', Roxbury mall parking lot, in front of the Reebok outlet, nine o'clock sharp, don't be late." Crook stated.

"Aight, I got you!" Angel hung up.

"This muthafucka! Now I gotta find out if he killed Troy," Angel said to himself.

Angel went to his room and saw Jerome looking out the window. He went over to him and asked Jerome if he wanted to go out. Jerome didn't reply he remained quiet looking out the window. He wanted no part of social life. Angel lied on his bed and began thinking about how he would plan this out until he came up with an idea.

Gloria Sanchez kept tossing and turning in her bed for the past two hours. On this specific day she could not sleep; she was cold, her bones ached, and she had a migraine that had her head throbbing. Any other night she would be knocked out sleeping. She didn't know if it was her arthritis taking a toll on her body causing her bones to ache in severe pain or whether it was the cold winter. Whatever it was, she had to do something about it. The pain was so excruciating. It felt like someone was poking needle in her vertebra.

She got out her queen size bed slowly trying her hardest not to make the pain worse. She winced in pain after placing both feet firmly on the wooden floor. She put on her house slipper and walked out of her room. She went straight to her thermostat that was on the wall in the living room and turned the heat up to eighty degrees. *"That oughta warm this damn apartment up,"* Gloria uttered to herself.

She walked into the kitchen and put the kettle on the back burner and turned the stove on high; she was getting ready to brew herself some tea. She reached in the cabinet that was over the stove and retrieved the Lipton's tea, some sugar, and the bottle of lemon juice. She looked inside the dishwasher and took out a saucer, spoon, and her favorite coffee mug she got from the Dominican Republic back in '79. She carefully put a drop of lemon juice and a teaspoon of sugar into the cup. Then she put a dab of honey inside her cup that was sitting on the counter. The kettle started shrieking and she turned the stove off after hearing the cue to let her know the water was hot.

She poured her steaming hot water and then she stirred the spoon around gently. She thought she was hearing things coming out of Angel's room but paid it no mind. She left out the kitchen and started walking down the corridor towards her room. Gloria heard the noises again. She knew it was something the first time, for a minute she thought she was losing her mind. She stopped at her son's room and that's when she could hear the noises clearly. It sounded like Jerome was having a conversation with someone, but with who? Angel was gone for the night at his girlfriends house. Who could possibly he be talking to at one o'clock in the morning? All these thoughts kept going through her mind. She didn't know if he was on the house phone talking to somebody or talking to himself, but she was going to find out.

Gloria pushed the door open slightly to see what was going on. She didn't want to startle him know she was sneaking in the room. She was just being concerned and making sure everything was alright with the poor child. After hearing about both his parents getting murdered, it was only right she took the orphan child into her home like she was the biological mother. She felt sorry for the kid. She liked Troy and Karen since the day they moved into her apartment building. She would even babysat from time to time whenever Troy and Karen would want to get away for the day. She loved Jerome like he was one of her own kids. Who in their right state of mind would murder an eight-year old boy's parent in cold blood, right in front of him leaving him traumatized? She asked herself that question over and over the last couple of weeks. She peered to her right and Jerome was covered in perspiration. He was tossing and turning talking in his sleep.

"Please don't kill me . . . . I don't wanna die! Mommy help me!!" Jerome had another flashback of the horrific murder he witnessed on Christmas Eve. Just about every night he was having these horrible nightmares. Gloria sat her cup of tea on the nightstand and rushed to his aid waking him up out of his nightmare. She hit the switch on the lamp and the light came on. She looked down at Angel's bed and it was soaked; Jerome had urinated on the bed. She felt so bad for him seeing him going through this ordeal.

"Rome, are you ok baby? . . ." she said, with the concern like a mother who's looking after her child. She looked at him and saw tears trickling down his cheeks. He kept turning his head left and right looking around the making sure there was nobody trying to kill him. He was petrified. She could see it all in his eyes, and right away she could see the pain he was in.

Jerome did not respond to her. He been incommunicado for the last couple of weeks; he wouldn't speak with anyone. He sat there in the bed crying and shaking like he seen a ghost, he had sweat coming down his face. She picked him up and carried him into the bathroom so she could bathe him. She stripped him out of his superman pajamas and underwear and discarded them into the hamper. She pushed the button down in the bathtub and plunged it up so the water wouldn't drain.

Gloria turned on the hot water faucet and the cold water simultaneously so it could be warm. She put her hand under the water to check the temperature, the water was just right. She squirted a dab of bubbles and bath into the bathtub and watched the bubbles form. She sat him inside the bathtub and a few minutes later it was half way full. She turned off the faucet and walked over to the bathroom closet, she took out a towel and washcloth. She sat the towel on the back of the toilet seat. She cracked open a bar of dove soap and began washing him up. After lathering his body up three times and rinsing him off—she took him out the bathtub and started drying him off.

She lathered his entire body with lotion and then she put him in some fresh garments. She lied him down in her bed afterwards and tucked him under the blankets. She held onto him with both her arms wrapped around him until he drifted off to sleep. He felt safe and secure lying there in the bed with her comforting him. She watched him fall asleep, and saw how easily he dozed off. In less than five minutes he was sound asleep. She knew it would probably be a while before the child started speaking again, but until then she was going to take it one day at a time. Gloria got out of her bed and went to Angel's room and put clean linen on his bed. She knew if he would've came home and seen his bed with pee in it—he would've been furious.

Beep, Beep, Beep! Angel woke up of a deep sleep once he heard his pager going off. *"Who the fuck is this blowin' me*

up dis early," he uttered to himself still half sleep. He rolled over and grabbed his pager off the nightstand and looked at the number. He sucked his teeth after recognizing the number. It been the same number blowing him up for the last couple of days; one of his customers needed some coke, but he was still dry with nothing. When Troy was alive he never had that problem. Troy always blessed him with coke on consignment without an issue. Angel was loyal to Troy when he was alive, Angel wouldn't deal with anyone but him. Now he wish he'd not taken Troy for granted.

Angel looked at the clock that was on the entertainment center, it was 8:07 in the morning. He got out of bed right away and went straight to the bathroom to urinate. He pulled his penis out but couldn't pee 'cause he had an erection and didn't want to pee all over the place. He stood there with nothing on but his boxers holding his penis waiting for it to go down. "Ahhhh . . . ." Angel said while he was peeing. After washing his hands and brushing his teeth, he left out the bathroom and went back into his girl's bedroom. He started getting dress right away. He didn't want to be late to the rendezvous he had with Crook.

He sat on the edge of the bed and was bending down tying his all black suede Timberland's. While he was his tying his shoe he felt his girl kissing him on the neck. He turned around and looked at her smiling at him. She wanted to make love again and he saw it all on her face. He wanted to have sex too, but couldn't 'cause he had things to do.

"Papi . . . . where you goin' this early? I want you to stay here wit me and fuck me good like last night," Carolina cooed.

"Baby I gotta go handle somethin' real quick, I'll be back in a minute," Angel told her.

Carolina Gomez was his heart; they've been together since they were twelve-years old and going strong. She been with him when he was down and out with nothing but a school bus pass. Carolina was beautiful with long sandy brown hair that came pass her shoulders stopping at the arch in her back. Her smooth golden brown complexion made her voluptuous body even more astonishing. She was 5'8, 160 pounds, and had ass and hips that held up traffic.

"Papi, be safe out there for me please."

"Baby, you know I'm good." Angel reached in the nightstand and grabbed his black .380 Lawson and put it inside his Avirex leather jacket. He kissed her on the mouth and was on his way out the apartment. Carolina got up and locked the door behind him.

Soon as he stepped out of her building he saw snow coming down outside. The snow was coming down hard and sticking to the ground. That still didn't stop the dudes that were outside hustling inside the Cathedral Projects. He observed a couple of drug transactions that were going down while children were standing around waiting for their school buses to arrive. He hopped in his Honda Civic and started the ignition and let it run for a few minutes so it could warm up. He was in deep thought sitting there watching the snow fall, he still couldn't believe his connect Troy was dead. Now all of a sudden Crook had bricks for sale, nothing was making sense to him. He put the car in drive and rode off. Driving through the South End between seven and eight o'clock in the morning was always heavy traffic; in fact, the whole city had traffic early in the morning. Angel didn't mind the early morning traffic 'cause he liked to blend in with the working citizens who were commuting to work. Plus, the police didn't really notice him either and he stayed low key. He sat on Harrison Ave at the red light waiting for the light to change. He looked at the clock on the dashboard and it was 8:26 A.M., he had plenty of time to get to Roxbury.

Going pass Boston City Hospital he saw all the different ethnic backgrounds of Doctors going to work; there were African Americans, Caucasians, Asians, and Spanish Doctors going inside the different entrances the hospital had. Angel got caught at another red light at the Mass Ave and Harrison Ave intersection. There was guys running up and down Mass Ave hustling getting their money legally. There were panhandlers out there stopping at every vehicle begging for change. There was a man selling newspapers, another man was selling cologne, and there was guys out there selling flowers to people who were stuck in traffic. The light turned green and Angel drove off down Harrison Ave.

He drove through all back streets the rest of the way trying to avoid traffic., Fifteen minutes later he pulled into the Roxbury Mall and hit the drive thru at McDonalds. He ordered two egg and cheese mcmuffins, and a large orange juice and went to go find a parking space. He pulled up at the Reebok Outlet and found a parking spot by the wall next to Warren street. He sat there with engine idling eating his breakfast waiting for Crook to arrive. Angel devoured both sandwiches and threw the rubbish in the backseat. He was not trying to be littering in public with a felony on him. He glanced to his right and observed Crook entering the parking lot in a red Cadillac. Crook pulled up and parked adjacent to where Angel was.

Angel shut the engine off and exited the vehicle. He kept his right hand inside his jacket with his hand on his pistol. He wasn't about to be caught slipping, he was alert 'cause he didn't trust Crook. In the back of his mind for some apparent reason, he thought Crook murdered Troy.

Crook hit the button and the door automatically unlocked. Angel got inside the car and right away he noticed the gold chain Crook had around his neck. Then he looked at his fingers—he had diamond rings on all his fingers.

"Angel . . . . what up my nigga!" Crook said, with emphasis. Angel glared at him for a few seconds before responding. He saw right through Crook and could tell he was being phony. "Whats's good Crook," he replied calmly.

"Listen, I got two bricks for you in my trunk. After you move all the work come re-up off me—I got bricks for days Angel, this Columbian connect I'm fuckin' wit in N.Y. is showin' a nigga love! I might even come down on my prices after you start fuckin' wit me for a while," Crook stated.

"Aight, I'ma fuck wit you my nigga you already know, you just better show a nigga some love."

Crook started grinning and said, "Hol' on real quick, lemme go get 'em out the trunk."

Crook hit the trunk release button under the steering wheel on the dashboard and the trunk came open. Crook stepped out the car and went to the trunk. Angel pulled out his pistol and cocked it back putting one in the chamber. Angel wasn't scared, he was just being prepared. He kept the safety button off and put his pistol back inside his jacket.

He kept his finger firmly on the trigger waiting in case it went down.

Crook stepped back inside the vehicle with a book bag in his hand. He unzipped the bag and revealed two plastic white squares with duct tape around them to Angel.

"Two birds of that Columbian flake, you could even stretch a lil extra 'cause the shit is that fire! Make sure you get wit a nigga soon as you finish, Angel."

"I got you dog." Angel took the kilos out the bag and started examining the packages to make sure it wasn't tampered with. The last thing he needed was some stepped on product. Angel put both kilos back into the book bag and said, "I'll take 'em and move 'em quickly, give me a couple days and I'll get wit you."

"Jus make sure you do—I'm goin' to the city dis weekend to get right," Crook declared.

"I got you, Crook. Oh yeah, I almost forgot—I got a couple pairs of Jordan's in my trunk, I got 'em from this dude who owes me, they size ten and a half's and I can't fit 'em."

"Word, lemme get those youngin', dog I can fit those," Crook assured him.

"Aight, lemme go snatch 'em out the trunk." Angel hit the trunk button on his alarm key chain and the trunk opened. He retrieved three Footlocker bags out the trunk and walked back to Crook's vehicle.

"Gemme three hunnit for these exclusive Jordan's," Angel demanded.

"Aight my nigga, I got you." Crook reached inside his jeans and pulled out a wad of money, he peeled off three hundred dollar bills and gave them to Angel.

"Lemme get goin' Crook, I got people waitin' to get right." Angel clasped hands with him and departed his vehicle with the book bag.

Angel could not believe what his eyes was seeing, Crook actually wore a size ten and a half. And on top of that he was lying about Troy fronting him bricks. He hopped in his Honda Civic and pulled off. Something wasn't right with Crook and knew it, he was going to do his homework and get to the bottom of the situation.

In the back of his mind he felt as though Crook killed Troy. Plus, Crook all of a sudden had kilos for sale and he caught him lying. But without any proof he could not assume anything. He drove straight to Carolina's apartment, he had work to do; he had some serious networking to accomplish. In a way he felt good being back in business with some product. Now it was time to play Crook close and rock him to sleep.

Chapter 5

Angel moved swiftly through Cathedral Projects with his right hand inside his jacket. He stayed alert glaring around watching his surroundings for stick-up kids and undercover police who were sometimes disguised in plainclothes. He stayed on point looking over his shoulders every couple of seconds, he was not trying to get ambushed by nobody so he remained vigilant. Angel was not trying to go to jail nor was he going to let somebody rob him; if it came down to him shooting his way out of a situation that occurred, he would not hesitated to let all ten hollow point bullets into somebody.

The snow was coming down harder than it was earlier in the day. It had to be at least three to five inches on the ground by now. Angel was slipping and sliding in the snow as he was trudging through the projects. He parked on a side street outside of the projects and it felt like he been walking for a while. Usually he would park inside the projects, but since the parking lot was full with tenants vehicles, he had to find the nearest side street with parking spots available. Most of them were reserved with trash bins by residents who would shovel a spot out. Finally he reached his destination, he walked inside the project building fifty-seven, which was a high rise. He walked into the elevator and pushed number seven and the elevator began ascending. He loathed elevators; every time he rode them his stomach dropped and he would get an eerie feeling, being claustrophobic did not help either.

The elevator came to an halt on the seventh floor and he got off. Three doors down the hall on his right at apartment fifty-five he stopped, knocked on the door three times, and waited for a response. "Who is it . . . ?" A female's voice answered from behind the door. He sucked his teeth and started getting frustrated, he could not fathom why she just didn't look through the peephole. He was not in the mood for any games, he had work to do, and people to supply. "Baby it's me, open up the door!" The door came open and Carolina was standing there behind the door with her bra and panties on. She had a smile plastered on her face. "You always think this shit is a game! Next time jus' look through the fuckin' peephole!" Angel walked into the apartment and she locked the door behind him. "What the fuck is wrong with you . . . ? Nigga don't be spassin' on me like you my daddy." Carolina retorted, with her arms folded in front of her. "Ain't nothin' wrong—go grab me some baggies and those latex gloves, I got work to do." "Yesssss Papi . . . ." Carolina replied seductively.

He stood there watching her ass jiggle from side to side as she sashayed down the corridor. Angel took off his jacket and threw it on the living room sofa. He pulled out both plastic squares and sat them on the glass kitchen table gently. Now it was time to get to work and get everything done before her mother came home. He pulled the kitchen drawer open and retrieved three brand new razor blades. Then he reached inside the cabinet over the counter top, and took out a triple beam scale and a hand held digital scale; then he sat them both on the kitchen table. He sat one square onto the triple beam scale and weighed a thousand and fifty grams, a smile crept across his face when he saw it was proper. He did the same thing with the other kilo and it weighed the same. Now he just hoped the cocaine was some good and some cut.

Carolina entered the kitchen in her bra and panties with some latex gloves on. She passed Angel a pair of gloves and gave him the Glad sandwich bags and Ziploc bags. She sat down at the table and started helping him bag up the product. She been around drugs all her life since she was six-years-old; so the game was in her blood. Her father Castro used to bag up kilos in front of her mother Veronica. Her mother Veronica used to help package up the product and distribute it sometimes, she even took trips out of state with bricks taped to her body. Veronica did anything for her man Castro, and now Carolina was walking in her mother's foot steps.

Those were the good ole days in the early eighties down in Fort Lauderdale. Castro had his baby's mother and daughter living the good life; they lived in a mini mansion, drove three luxury vehicles, and had a big yard with a massive pool. Carolina was a jubilant little girl that got anything she desired, life was beautiful. Until her ninth birthday at home with both her parents—she watched the DEA and FBI come swarming into their home arresting her father, for having business ties to Pablo Escobar, a famous Columbian drug lord. Carolina never got to go to Disney World that day. They charged Castro with trafficking kilos and kingpin status. He was sentenced to a thousand months in Marion Federal Penitentiary.

Angel sat at the kitchen table in Carolina's two-bedroom apartment she shared with her mother Veronica breaking down both kilos. He had on latex gloves so he wouldn't have any residue on his fingers. He sat there patiently breaking down the product into ounces, half-ounces, and quarter-ounces. Then he packaged up a few kilos and few eights of a kilo, those were for a couple of his closest peoples. He scooped cocaine up with a card and gently placed it on the digital scale to confirm his theory, he could not assume they were all twenty eight grams, they had to be precise; he did not believe in short changing his customers 'cause it was bad for business. He was taught by one of the best on how to get money and conduct business, it was instilled in him as an young adolescent. Troy gave him the game and he absorbed it all in like a sponge.

He had to hasten and get everything packaged up and ready to be distributed, Veronica would be home by quarter to four in the afternoon, so they had precisely a little over four hours to get everything done. Well actually, they had more than enough time, unless someone paged him and needed something cooked up. Majority of the time his customers didn't buy it ready, they just purchased cocaine. The cocaine was so strong it had a vile odor that was lingering in the kitchen, he assumed it was some descent quality cocaine 'cause the good shit always had a stinky smell. Angel looked at his girl and started snickering to himself when he saw how dedicated she was selling drugs with him. She took her eyes off the product and caught him staring at her with a sly smile. "What papi . . . . why you laughin' at me?"

"Nothin' bay, let's jus' hurry up and get dis shit done before Veronica gets home."

He loved everything about Carolina, from her looks to her personality, she was the perfect match for him. They understood each other to the fullest, and they were loyal to one another as if they were married. Angel took her virginity from her when she was sixteen, and ever since then they've been inseparable. She was right by his side when he used to out there on the block serving fiends trying to double up and get his money right. She used to help sell his product and never once asked for money. Angel took care of her without her asking. Carolina was hood and down to get that money by any means necessary for her boyfriend. She was far from a hood-rat who hung around broke gangbangers all day, she rolled solo or hung with Angel. Almost every female in their neighborhood wanted to fuck Angel, they would even throw the pussy at him like it was nothing. Even her friends tried fucking him, but he would pass every time. Angel wasn't pussy whipped or nothing—he was just faithful and loyal to Carolina; she was his heart and soul mate.

They finished bagging up all the product three hours later. He put all the cocaine back inside the book bag and then he went and put it inside her bedroom closet. He walked over to her window and stared at the snow coming down outside; it just kept falling.

"Damn! I can't even ride in that fuckin' snow right now," he uttered to himself. He was right, the little Honda Civic was not a good vehicle to drive around in the snow. It was definitely time to get a new car and give the Honda to Carolina after he sold both bricks. He had two free kilos and some money stashed. He knew Crook couldn't be

trusted so he had to be real careful doing business with him. Eventually he would have to find a new connect and cut Crook completely off, and not buy any more product from him.

Carolina stepped into her bedroom and walked up behind him wrapping her arms around him. She startled him a little bit taking him out his train of thought. He turned around hugging her then gripping her ass with both hands. She gazed into his dark brown eyes and smiled revealing her pearly white straight teeth. They both stood there for a brief minute gazing into each other's eyes before saying anything. Angel had a lot of things on his mind concerning money and other serious issues, but staring into Carolina's light green eyes made him stop worrying and stressing over everything. She always put his mind at ease and tried to cater to him every chance she had. Carolina was taught at an early age that if you have a man—and you're deeply in love with him, you go all out for him. She constantly did that for Angel. Even when they broke up temporarily for a month, she wouldn't even fuck nobody nor would she date new guys. Angel was her heart, and no other guy had that effect on her life.

"Papi, I need you here with me tonight, stay with me please . . . . ?" Angel pecked her lips while massaging her ass cheeks with both hands. She started blushing right away and then grabbed his penis caressing it through his Guess denim jeans. Angel knew what time it was, she wanted to have sex.

"Papi, you makin' me horny, when you touch my body like that it makes my pussy wet," she stated.

"Oh yeah . . . . well, I'm in the mood to fuck right now lil' mama. I'm gonna lick you from ya head to ya beautiful manicured toes," Angel said.

"It sounds good papi . . . . you gonna have to make me a believer."

"I don't be talkin' jus to talk, I can show ya better than I can tell ya."

Angel picked her up off her feet and then lied her down on her bed. They French kissed passionately and their lips stayed locked while he unbuttoned her bra strap and tossed it on the floor. He cuffed her firm perky c-cup breast into the palm of his hand and began sucking on her nipples and biting them gently. The more he caressed her breast sucked on them, the more aroused she became. She was getting wet and wetter from Angels touch, her vagina was yearning for his penis. She became so aroused that she was on the verge of climaxing and he didn't even fuck her yet. He was taking his time exploring her entire body like it was the very first time they got intimate. That was what she enjoyed and loved about her man, he took his time and made sure he did it right. He licked his tongue down the center of her body slowly exploring every crevice in her body. He was running his tongue inside her belly button, and then down to her navel. She exhaled after holding her breath and began to snicker a little bit, once he made his way down to her vagina. He said her panties off nice and slow while giving her little pecks on her inner thighs right near her vagina, she started getting wetter than ever. She started squirming, anticipating for his tongue to lick her vagina. He took his time making her fiend for him like a junkie needing a fix.

"Make love to me papi . . . . lick me chocha," she cooed.

"You want me to suck this pussy huh?" Angel continued pleasing.

"Yeeesssss! Please baby don't stop . . . ." she begged.

Angel put the tip of his tongue on her clitoris, and began rotating in a circular motion sending thrills through her entire body. He licked her vagina and sucked on her love boat sending her ecstasy. The more aroused she became, the bigger her clitoris got, he licked and sucked on her pink lips gently. Her vagina was well trimmed, so he never had to worry about hair in his mouth. He made sure his girls vagina stayed groomed, and smelling good, she tasted so sweet like a piece of candy. She always bathed herself in the fruity bath and body products; it was a ritual to her bath in her Victoria Secret products. She climaxed after getting her vagina pleased for fifteen minutes straight.

"Put that dick inside me, I need that shit!" she demanded.

"You want some of this dick bad, huh?" Angel said, while taking all his clothes off. His penis was hard and ready to be inserted inside her vagina.

"Yeesssss, please daddy, I need it now . . . ."

Angel rubbed his swollen penis across her clitoris slowly making her ooze out more fluids from her vagina. She was her patience and needing him badly, she grabbed his penis and began inserting him inside slowly. Angel couldn't help but smirk a little bit at the way she reacted desperately. He knew she was horny and needed every inch of him badly, he wanted to tease her some more but it was too late.

He was completely naked, the only thing he had on was some socks. She lied there on her back biting on her bottom lip, while he dug inch by inch inside of her. His loving was so good that tears started trickling down her cheeks as he pumped in and out with ease. He took his time with her, 'cause he was trying to nut fast inside of her. He was hitting the bottom of her vagina with each long stroke. Carolina moaned out of pure pleasure, and unwilling to hold the good feeling back. "Uhhhhhh . . . . yeesssss . . . . baby! . . . Please don't stop," she begged.

The more she moaned out and yelled his name for him to go harder, the more faster he went. That turned Angel on even more, he loved when his woman moaned. He propped her legs on his shoulders and dug deep inside, stroking her with something fierce. They went at it over an hour and switched into numerous positions. They both climaxed from the amazing sex that they had and dozed off to sleep.

The very next day, Angel went by Money Bags apartment on Ruggles street and dropped him off a quarter kilo. All he expected in return was nine thousand for fronting him the product. Usually he'd only charge seven thousand, but since Money Bags didn't have the full amount of money, he had to tax him for the consignment. Money Bags didn't mind paying the extra cash 'cause he was going to cook all the powered drug into crack, and then sell grams and half grams so he would make a descent profit. Angel explained to Money Bags that he was going to have weight for sale consistently now. He also convinced Money Bags to cut Crook off and purchase more often from him. Money Bags agreed that he would strictly deal with Angel more often, plus he knew Angel too long to not show his Spanish brother some love. Money Bags only dealt with Crook due to Troy's death. Now that Angel had cocaine for sale, Money Bags vowed to stay loyal and business. Everything was starting to fall in place for Angel.

Right after he left Ruggles street, Angel drove straight to Dorchester. He went to meet up with his man on Homes Avenue to drop off some product. Angel was spreading his product around the city, so that way he could get rid of it much faster. The faster he got rid of the work, the faster he could get another batch. He gave his Cape Verdean man "Montana" four and a half ounces, and told him he wanted five thousand back. Montana didn't complain, he used to getting consignments all the time. After leaving Homes avenue he made one more stop to Westville street a few minutes away. He dropped off nine ounces to his cousin Gee who just came home from upstate. Gee was shocked at how things had changed since he been up the way at Shirley Max, doing a five year bid for a shooting at Good Times in Somerville. He once the man that his little cousin Angel was now. Gee couldn't cry over spilled milk it was part of the game.

After making all his rounds through the city and dropping off product to his peoples, Angel went to his mother's house. It had been three days since he went home and checked on her and Rome. He knew she was probably worried sick about his whereabouts. Angel knew his day was coming soon where he'd be the man networking behind the scene and stacking money. He knew he would have to move strategic, and stay on the low if he ever expected to prevail in this game. Angel knew the dope game was like playing chess, one wrong move and he would be out the game. *"Life is crazy out here in the hood . . . ."* He uttered to himself as he drove down Dudley street.

Chapter 6

Wally sat on the edge of his queen size bed taking sips from a pint of E&J Brandy. The taste was bitter as he drank the liquor strait with no chaser. He was dressed in a pair of black army fatigues, and some all black Timberlands with a matching Champion hoodie. He was sitting there in deep thought as he swallowed the last of the liquor with one gulp. His chest started burning from the strong cognac. He was an imperative drinker who had to have his brown liquor on a daily basis. Just to function and go on about his day, he had to pick up a drink first. He never made wise decisions due to the fact his judgment was clouded.

Life was a struggle for a man who just came home from prison. Wally couldn't deal with going to work every day like a normal citizen. Normal to him was picking up a pistol and going to take money from someone. That's why he'd drink all day just so he could numb all the pain away he been through in life. Sometimes he felt as though he had the worst luck in the world. Nothing was going right in his life, so every chance he got he got drunk. He discarded the empty bottle in the trashcan beside his dresser.

Sitting there watching the ten o'clock news on Fox 25 had him feeling down after seeing the late breaking news. A twelve-year-old boy was killed in a drive-by shooting that occurred on Humboldt avenue in broad daylight. He shook his head in disbelief after hearing the devastating news. His heart always went out to the kids who fell victim to the streets. At that moment he realized that the streets were spiraling out of control. Young kids were ending up casualties over disputes between street gangs. The streets were in a uproar and different crews were warring with each other over territory. Wally didn't condone in none of that gang activity. He only cared about making money the fast way, and getting by any means necessary. He pulled out a pack of Newport's, lit one up, and sat there contemplating on his next move.

Time was flying by and Wally still couldn't believe he was still at his mother's house after being home for two-years. He sat there regretting what happened in the past. He still kept wondering if he didn't go to prison would he still be broke? He was dwelling on the past constantly, he wanted to be the man who used to be successful. The money he was seeing from robbing was descent, but it was nothing like when he sold drugs. The problem was he was spending the money as fast as he made it. He didn't save nothing. So every time he turned around he was broke. He lived off one stick-up to another never really knowing when his next dollar would come from. He was playing a dangerous game, he didn't realize sooner or later he could be back upstate, or even dead.

Before Wally went up the way and did his five to seven-years in Shirley Maximum State Prison—he was doing good on the streets. He had an apartment, a descent car, and some jewelry. He ran with some hustlers from the South End who were certified earners. Selling crack 24 hours a day was all he did with his comrades. He was pulling in substantial amounts of money from hustling all day every day. But the same individual he hustled with years prior, was now the man and on a whole another level controlling the streets in the South End. Wally was even offered a job hustling for him on one of the blocks, but he refused to hustle for him. Wally let his pride get in the way and didn't see the big picture. He thought just 'cause his name rang bells back in the day, and he used to get money with his homey, he was supposed to get a handout. But what he failed to realize, no one owed him nothing and no one was giving him anything for free.

Therefore, he had to go back to doing what he knew how to do, which was rob everything moving. After realizing that he wasn't going to get blessed with a package on the strength of his name, Wally did whatever it took to get paid. He wasn't even out a week when he decided to go back to the streets. He been out there for two-years now committing felonies every other day since he been home. The streets was in his blood, he loved fast money. He never even gave himself a chance to go and get a job to fall back legitimately. It was all about playing catch up and keeping up with the joneses.

Wally inhaled the last of the cancer stick and put the butt out in the astray on the nightstand. He exhaled the smoke out through his nose and snickered when he glanced to his right and noticed Coco walk into the room. Coco was a bad ass bitch and sometimes he wondered how he even knocked her. Wally had low self-esteem 'cause he was so big black and ugly. Being over weight was another one of his insecurities.

Coco was a walking beauty with her chinky eyes and full lips. Her thick thighs and fat ass turned heads whenever she walked down the street. She had long jet black hair that draped passed her shoulder and hung down the arch of her back. She got the name "Coco" 'cause her complexion was the same color as a cocoa butter stick. Her 5'7 frame and double DD's accentuated her body impeccably. She was one of the prettiest bitches he ever fucked. Wally sat there licking his lips while watching her stand in front of him with her T-shirt and panties on. Coco scooped her blue jeans off the chair and started squeezing inside them. Then she sat on the edge of the bed tying her white Nike's.

"So you still ain't gonna help set dis nigga up? Coco, I don't know why you frontin' on me like that for . . . . Ma you know I'ma bless you with half of everything I get . . . . come on help me out dis one time. If you help me get dis nigga we could be sitting right," Wally said, trying his hardest to persuade her.

Coco sucked her teeth and rolled her eyes after hearing him talking. For the past couple of weeks he been kicking the same shit to her. She felt bad for Wally and understood what he was saying—but she wasn't the one to be setting somebody up and getting them robbed. Coco had to let him know what it was.

"Wally, you already know I don't even get down like that baby, I don't know why you keep asking. Them niggas is my people's jus' like you is. I'm not that set up type bitch, Wally, I'm sorry . . . ." She stated, firmly with a serious look on her face.

Wally could tell by the look on her face and by the tone of her voice she was being sincere. Even though she stood her ground and told him she wasn't doing it, Wally still figured he could change her mind.

"Damn Ma, I thought you was my ride or die bitch . . . . Now you gonna tell me that you don't get down for me and he ya peoples. Coco me and you go way back since middle school, you don't even know them bustas like that. I thought you was down fo' whatever and willing to get dis dough wit me? Come on sexy, can you make it happen for me." Wally tried reasoning with her.

Coco got up off the bed and stood over Wally looking him in the face. She wanted to make herself clear so he could get the message. Coco was getting tired of him asking her to set her peoples up.

"Nigga first of all, I ain't ya muthafuckin bitch! Yeah you got some good ass dick and all—but you ain't putin' no bread in my pockets. The nigga takes good care of me and makes sure I stay wit stacks, so I'll be damn if I set up his man, Angel. I don't give a fuck if we went to school together when we were younger, I'm not setting that nigga up. Bottom line Wally, take it how you wannna . . . ." Coco said, sternly and then turned her back on him.

Coco stood in front of the mirror feeling agitated by Wally being so persistent. She threw her hair in a ponytail with a scrounge and then grabbed her purse off the dresser. Coco was fed up with his bullshit and was getting ready to leave the house. She turned around and Wally was standing behind her blocking the exit.

"Yeah it's all good hoe, I don't need ya stankin' ass anyway breezie. Go ahead and suck that nigga dick like you been doin'. I knew you wasn't down for me anyway, you dick ridin' ass bitch! You stay on them niggas dicks . . . ."

Coco turned around and smiled at him. She couldn't believe Wally was coming at her on some disrespectful shit. Coco applied some red Mac lipstick to her lips and put it back inside her purse, then she turned around to let him have it. "It's alrigiht, at least he ain't no broke ass nigga still livin' with his momma . . . . you big fat stankin' ass nigga, what bitch would want you. I should've never fucked with ya busted ass!" Coco retorted and then walked out the house.

Back in the days Wally would've smacked the dog shit out of C oco for disrespecting him like that. But since he was still on Suffolk Superior Probation, he had to fall back and let that slide. The last thing he needed was going to prison for a 209A. Those last words she said to him hurt his pride. Wally knew it was the god's honest truth what she said, but her saying it so harsh made him feel less of a man and like a sucker. He left out the room to let her hear the last word before she got in the car. Coco was halfway down the stairs when Wally opened the door and started running his mouth.

"Yo, don't even hit up my horn no more you funky ass bitch! I'm good on that stankin' pussy!" Wally said, with a smirk on his face.

"My pussy wasn't stankin' when you had ya face in it, you nasty ass nigga. The only thing I'm gonna miss is you eating my ass and pussy!"

"Bitch shut the fuck up! You ain't got no walls left on that pussy! You got more miles on you than that rental you ridin' in," Wally yelled out loud enough so the dudes next door shooting dice could hear him.

The crowd of people next door that were shooting dice diverted their attention to Coco and started laughing. Coco felt embarrassed after he made a fool out of her. She hopped inside the Pontiac Grand Prix and pulled out her cell phone and placed a call. She looked up on the porch, smiled at Wally, and pulled off down St. James Street. "Hello, hey baby . . . . you ain't gonna like this," Coco said, as she put on her right blinker to turn onto Washington street.

Wally shut the door and walked back into his bedroom. He felt good getting that bullshit off his chest. But little did he know he just signed his own death warrant for running his mouth. Tonight was the night he been patiently waiting for. He been watching one of Angel's money spots and been plotting for the right time to capitalize on the situation. The more he observed Angel's worker's, the more he noticed how vulnerable they were. He knew anyone of them were easy to touch. Everyone bled just like him, so he feared no man.

He knew precisely how he wanted everything to transpire. Wally was no dummy nor was crazy; he had to scheme and do this robbery right. Angel was nothing to fuck with when it came to his money and he knew it. Wally done heard plenty of stories while he was upstate about how Angel had the South End on lock. So he couldn't half ass when it came to robbing Angel's workers.

Wally lifted up his mattress and retrieved a black Glock 9mm with an extended clip. Inside the magazine it held sixteen hollow point shells. Wally pulled the magazine out the pistol and double checked it to make sure it was fully loaded. After realizing he was working with a full clip he cocked it back and threw the safety on. He put the pistol in the small of his back and stepped out the house with money on his mind. Wally hopped inside his burgundy Nissan Maxima and made moves to his destination.

Wally parked on Shawmut avenue and killed the ignition. He looked threw his windshield and noticed it was a full moon outside. It was drizzling outside as he sat there puffing on a cigarette. He reclined the seat slightly and scoped out the area. The weather was perfect for Wally, he loved when it rained or snowed outside, it usually meant less cops were out on the prowl. Wally sat there glaring at building 255 that was diagonally across from him in the projects. Out in front of the project building were two black males in dark clothing conducting drug sales. One was the lookout for the police, and the other one collected the money and then sent the fiends into the project hallway to see the third man with the drugs. It was like clock work with the trio who hustled inside Lenox Street Projects. Wally been watching this spot for the last three weeks and observed how they networked. Wally just didn't realize he wasn't the only one watching them.

Wally put on his hood and tied it so he could conceal his identity. He left the keys in the ignition so he could have an easy get away from the scene. This was his time to strike like a cobra since they were occupied with a line of fiends waiting to purchase crack. Wally stepped out the car and shut the door gently not trying to bring any unwanted attention to himself. He glared around doing a double-take on his surroundings before pulling out his pistol. Furthermore, the last thing he needed was for a squad car to ride by and see him pulling out a pistol. The area couldn't been any better, two street lights were out so it was darker than usual. After feeling as though nobody was in the vicinity, he pulled out his pistol and crept across the street.

Something about this stick-up wasn't right, he had an eerie feeling about this one. Beads of sweat started forming on his forehead as he walked in the muggy weather. Wally took a deep breath and shook the thought off to clear his mind. He kept his eyes on his two victims as he moved hastily across the street. They never saw wally creeping up on them until it was too late. The lookout man was looking in the opposite direction staring at a female coming down the street. Wally emerged from behind a parked truck and grabbed the dude who collected all the money by the shirt and put the pistol in his mouth.

"Don't even run or I'll blow ya man's fuckin' top off! All I want is the bread and all the work dawg. Walk inside the hallway and tell ya man to give me all the work or ya man's dead," Wally demanded.

Wally kept the gun to the side of his head while walking up the stairs into the project hallway. The dude with all the product was shocked when he saw Wally walk into the hallway with a gun to his partner's head. He reached inside an empty mailbox to grab a brown paper bag. He passed the brown paper bag over to Wally. He wasn't taking any chances risking his partner getting killed. The brown paper bag was filled with crack.

"Dis all the work homeboy?! Don't fuckin' lie either 'cause I'll murk ya man."

"That's everything right there dawg, no bullshit fam . . . ."

"Pussy ass nigga I ain't ya muthafuckin fam! Empty ya fuckin' pockets nigga! Now you bitch ass nigga before I put two in ya dome," Wally snarled, gritting his teeth.

"Aight . . . . jus' don't shoot me man." The dude with the gun to the side of his head said pleading for his life. All three of them emptied their pockets pulling out stacks of money and handing it to Wally.

"Y'all bitches have a nice day," Wally said, grinning while walking backwards outside the building with his pistol aimed at them.

Wally never saw it coming and by the time he turned around it was too late. Soon as he stepped out the project hallway, four Narcs were running down the street swarming in on him with their guns drawn. The whole time Wally was robbing them, they witnessed everything from down the street in an unmarked vehicle. When he saw them four big white boys with "BPD" jackets and hats on, he almost pissed on himself. Never in a hundred years would he ever expected to get caught red handed robbing someone. He really felt as though he had bad luck now. *"Ain't dis a bitch, fuck!"* Those were the words he uttered to himself.

"Freeze! Get down on the floor now! Drop the weapon and put your hands up over your head! Now got damn it!" One of the officers bellowed, with a pistol trained on Wally.

Wally was surrounded with guns drawn on him. He thought about running but realized he wouldn't get far. He complied to their demands and dropped his pistol and lied prone to the ground. He could not believe the police caught him in the act of committing an armed robbery. Now he was on his way back upstate. Being a three time felon did not help either. They cuffed him and escorted him back to the Ford Windstar minivan with tinted windows. They took Wally straight to C-6 police station a few blocks up the street where he was booked and processed.

After getting booked and finger printed, Wally was escorted to a filthy holding cell in the back of the police station. He was charged with five counts of armed robbery, possession of a lawful firearm, and possession of class B. He was stressed out sitting there with his head in his lap. Everything happened so fast he couldn't believe he was arrested. All he kept thinking and wondering did Coco set him up with the police. For some reason he thought she had something to do with him getting apprehended. Wally knew one thing for certain, if she did call the Dicks, he was going to kill her.

Hours done went by since he first got apprehended. How many to be precise, he did not know. All he did know was he was in a world of trouble. He sat there looking at the floor not knowing what to do next. He didn't have no bail money put away, so he wasn't going nowhere. He refused to call his mother and ask her to come and bail him out. Now he wished he never left the house. The cell door opened up bringing Wally out of his train of thought.

"Detective Anderson wants to see you in the back room," the uniformed police officer stated.

"For what?! I don't wanna talk to that muthafucka! Tell him I said suck my dick!" Wally retorted, with hostility in his voice. Wally looked at the officer and then turned his head and spit in the toilet. "Muthafucka you can't hear? Tell him I said go fuck himself!" Wally was furious.

"Listen you little street punk! I don't know what he wants, and personally I don't give a fuck! Now just go see what the hell he wants . . . ."

Wally looked at the white man that stood in front of him with the big red nose and shook his head. He got up and followed the cop into interrogation room. Soon as he stepped inside the room he saw the two Narcs that arrested him sitting at the table. Immediately he knew they wanted him to talk and tell them some information. He figured one was going to play the bad cop, while the other one was going to play the good cop.

"Mr. Peterson take a seat buddy," Detective Anderson gestured for Wally to sit down. "I got some things I want to ask you . . . ."

Wally took a seat in front of both Detectives at the table. He was nervous sitting there inside that room. Detective Anderson had a grin on his face and it made Wally uneasy. "What y'all wanna talk to me about? I got nothin' to say to y'all . . . ." Wally stated.

"You sure you don't want to talk to us? Remember your still on probation for that armed robbery . . . ." Detective Anderson smiled and continued, "You don't want to go back upstate, Wally. Come on think about it—this is your second gun charge, you looking at numerous counts of armed robbery, plus a drug charge, let's just say you're looking at a minimum of ten-years at least. So if you don't want to talk that's cool, well just bring you back to the holding cell, and transport you to court tomorrow. Or, you could do the right thing and tell us some things we don't know," Detective Anderson said, calmly making sure he clearly understood the consequences.

Wally held his head cupped in both hands staring down at the table.

He sat there elaborating not knowing what to do, he was in a tight situation. One thing was for certain, he did not want to go back to Shirley Maximum State Prison. Detective Anderson was sitting back watching Wally sweat from being distraught. Both Detectives knew it was only a matter of time before they flipped Wally and turned him into a fink.

"Wally, you want a smoke?" Detective Anderson held out a pack of Marlboros.

"Yeah . . . . lemme get one of dem squares," Wally uttered, and took two cigarettes out the pack. He got a light from Detective Anderson and said," Do you remember those two murders that happened on Christmas Eve?"

"Yeah, that was Troy Jenkins and Karen Benson," Detective Anderson replied.

"Well, I know who killed them. But before I tell y'all anything, I want a guarantee that I won't get prosecuted."

"You got my word on this one here, Wally. But if you turn out to be blowing smoke up my ass, Wally you are fucked! Remember, I got the firearm with your prints all on it, and I'll make sure you don't see the streets for a long, long time if you fuck wit me!"

"Man you got my word, dis here the truth."

"Alright, Wally, I hope you ain't stupid enough to fuck me. Hold on give us a couple of minutes and we'll be right back," Detective Anderson said, and then left the room with his partner.

"Mark, you think this piece of shit is blowing smoke up our ass?"

"Brad, I really don't know to be honest with you, it's only one way to find out . . . ."

"Yeah, I know your right, I'm going to give Roy a phone call. He's going to love this information we have, Mark. You go back in there and keep an eye on the kid."

"Alright I'm on it right now, Brad."

Detective Anderson pulled out his cell phone and placed a call. The phone rang five times before a familiar voice answered.

"Hello, Roy, how's everything going . . . . sorry if I woke you up out of your sleep. I had to call you and inform you on this one. Roy, are you still there?"

"Yeah, I'm here, now tell me what's so important that you had to call me at one o'clock in the morning and wake me up outta my sleep."

"I got someone down here that has some good information to share with you."

"What're you talking about, Brad? You callin' me in the middle of the night talking about someone wants to speak with me!"

"Roy, I got this kid Wally down here. I just picked him up on some armed robbery charges—"

"Alright get to the fuckin' point, Brad! I'm tryna get some zees . . . ."

"If you just shut up and listen I could explain! The kid Wally knows about the Christmas Eve massacre . . . ."

I'll be there in ten minutes . . . . Brad, don't let that muthafucka leave your sight."

"Don't worry he ain't going nowhere, Roy. I'll be waiting for you in the interrogation room." Detective Anderson assured him.

When Homicide Detective Roy Barros walked through the C-6 police station in the South End, all the officers in the building acknowledged his presence. Majority of the officers waved at him while some conversed in small talk. He ascended two flights of stairs and turned left at the end of the corridor going into the interrogation room. Inside Detective Anderson was to the left, and his partner was on the right. Detective Barros shook both their hands while glaring at Wally.

"Good to see you Roy . . . . how's everything down at Headquarters?"

"It's alright, so what's going on in here?" Roy Barros asked inquisitively, wanting to cut all the small talk. "This the guy you was talking about, right?"

"Yeah, he said he knows about the double Homicide that happened on Christmas Eve. Tell him what you said you know, Wally. Remember if you fuck me—I'll make your life miserable," Detective Anderson assured him.

"Come on Mark, let Roy handle this one on his own."

Both Detectives left out the interrogation room. Homicide Detective Roy Barros didn't waste no time heckling Wally for information. He got every piece of information up out of Wally. After hearing everything he needed to hear about the double Homicide and who was responsible, he felt a whole lot better. Now he felt as though he was on to something, however, this was just the beginning of an on going investigation.

"So you said "Crook" had something to do with this, huh?" *I knew that muthafucka had something to do with Troy and Karen getting killed,"* Homicide Detective Roy Barros said to himself.

"Yep, every nigga on the street know he had something to do with it. Crook is known for laying niggas down and putting 'em to sleep."

"So how I know you ain't lying to me Wally—for all I know you could be making all this shit up just to get out of jail."

"Listen, one of my man's fuck wit Crook hard body, he tol me right out his mouth how it all went down."

"Alright listen and listen closely, I'm going to give you a wire to wear and I want you to get your man to admit to everything he knows. Once he says all that over the wiretap, I'm going to need you to go down to the courthouse and go in front of the grand jury. Do I make myself clear?"

"I'm willing to do whatever it takes to stay out of jail," Wally stated.

Homicide Detective Roy Barros looked at him and smiled, "Don't worry boy, you ain't going to jail. Just remember don't try and play with my emotions. Hold on I'll be back in a minute. Oh yeah, I almost forgot, take my card and call me soon as you get out."

Homicide Detective Roy Barros gave Detective Anderson the word to release Wally. Detective Anderson released Wally thirty minutes after talking to him. Wally was officially a snitch now and worked for the police. Now he just prayed that nobody ever found out about it.

Chapter 7

The South End was flooded with coke and heroin on every street corner. Any street you walked down or drove you would see a drug dealer out there conducting business and getting money. The jobs in the city were at an all time low. A host of employees were getting laid off from work and losing their apartments and homes due to these dire times. So it was evident that your average law abiding citizen turned to the life of crime. No employees were trying to hire an ex-felon who just came home from being incarcerated. That was why eight out of ten convicts in the city, were right back to square one: living the life of crime again.

The crooked Boston Police even attempted to thwart the drugs that were being sold in the hood. They were arresting people left and right trying to clean up the streets and get convictions. Some of the cops were even setting up drug dealers and planting drugs on them. The cops were doing any and everything to try and make the streets safe again for the citizens to walk on. It seemed like the more arrest they made—the more complaints people made to City Hall. It was a war on drugs and the cops were not accomplishing anything; they would lock one drug dealer up and then there would be ten more back on the block hustling.

Mayor Thomas M. Menino was all over the Boston Police urging them to get the city cleaned up. The last four years over four hundred murders were committed in the city alone, not mention the nonfatal shootings. Seventy-percent of those murders remained unsolved. The mayor was demanding Homicide to solve murders and insisting gang unit police to bring in anyone affiliated with gangs. The cops were on a prowl conducting sweeps and raids on a daily basis. Each gun they took off the streets was a bonus and three days off with pay. Bu still, that didn't hinder the drugs being sold, nor did it stop people from getting killed. Just about every day someone was getting killed over some drug money or their street corner. Homicide were on the scene just about every day asking questions. It was so many senseless killings that all it did was make the block hot for drug dealers to hustle on. When someone got killed on the block, no drugs were being sold after that for a couple of days; Homicide would come through and shut everything down. Majority of the time the police wasn't worried about the drugs being sold, they just wanted to solve the murders promptly.

Angel stayed low-key and out the eye of the law who were harassing everyone on his blocks. He had the South End under control and made sure his customers were well taken care of. Everyone loved his cheap prices, he was wholesaling his product just to keep the flowing like water and the drugs on the streets. No other dealer on the streets were selling their product as cheap as Angel, anyone that had his pager number preferred to beep him before the next dealer. He was always around for his customers and he'd always made sure he gave them good quality product consistently. He was showing love and breaking bread with all his people. Once he started flooding the streets with product, other dealers migrated somewhere else 'cause they wasn't eating no more. No other street hustlers could compete with his prices, and their crack wasn't better than his. Angel made sure his product was good and didn't have all that extra baking soda to it. The last thing he needed was people on the street saying he had garbage, 'cause then that would make it hard for him to get rid of it. So that was one of the main reasons why so many people fucked with Angel, no other dealer could lower their prices like him and have bomb coke.

Everything was falling into place and moving accordingly with his enterprise. He was picking up six kilos every week and spreading it all throughout the South End. Angel was the main reason why a lot of dudes were getting money in the city, he made sure none of them were broke. He had four runners that hustled on different corners for him, and paid all them fifteen-hundred a week. Plus, he paid for their insurance on their cars, paid their rent, and bailed any of his workers out if they got arrested. It was all an investment in Angel's eyes. The money he was pulling in weekly off them was lucrative. Angel made sure his workers were well taken care of, and in return they sold all the product and never once shorted him on his money.

Angel was the man to see on the streets, every hustler who was getting money knew that. His name was buzzing in the streets and he was known for having that fire coke. Niggas in the street knew his shit always came back right and was never stepped on. There was never a drought with his product, and whenever you needed something, he always there to meet their demand. The only thing you could not page him after a certain time 'cause he wouldn't deal with you, after seven o'clock he stopped selling weight.

The money was coming in fast and in bulks on a daily basis. Angel was saving every dollar and selling out quickly. On a good day he'd make twenty-thousand easily, he kept all his money neatly wrapped in rubber bands inside duffle bags. Angel didn't splurge on anything unnecessary just 'cause he had money, he only bought things that were essential. He wanted to do some serious stacking before he started buying jewelry and cars. The following year he gave Carolina his Civic and brought a brand new Chevy Trailblazer. He left everything factory and drove it as is. He didn't care about being flamboyant at the time, he was in the game to win.

Angel surrounded himself around go-getters and true hustlers that was all about their money. Every nigga around him was an earner, he seldom hung around hard headed and careless dudes. Nobody in his circle did senseless shootings; if he didn't give one of his goons the word to shoot someone, then they wouldn't do nothing to anyone. Everything was strictly business, the way he orchestrated things was like running a business. Angel was the employer—and his boys' were the employees—he made sure they were financially strait. It was all about making money with Angel. If it didn't make dollars then it didn't make sense, was his motto.

After getting so much money in the hood and letting it accumulate—Angel was running into problems with dudes he knew from when he was a kid. Angel couldn't believe that one of his homeboys that he grew up with from the sandbox had betrayed him. Angel got wind of the whole situation and had to do something about it promptly. Angel could not let nobody exploit his workers and get away with it, then niggas in the hood would think he was frail. He couldn't allow the wolves in the streets to think he was fresh meat, he was going to put somebody in the dirt to make a statement. He was determined to solve the problem he had by any means necessary.

Angel was riding down Shawmut Ave making his rounds through his hood. Every day he would come through all his trap spots and collect from his workers, it was like clockwork. He liked to let his workers know he was watching them, so that way they made money and did what they was supposed to do.

"There go ya man, Wally, comin outta the pawnshop," Money Bags said.

"Where the fuck you see him, at?!" Angel was vexed.

"The nigga right there walking to his whip," Money Bags pointed to the left of Angel, and from there they could see Wally walking to Burgundy car.

"Let's get dis fool befo he get away," Money Bags said, with a grin.

Angel made a U-turn in the middle of the street and parked a few cars behind Wally's burgundy Nissan Maxima. Angel glared at the dark-skinned over weight man as he opened the passenger's side door and reached into the glove compartment. Wally then walked back across the street with a gold rope chain in his hand and headed towards the Suffolk Down Jewelry. Angel sat there patiently tapping his fingers across the dashboard. They sat there watching Wally from across the street like a lion watching it's prey.

"You rapped up right now?" Angel asked.

"Yeah, why? We ain't finna murk dis nigga in broad daylight, on hot ass Washington street," Money Bags replied.

"Who said we gonna wig dis clown here, I'm not tryna make the block hot. We gonna follow dis nigga and get the drop on him," Angel added, "And if he goes down a side street, we gonna do dis nigga!" Angel declared.

"Aight, lemme peel dis nigga, A, you don't need to be gettin' ya hands dirty.

"Nah, you do enough shit fo' me as it is, I got dis one here dog."

Money Bags shrugged his shoulders, "If you say so my nigga . . . ."

Angel took out his black .380 auto and cocked it back putting one in the head, then sat the gun on his lap, and released the safety button. Money Bags followed suit by taking out his .50 caliber and cocked it back.

"I can't wait to light dis pussy up!" Money Bags sniped.

"We gonna light him up somethin' proper, ain't no nigga gonna lay down my workers and I don't do nothin'," Angel replied with a screw face.

Money Bags lit up a Newport while they sat there waiting for their mark to come outside. Angel tried to stay focus on the mission they were about to do, but the two redbone females walking by Derby park were looking enticing to him. Angel had to shake the thought off of getting his dick sucked and stay focus. Money Bags kept staring at the females with lust in his eyes. Angel noticed he wasn't focused and something quick.

"Dog fuck them hoes . . . . always thinkin' bout some puss," Angel quipped.

"Yeah, ya right—fuck dem hoes!"

"Here dis clown come now," Angel informed him.

They both sat there anxious and ready to fill the Nissan Maxima up with slugs. Angel wanted him dead badly 'cause he would eventually end up becoming a problem if he let Wally live. They watched as Wally got inside his vehicle and drove off. Angel pulled off slowly following him staying three to four cars behind.

Angel followed Wally through Dudley square and then up Dudley street. He followed the Nissan thru Roxbury taking different side streets and staying a safe distance behind. Angel took a left turn down Magazine street bypassing Saint Patrick's Catholic church on his left and proceeded following behind his mark. Then Angel turned right onto George street and slowed down once he noticed Wally pulling over and parking. Wally parked on the left near the corner of Shirley street in front of a triple-decker. Angel turned right up Shirley street and circled the block. Angel hit Dudley street again and drove two blocks and turned right down Clarence street. He came to the end of the street and took a quick right and another right onto Langdon street. Angel parked behind a Jalopy Toyota Camry and killed the ignition.

Angel observed the area and noticed the street was quiet and deserted. This was the perfect place to kill somebody at due to the location. Angel was parked a street over from Wally and had to move fast. This was Angel's best opportunity so he had to capitalize off the situation. They heard somebody beeping a horn from the next block over and assumed it was Wally. Both of them concealed their pistols inside their jeans before stepping out the truck. Angel pulled his blue Red Sox fitted down his forehead trying his hardest to disguise his identity. Money Bags put on his black shades and looked at Angel.

"Come on Bags, let's go get dis nigga . . . ." Angel said, solemnly while they both stepped out the truck.

They both were speed walking around the corner not wanting to let Wally get away. Time was not on their side so they had to move fast. Angel glanced to his right and saw a sick grin on Money Bags face. Angel just shook his head in disbelief and kept walking down the street. He couldn't understand how Money Bags always would be grinning before he put in some work. Angel scanned the area carefully making sure nobody was outside watching them. They looked like they were up to no good walking fast down the street with their hands on their waistline.

Angel observed a light-skinned female descending the stairs on the house where Wally was parked. Angel and Money Bags whipped out their pistols simultaneously as they walked up behind Wally's car. The girl walking down the stairs started screaming out the top of her lungs and ran back upstairs into her house. The elderly lady across the street dropped her groceries when she saw them pistols come out, she stood there in shock not knowing what to do. Angel walked up on the driver's side of the car and Money Bags did the same. Wally never had a chance, he tried reaching for his pistol under the seat, but it was too late. All Wally saw was the sparks and then his life was gone. Angel and Money Bags emptied both clips on him riddling the car with over twenty slugs. Shell casings were all over the ground next to the Nissan as Wally's head was slumped on the steering wheel causing the horn to go off.

Chapter 8

It was hard for Jerome trying to deal with both his parents dead. All his life he looked up to his father and admired the way they would play together and spend quality time. He missed his father being in his presence. He missed his mother's love and how she always pampered him and how much she told him he was special. Jerome felt lost without having no parents to come home too and talk with after school. Jerome's whole outlook had altered and he was messed up in the head. After going through that ordeal, Gloria went and signed him up for counseling. Gloria figured that was the first step into getting help for Jerome so he could progress.

After three years of counseling by special rehabilitation doctors from the Children's Hospital, and Gloria consoling poor little Jerome—he was now speaking eloquently. He was trying to get on with his life and live as a normal kid. Gloria had enrolled him into the Blackstone elementary school that was five blocks away from her apartment. Being in school there the first couple of weeks only made things worse for Jerome. After being in school for only two weeks, he was suspended for fighting with another boy in his math class. When Gloria asked him why'd he fight the kid, his response was: "The kid started talking trash about my mommy and daddy." Gloria couldn't even blame him for reacting off impulse nor could she chastise him; it was not his fault for fighting, both his parents were dead and gone. Jerome had a flashback and snapped on the kid.

Jerome was very quiet, shy, and always to himself most of the time. He wouldn't participate in anything at school. Jerome wouldn't play kickball, he wouldn't do no relay races in the schoolyard, he didn't socialize with no other kids and he hardly spoke to any of his teachers. Right away he was labeled an outcast at school. The kids at his school tried so many times to talk with Jerome, but he would not talk to the kids. He would speak to his teachers and stay antisocial towards his classmates. Jerome didn't want to have any friends after witnessing his father's best friend killing his father. He couldn't trust no other kid he thought everyone was out to get him. All he ever wished for was his parents to come back. He still couldn't understand why people have to be taken away from their loved ones when someone died. depressing for him as a child.

But as time progressed, Jerome began improving in his work ethic at school. He excelled in all his major subjects and his conduct improved dramatically. All his teachers were in awe and could not believe how much of a prodigy child he was. The same kid who was constantly fighting and being suspended from school—was now achieving school spirit and the honor roll. The majority of his teachers were surprised when they realized he was not a problem child, he was just a child who'd seen a lot and had been traumatized. Jerome excelled out the Blackstone elementary school without any further problems. Gloria was right by his side along with Angel to watch him walk across the stage in the auditorium to attain his Diploma. They were there to give Jerome their love and support. They all went out to eat at Pizzeria Uno's afterwards.

Chapter 9

Roy Barros stared at the photo that was on the wall hanging above his fireplace in the living room. Very often he would stare at the picture and start reminiscing about the good old days when he was younger. It was an old photo of his ex-partner Moses Jenkins and himself on the day of their graduation at the Police Academy back in '68. They were both smiling in the same picture and excited about joining the force. After they became partners, they quickly became the best of friends and did everything together. If one went on a date it would end up being a double date. Roy missed his best friend daily and now he had to solve his ex-partner's son's murder. He was devastated over the Christmas Eve massacre case, he wanted the perpetrator badly.

He was losing a whole lot of sleep over the murder case that happened nearly six years ago, he hardly got five hours of sleep a day. He was still going hard on the now profound cold case. He didn't care if it took him the rest of his career to catch the person, he was going to get to the bottom of it one way or another. Roy Barros was the sole Detective who spent a tremendous amount of overtime on murder cases; once he picked up on a case, he would hardly sleep. He would be up sometimes twenty hours a day looking for evidence and leads. That was one of the main reasons his wife left him back in 1980, he never spent enough time at home with his family. He was a nonstop workaholic who was constantly working to solve cases. Roy Barros loved his job and never once did he get suspended from work or demoted.

After ten-years of being happily married to the love of his life, Elma; she filed for divorce and left him. She could no longer put up with his long working hours no more. He put his career before his family and his wife couldn't put up with it anymore. Roy Barros hardly spent any time with his wife anymore, when they first got married they did everything together. Elma warned him numerous times that he needed to start spending more time at home with her and their two daughters, but he needed to start spending more time at home with her and their two daughters, but he needed to start spending more time at home with her and their two daughters, but he didn't take heed to what he was saying. Elma stopped getting intimate with him and no longer could be with him. He was rarely home and when he was—either sleeping or watching sports. Elma took custody of their two girls and took the house on Blake street in Hyde Park. Roy Barros moved out and bought another house on Harley street in Dorchester. Till this day he pays his wife child support and alimony every month. He's been doing it for the past fourteen-years.

He sat down on his suede love seat and started flicking through all the cable channels. He was hoping he could find something to watch before he went to work in two hours. There was nothing on but soap operas and the daily shows and re-run movies that he seen a hundred times. He settled for Sports Center and started watching all the highlights of last night's games. The Red Sox won with a game winning homerun by Mo Vaughn in the bottom of the ninth inning. Roy Barros was delighted that the Red Sox won, he was always proud whenever the home team won.

Roy Barros grabbed his pack of Kool cigarettes off the coffee table and took one out the pack. *"These things gonna be the death of me,"* he thought. He sparked up the cigarette and inhaled it deeply, and then blew out smoke circles. He been smoking cigarettes for over twenty years now, and even though he knew cancer ran deep in his family, he constantly smoked them anyways. The phone started ringing in the house bringing him out his train of thought. He got up and walked into the kitchen to go answer it. By the time he got to the phone that was hanging on the wall—it was too late, the phone had stopped ringing. Soon as he started walking down the hallway the phone started ringing again. *"Who the fuck is this calling me!"* He thought.

"Hello! Who the hell is this calling me?!" he shouted into the receiver.

"Roy, is everything alright? Why are you answering the phone like that?" A female's voice said over the receiver.

"I'm alright Sarah, just a little frustrated right now I guess," He continued, "Why, what's going on sexy? I been doing some serious thinking about the other night and—" Roy Barros got cut off.

"Now is not the time for that Roy, we can discuss that issue another time. You're not going to like this Roy." Sarah explained.

"Sarah, what are you talking about?" Roy Barros stood there confused running his hand threw his hair.

Sarah sighed, "Remember your informant on the Christmas Eve massacre case . . . ?"

"Yeah, why? What about it? Roy Barros was puzzled.

"He was found dead in his vehicle a little over an hour ago. I'm at the scene right now," Sarah informed him.

"Ain't this a bitch!" Roy Barros was furious, "Where you at right now?"

"Eighty-three George street, get down here pronto!" Sarah hung up the phone.

Roy Barros hung up the phone feeling disgusted. His main witness on the Christmas Eve massacre case was now viciously murdered. He had to do some more investigating and start from scratch all over again. All his leads he had attained were now obsolete because his key witness was dead. Now he wondered if it was related to the case he'd given his heart too. Roy Barros did not like this feeling at all. Every time he thought he was onto to something, he ended up running into a dead end. He went upstairs to his bedroom and retrieved his police edition Glock seventeen, and threw on his bulletproof vest. He put his pistol in its holster on his waist, and put on pair of Stacy Adams shoes. He grabbed his set of keys and left out his bedroom door. Roy Barros was smooth detective who always dressed casual on or off duty. He went down stairs, activated his ADT alarm system, and departed from his home.

He jumped in his black Crown Victoria and was gone. He activated his emergency lights and pushed the pedal to the medal down Dorchester avenue. Roy Barros drove fast running every red-light and stop sign until he reached his destination on George street. Soon as he got to the crime scene, he observed yellow caution tape everywhere; half the street was blocked off with police cruisers and ambulances'.

He stepped out his vehicle and saw his partner Sarah Thompson walking towards him.

"Show me the body, Sarah." Barros was frustrated.

"Right this way, Roy."

Sarah walked him to the location of the body and unzipped the black body bag for his observation. He knelt down beside the dead body and examined the gunshot wounds. Wally's body was riddled with numerous bullet wounds. He shook his head in disbelief and zipped the bag back up. Roy Barros signaled the paramedics over to him.

"Bring the body to the coroner's office, then leave the ME do an autopsy."

The paramedic nodded his head and did what he was told.

"Sarah, any leads on this case?" Roy Barros asked.

"We could be onto something—but right now it's really hard to tell, Roy."

"What do you mean . . . ? Do we have any witnesses?"

"We might have two witnesses who could eventually come forward. I interviewed both of them, and neither one of them were cooperative. They both said they couldn't recall what the shooters looked like . . . ." Sarah Thompson sighed, "I think they know something but are too petrified to come forward."

"Who are the two witnesses?" Barros asked while rubbing his beard.

"One is a young girl, probably no older than sixteen or seventeen who lives on the second floor of eighty-five. The other witness is an elderly lady who lives across the street from the young girl. They both claim they didn't see the shooter's faces."

"Well, I still want to speak with them, Sarah. I got some questions I want to ask them, and maybe I'll get something out of them," Roy Barros insisted.

"Ok, let's go speak with the young girl then first."

Roy Barros followed her up two flights of stairs into the triple-decker. She pushed the door open and went up another flight of stairs through the house to the second floor. Then she knocked on the door twice and waited for a response. Roy Barros listened closely and heard people speaking in Cape Verdean language inside the apartment. Right off top he was familiar with island accent. The door came open and an elderly lady with salt and pepper hair stood in the hallway at the apartment entrance. She wore rosary beads around her neck and chewed on tobacco. Both her wrist were covered with Cape Verdean bracelets. The lady gawked at both detectives. Sarah Thompson stepped in and said something before her partner could.

"Ms.—I'm homicide detective Sarah Thompson, and this is my partner Roy Barros, we have a few questions we want to ask Nadia. Do you mind if we come inside?" Sarah inquired.

The elderly lady nodded her head in approval. Both detectives walked inside the house. Roy Barros looked around the house and noticed all the African souvenirs on the walls. The house was immaculate and well furnished. Roy Barros peered to his right and saw a light-skinned female, walk into the living room. The first thing he observed was tears coming out of her eyes and her nose was running. The elderly lady spoke to the girl to inform her about the detectives questioning.

"Hey, Nadia, this is my partner Roy Barros, he's with Homicide also. He wants to ask you a couple of questions about the murder of your boyfriend Wally," Sarah Thompson told her.

Nadia nodded her head in unison. Roy Barros started asking questions immediately and he was pleased she was being cooperative. "Nadia, what happened out there earlier today? Can you tell me what the guys look like? You know . . . . were they tall, fat, what was their skin complexion? Roy Barros asked.

Nadia looked at the elderly lady and back at both detectives who were waiting for her response. The elderly lady stepped forward speaking Portuguese.

"I can't remember what they look like, I'm sorry . . . ." Nadia exclaimed.

"Kes diabus bazzal tiru . . . . un di es e parce spanhol ku kabelu kumpredu."

(Those devils shot him . . . . one of them looks Spanish with long hair.)

Detective Roy Barros stood in shock because he understood the Cape Verde language slightly, but he did not know how to speak it. His mother and father were from Praia, the capital of the Cape Verde Islands.

"Mama bo e di mais!" Nadia said.

(Mama you're too much)

Roy Barros realized he wasn't getting anywhere with all the heckling he was doing. He had to take another approach at Nadia and hope she insisted on calling him.

"Here's my card Nadia, that's my cellular number and office number right there, if I don't answer then just leave a message. It's very important that you call me if you hear anything," Roy Barros emphasized.

Sarah Thompson also gave Nadia a card with her contact numbers and one for Nadia's mother also. "Nice meeting you Nadia—and you to Ms.—" Sarah Thompson shook both their hands.

"Her name is Filomena Barbosa," Nadia proclaimed.

"Nice meeting you Filomena." Roy Barros departed from the apartment with his partner. When Roy Barros and his partner went back outside to the crime scene, there were news reporters everywhere. Roy Barros avoided them all and walked down the street to his vehicle. He jumped inside and Sarah Thompson signaled the cruiser who transported her to the scene to proceed and leave as she got into the passenger seat.

"That girl knows something, Sarah, she's just not talkin'."

"I believe that too. I've had that same feeling in my gut, she definitley knows something."

"Now I'm back to square one; no witness on the Christmas eve case, and Jerome still won't talk to me. Fuck!" Roy Barros banged his fist on the dashboard out of frustration.

"Roy, take it easy . . . . I got something I've been waiting to show you. It's Wally's phone," said Sarah with a smirk.

Sarah Thompson pulled out a cellular phone and passed it to Roy Barros who was now furious and frustrated with himself. He observed the cellular phone and scanned through the recent calls and time. As he went down the list he became amused at what he was seeing.

"What a fuckin' coincidence, Sarah."

"Why you say that?" asked Sarah Thompson.

"Christopher Walker aka "Crook", was just the last person to call Wally before he died. I bet that snake muthafucka had something to do with this murder! We gotta nail this muthafucka soon. This is getting way out of hand—I he killed Troy and then found out Wally was under the Grand Jury Investigation in that case so he kills him . . . . snake muthafucka!" Roy Barros sat there in deep thought staring at the road ahead of him.

"So let's just keep a close eye on him. Let's watch him and soon as we get enough evidence on him, we can fuck him in his own tracks. Plus, it shouldn't be hard if he's a kingpin running loose like he's untouchable or something." Sarah Thompson explained.

"Exactly . . . . now you're starting to see the big picture. Say—you in the mood for some drinks tonight? We can stop at the Dublin House?" Roy Barros asked.

"Sure, Roy, why not. I would love to go out have a few drinks . . . ." Sarah Thompson replied, with a seductive smile on her face.

Roy Barros started grinning to himself. He turned his car on and drove off. He was listening to the Temptations and humming to the melody. "Said it was just my imagination . . . ."

"Somebody's in the mood tonight I see . . . ." Sarah Thompson flirted.

Roy Barros and Sarah Thompson were among the few detectives in their divisions that were dating each other. He was completely attracted to her the minute she was assigned to his unit. The two partied every time they were off duty so much that they were better off moving in with each other.

Sarah Thompson had suggested it a myriad of times, but Roy Barros would always disapprove. He wasn't scared to move on; in fact, he just didn't want her to go thru the same things his wife had with him. At times he thought about it because she lived the same busy life as him every day. So what's the chances of that happening? He always debated that thought on the regular.

It was close to two o'clock in the morning when they stepped out the Dublin House. The night was nice and soothing. The streets that were usually busy during the day were now completely dead. Nobody was walking their dogs or nothing, all that could be heard was the loud music thumping loud from the Dublin House. As the two walked to Roy's vehicle, they were laughing at the cars who ignored the traffic red lights and drove straight through not acknowledgeing that they were two detectives. They just followed one another right through the traffic lights, but Roy and Sarah weren't in the mood to issue traffic violation tickets. They were tipsy and feeling each other too much.

"Where to Sarah?" Roy asked.

"Roy, every night we do this, for the last time just drive to your place. It's like I don't end up there every night," Sarah replied, while running her hand across his manhood.

"well I just thought—" she cut him off.

"Your thinkin' too much Roy, and half of my working attire are at your place. You kill me every time you ask me where I'm staying for the night, and why you tryna front like you ain't tryna get this pussy?" Sarah turned to him smiling.

"Whoa! I wasn't expecting that to come out your mouth," Roy replied laughing.

"So you tryna say I'm lyin'?"

"Nah! I didn't say all that—I jus'—"

"Yeah, I know, you know what Roy . . . . shut up and drive we got things to do and somewhere to be," Sarah demanded as she activated the emergency lights on the Crown Victoria.

"Yes ma'am," Roy complied as he sped through the streets of Dorchester speeding to get home.

It had been about seven years since Roy and Sarah had became intimate with each other. Sarah was actually right, most of her belongings stayed at Roy's apartment. Roy earlier that day had been thinking about the previous night and he wanted to surprise Sarah by telling her she could move in. The two had agreed about the issue plenty of times. Sarah had deep feelings for Roy and certain times, she believed Roy was just using her as a booty call due to their seven year affair. As they cuddled peacefully in his bed after having sexual intercourse, he woke up.

"Sarah, I got something to tell you."

"What Roy, can't it wait till the morning?"

"Well—it is morning, if you wanna get technical."

"Fuck! We got to get to work in two hours," Sarah cursed.

"I've been giving it good thought and I been seeing you for seven years now. It's official I love you, and I'm not scared to say it. I think it's time you really move in," Roy gazed into Sarah's eyes waiting for a response.

"Roy, I love you too!" Sarah replied with tears in her eyes.

"Well, since you're going to be staying here now . . . . you might as well get my coffee ready," said Roy being sarcastic.

"You jerk . . . ." Sarah punched him playfully on the arm.

"I'm not a jerk, I'm your sweetheart," Roy stated.

"I know—that's the only reason I'm about to get up and actually do it."

Sarah and Roy drank coffee and had a few toast before leaving for work. This had been the first time Roy had accepted another female to reside with him since his ex-wife Elma. For the first time Roy had a good feeling about this relationship, because Sarah could relate to his job and how stressing it was. After they planned the moving date, they showered and headed down to the police headquarters for another long day of work.

Chapter 10

Jerome was spoiled by Angel massively from video games to name brand clothes. Angel kept his protégé updated with the exclusives; jewelry, Jordan sportswear, new video games, all the things that a simple kid would like. Angel had more expectations from Jerome, he wanted Jerome to be well educated. Angel never went to College, but he did graduate from Madison Park Vocational School. At the time, he was trying to get a career in the mechanics field. He loved anything with wheels on them, but making money on the streets got in the way of his dreams. Education was very important to him so he made sure Jerome was getting his education.

Jerome started his ninth year of school at Charlestown High School in Charlestown, Massachusetts. He was excited, but also shy. In Boston, first days of school represented everything about you. Hair well groomed, new clothes, and you had to be dressed to impress. Everything had to be coordinated and Jerome indeed was. A crowd of teens various ages lined up outside the school waiting to get their schedule, as Angel pulled up in one of his project cars, a '74 pearl black Chevy Nova. Jerome looked nervous feeling all eyes on him. He dapped Angel up and stepped out the car.

"Good luck lil' daddy, make me and momma proud!" Angel stated.

"No doubt," Jerome replied.

"Later homie!" Angel yelled as he sped off.

Jerome started walking to find a spot in the long line outside of school. He noticed everyone staring at him and he making a big impression. He stood in line nervous. Jerome was accustomed to his surroundings. He had just left junior high school and got recruited for basketball. He was the man in junior high school, but this was different. This was a whole new league.

As Jerome walked in his first assigned class he felt kind of weird. Most of the students were smokers, and there wasn't any teachers make them get to class. High school was kind of free to him. He felt more mature. He spent his first hour in mathematics in unit C. He noticed the students showing their clothes off and talking about fashion, but he never spoke to anyone.

"Welcome to Charlestown High School! My name is Mr. Carter, and I will be your math teacher for the semester. I want to know your full name, you want to be, and what your parents do for a living." Mr. Carter requested.

Jerome had recaps about the incident and he was startled by the request. Three students recited their information to the class, and when Jerome's turn was up he became stiff; you could hear students whispering as Mr. Carter requested the class to calm down. "Guys! Guys! Please respect one another!" He bellowed. The whispers became low but some students continued talking to each other about their summer vacation while Mr. Carter requested Jerome to continue.

"My name is Jerome Jenkins, I'm tryna play pro basketball." As Jerome informed the class about himself, he had nobody's attention except for one girl who actually seemed interested to know what he was about.

"Jerome, can you please tell us what your parents do, starting with your mother?" Asked Mr. Carter.

"My mother is dead." Jerome said, and then looked down to the floor.

The class got completely quiet. It was so quiet, you could hear a pin drop. The girl stood shocked with her hand over her mouth as she emotionally became sad for Jerome's loss.

"Sorry about that Jerome. Would you like to tell us about your father instead?"

"He's dead too." Jerome replied, coldly.

"I'm sorry to hear that Jerome . . . ." Mr. Carter felt bad Jerome due to the fact he didn't have any parents. All the kids in the class had both parent figure so they could not possibly feel how Jerome felt. Jerome took a seat and waited for the periodic bell to sound signaling for the next session. When the class was over the students stormed out the classroom, except one girl as she approached Jerome with her soft voice.

"Hey, ummm . . . . i don't know how your feeling right now 'cause I have my mom and dad, but I feel sorry for you. If you ever need somebody to talk too I'm here." The unknown girl stated.

"Thanks shorty, I appreciate it." Jerome replied.

As the girl walked away, Jerome ran out of words. He was a virgin and didn't have much experience with girls. Jerome went to his next class and all he kept thinking about was the girl who spoke to him. *"She ain't gonna be hard to find,"* he thought to himself. He couldn't stop thinking about this girl. Her eyes were hazel, her lips were glossy, plus she smelled good. He had a thing for this unknown girl. Her mean walk down the hallway was the last of his faint memories of her.

Jerome started walking through the school and getting familiar with where everything was at. He seen drug transactions, girls on their cell phones, dudes rolling dice, he was already accustomed to the street life and drug game. Angel was the man on the streets and basically a father figure to Jerome. Angel put him under his wing and schooled him to the game. Jerome knew a little about drugs. He continued walking through the halls when his Nextel started going off.

"Who the fuck is this blowin' me up . . . ."

Jerome started to answer his phone the school police told him turn his phone off. He continued to walk to his class. Charlestown high school was very big and known as outstanding performing basketball team. Jerome wanted to be part of it, he was a phenomenon in the making. He always won the city's BNBL (Boston Neighborhood Basketball League) with Mission Park teams. He was already recognized around the city and that's why Charlestown high school wanted him to come to the school.

As Jerome approached the class he was assigned too, he recognized his tardiness and there was only one seat open. It was next to the girl he'd just met, so this was the perfect chance. He took out his three subject notebook and caught up on the notes he had missed. After his notes, he began to pay attention to the teacher when he was spoken to by the girl who he'd forgotten to ask for her name. She was astonishing and flawless. Her beauty was so intriguing that every time Jerome spoke he got lost in her eyes.

"So we meet again Jerome!" She started to converse with him.

Jerome was shocked she remembered his name. He had a feeling she probably was feeling him too. "Yeah, lil mama I guess so, but on some real shit I been wondering what your name was since you was so rude enough to let me have it." He laughed.

"So you were thinkin' about me?" She blushed showing her dimples.

"Nah not like that—" Jerome replied, as she interrupted him with a funny face.

"Right, Right you got me, ya fly lil mama. I was wondering, and I still don't know ya name."

"Well, I don't think you were interested in knowing! You should have asked." She replied with a snicker.

"What's ya name shorty?" Jerome asked.

"Lil mama!' She replied, being funny and complicated. "Sorry, I'm just messing with you Jerome, my name is Mercedes Walker."

"That's a pretty name sexy . . . ." Jerome added, with a smile.

They continued talking for nearly an hour getting acquainted with each other. Before they knew it the class was almost over. Jerome's phone went off again, this time he felt the vibration in his pocket. He decided to take a bathroom break leaving the class for five minutes. As he entered the bathroom, he noticed some other students smoking and just ignored them as he alerted Angel from his Nextel.

"Churp! Churp! What it do mane?" Jerome asked, as he spoke through the speaker.

"How is my lil mans first day comin' along?" Angel asked.

"Perfect, I'm working on dis lil shorty, Angel she's a dime fo' real . . . . her ass got a nigga all fucked up in here."

"Man, you don't know shit about girls, Rome. Get ya education first homie, oh yeah, am I picking you up from school or what?"

"Nope, I might walk her home . . . ." Jerome joked.

"Aight, get wit me later and stay safe, I love you."

"I love you too bruh." Jerome ended the conversation. As Jerome returned to the classroom Mercedes looked up to him as he was about to sit down and she made a smart remark. "Had to call your girlfriend?"

"Nah, I don't have one. That was my brother."

"Yeah, whatever liar." She sucked her teeth.

"Nah fo' real no bullshit, I ain't gotta lie . . . ." Jerome looked her in the eyes. "Plus I'm walkin' you home so you already know." Jerome added.

Mercedes twisted her face up at him like he was lying. "No you're not . . . . for real are you?" Mercedes asked, blushing.

"Yep . . . . where do you live at?" Jerome asked.

"I live around Fields Corner, you know where that is?"

"Yeah, I used to play basketball at Reebok Court at the park . . . . I got you lil mama, be easy I'ma get you there."

The two of them became extremely tight and they already had feelings for one another. They had no clue about their parent's involvement. After school they both continued talking as they boarded the MBTA Bus 93 to Sullivan station and hopped on the orange line train. While waiting for the Forest Hills train, they exchanged numbers and flirted all the way to Jerome's destination and Mercedes became mad because he wasn't going to bring her completely home. He was just putting her to the test and she already exposed herself. He had her wrapped around his fingers.

"NEXT STOP, NORTH STATION! CHANGE HERE FOR THE GREEN LINE!" The intercom on the train announced.

"That's me Mercedes!" Jerome teased.

"You're a loser, I thought you was gonna walk me home . . . ?" She whined.

"Somethin' came up, I can't lil mama." He lied.

"Like what . . . ? You know you're lying Jerome."

"It's alright lil mama. I got that kind of effect on girls . . . . I'll just see you tomorrow." Jerome quickly pecked her on the lips before the doors on the train closed. He stepped out and she could see him on the other side of the glass. She was smiling and laughing. She couldn't believe how aggressive he was. On her way home she could not get Jerome off her mind. After the kiss she waited impatiently for the train to come out the tunnel so she could have enough reception to call him. She didn't really know Jerome, but she was definitely feeling him. Jerome felt the same way, he was ready to come out his shell. Mercedes debated on calling him, then she wondered about what would happen if her over-protective father found out. She switched to the red line at Downtown Crossing and began running for the Ashmont train nearly missing it.

During school let outs there would be traffic everywhere. All of the Boston Public schools usually got out at the same time. Mercedes didn't have any service on her phone so she waited patiently to get out the tunnel to call Jerome. As the train departed from Andrew Square, she began to receive service on her phone and before she could dial his number she had an incoming call.

"Hello." She answered.

"Hey, lil mama, I was jus makin sure you got home safe." Jerome came through the receiver.

"I ain't home yet, but what was the kiss for?" She asked

"I don't know, I jus like you for some reason, why do you hate me now?"

"No . . . . It just happened too fast and I think I like you too." Mercedes replied.

"You think? Girl I need to know if you feeling me . . ."

"No! You know what I mean boy . . . . cut it out." She confirmed.

"Aight well . . . . hit me up when you get home so I know your safe."

"Ok I will . . . ." Mercedes hung the phone up smiling from ear to ear.

Jerome and Mercedes instantly became best of friends. They spoke on the phone all night, knowing they would see each other at the school the very next day. Jerome would even meet Mercedes Downtown Crossing every morning so they would commute to school together. Jerome started taking Mercedes to the movies on the regular and they became a couple. Jerome instantly fell in love with Mercedes, there was no way of keeping the two of them apart. It was love at first sight.

Chapter 11

Crook drove slowly down 143rd street in his black-on-black Range Rover looking at building numbers. Being that it was dark outside, he had to squint his eyes to be sure he was reading the numbers correctly. After finding the building he was looking for, he pulled over on his right and parked behind a random yellow cab. Crook parked directly in front of building three-forty-five and killed the igniton. He glanced in his rearview and observed a Chrysler Sebring pull over about fifty feet behind him. He pulled out his Nextel and hit the alert button on his phone and sat there and waited for a response. Crook's phone started beeping and he looked down and saw the name Keisha.

"Churp! Churp! Y'all don't move till I say so, ya heard?"

"Yeah, I got you daddy . . . ."

"Aight, I'ma call ya back in a minute, Keisha."

"Alright, don't have me waitin' forever."

Crook got off the two-way and placed a call. The phone rang once and went straight to the voicemail. Crook ended the call and waited two minutes 'cause he figured someone was on the phone. He dialed the number again and the phone rang five times and went to the voicemail again; now he was agitate. Crook sighed deeply and said, "Smooth, dis dude ain't even answering his horn . . . . I know he ain't make me drive out here for nothin'," Crook stressed.

"Be patient dog, Diablo ain't never stood us up—he probably on the horn doin some things," Smooth reasoned.

"I know right, lemme try and call dis dude again."

"Yeah, do that and stop trippin' . . . ."

"Smooth pulled out a pack of Newport's and tapped against his wrist to pack the cigarettes. After he finished packing his cigarettes, he peeled the plastic off the pack and lit one up. Smooth cracked the window slightly so the smoke could go out. Crook dialed the number again and this time someone answered on the third ring.

"Diablo, what's good man . . . . I'm out front papi," Crook told him.

"I'll send someone downstairs no my friend," Diablo replied.

Crook reached in the backseat and grabbed the Nike Duffle bag and passed it to Smooth. Crook pulled his P-89 Ruger from out the stash box and put it in the small of his back. Crook departed from the truck and Smooth followed suit with the duffle bag in his hand. They walked over to the building and walked up the stoop.

A short light-skinned man, with a thick mustache and curly hair, opened the door for them. Crook nodded his head at the Columbian man and walked inside the building. They walked up four flights of stairs and went inside apartment fifty-two, which was the first door on the right. Crook and Smooth took seats on the Ostrich couch in the plush living room. The apartment was immaculate. Crook looked on the wall and saw a descent size picture of Pablo Escobar and Manuel Antonio Noriega, both of them had cigars hanging from their mouths. Crook looked at the television and saw the front of the building outside and up the street on both ends. Diablo had cameras all around the building to keep an eye on the busy street.

A Columbian man with his hair slicked back in a ponytail entered the living room. He was tall, slender, and was clean with a toothpick in his mouth. He was a older man maybe in his early fifties. He wore gold on both wrist, and sported two pinky rings on each finger. He had on blue jeans and a white polo golf shirt with some white air force 1's. He started grinning the moment he saw Smooth and Crook. His comrade that stood behind him did not smile, he stood there mean mugging.

"Crook, what's goin' on my friend . . . ? I see y'all finally made it," Diablo stated.

"Jus' chillin' papi, takin' it one day at a time. We had to take it easy on 95, dem muthafuckin' staties were everywhere . . . ."

"How's life in Boston treating y'all?"

"Couldn't get no better—I'm lovin' it, Diablo! Dis coke I been getting from you been goin' fast, niggas in the hood iz lovin' dis shit!" Crook proclaimed.

"I see the game is treatin' you good my friend. You and Smooth came up a long way . . . ." Diablo continued, "I remember when y'all used to come see me and buy five kilos—now y'all buying twenty of 'em," Diablo said, with a slight grin revealing a gold crown.

Crook started snickering and said, "We've been stackin' and makin' moves, Diablo. It's 'bout time we stepped our game up, I've been waitin my whole life fo' dis day to come."

"We came up from rags to riches, Diablo. I member a few years ago when I didn't have a pot to piss in. I had to sleep in my car 'cause I ain't have nowhere to go. Now I got two cribs—we playin it raw in my city, we got it on lock," Smooth ranted.

Smooth could recall the days when he was down and out with no place to rest his head. He had to sleep in his car every night and wait for a fiend to call him, just to keep food in his mouth and money in his pockets. He showered at fiends houses, and sometimes wore the same clothes for a week straight; times were hard for him. Once he met Crook and started getting money with him, everything altered dramatically.

Diablo pulled out a cigar, lit it up, propped his Nikes on a Mahogany coffee table, and sat back blowing out smoke. He stared at them and didn't say anything, Diablo would get like that whenever he was in deep thought. Two of Diablo's goons stood in each corner of the room watching Crook and Smooth intently. Neither one of them took their eyes off Crook and Smooth. Diablo sat his Cuban cigar down in the astray and looked at one of his goons.

"Buscame los kilos, Tony." (Go get the kilos, Tony)

The short Columbian man with the thick mustache left out the room. Diablo sat there on the couch watching his surveillance on the TV. Tony came back in the room with the Gucci duffle bag and sat it on the floor in front of Diablo.

"Amigo, dis is straight from Bolivia—off each kilo you could make two or three easily," Diablo assured him.

Crook took that thought into consideration. Diablo unzipped the bag and inside there were twenty plastic squares with duct tape around them. Crook retrieved on out the bag and sat it on the coffee table. Smooth took out his shank and sliced open one of the squares and put a dab of coke on his knife, and then put some on his tongue. Smooth's face became numb instantly.

"Damn! That shit iz the real deal," Smooth proclaimed.

"Lemme get a taste of that partner," Crook stated.

Smooth placed coke on the knife for Crook and gave it to him. Crook put some on his finger and placed it on the bottom of his gums, he made a sour facial expression. "Mmmm-hmmm, I think that's the best we got thus far, that shit iz some fire!"

"I tol' you, Crook." Smooth closed his shank and put it back inside his pocket.

"Now where's me money at, Crook?" Diablo asked, cutting strait to the chase.

"My money iz good—I got it all right here inside that bag," Crook replied.

Diablo got off the couch, opened the duffle bag, and saw stacks of money. All the money was neatly stacked with bands around it.

"It's all there, Diablo, that's three hunnit and eighty thou right there in the bag," Crook continued, "I never come short wit the paper . . . ."

"We shall see, my friend. I count all my money 'cause it's business, it's never personal. Tony, go get me the money counter," Diablo demanded.

Tony nodded his head and left out the room. Diablo commenced to taking the money out the duffle bag and began stacking it on the table. Next he took the rubber band off the first stack of money and was prepared to run it through the machine. Tony entered the room with the money counter in his hand, he sat it down on the table in front of Diablo. Tony walked back to the opposite corner of the room and stood there watching Crook and Smooth.

Diablo sat there for twenty minutes counting money thru the money machine. He counted the money twice just to be sure it was all there. He didn't need no miscounts. Crook sat there twirling his fingers getting impatient, he was trying to get the kilos and get out of NY. Crook had people on standby waiting on him, he had money to go collect when he got back.

"Everything is all good my friend," Diablo confirmed, after counting the money.

"Word, now I'm 'bout to call my two home gurls up here," Crook took his Nextel off his hip and hit the alert button.

"Churp! Churp! Crook, you ready for us to come upstairs?"

"Yes, I am baby girl, hurry up please."

"We on our way upstairs, now."

"I'll be waitin," Crook flipped the phone shut.

Crook sat down on the couch and waited for his home girls to come upstairs. The room was silent it seemed as though it was empty. Crook sat there in deep thought thinking about all the times him and Troy used to take trips to NY to cop coke. Troy showed him how to hit the highways and how to transport the drugs. Crook had to snap out of it and focus back on the task that was ahead of him.

"Tony, ves para a bajo y dejas a las mujeres pasal a dentro."

(Tony, go downstairs and let the ladies in," Diablo said.)

"Jefe, ya yo voy para a bajo."

(Boss, I'm going to do it right now," Tony replied)

Tony left the apartment and went downstairs while Crook counted every kilo inside the Gucci Bag to make sure it was twenty of them. Diablo placed all the money back inside the bag and then lit back up his cigar while watching the front of his building on the TV screen. A blue Crown Vic with tints pulled up in front of Diablo's building. Crook got paranoid after seeing the car pull up and park.

"I know that ain't the muthafuckin' police, Diablo."

"That's jus a taxi cab, amigo. Take it easy—Crook, I run dis whole street my friend, nothin' comes down dis street without me knowing . . . ."

Crook stared at the television and observed a Spanish lady getting out of town Crown Vic with bags in her hand. Crook was relieved once he realized it was not the NYPD. There was two light knocks at the door; Diablo walked over to the door, peered thru the peephole, and opened the door after he saw who it was.

"Keisha, the work iz in the bag on the floor," Crook pointed and continued, "Me and Smooth gonna go down to whip and make sure y'all get downstairs safely. You know the routine ma—it's jus like how we do it every time, baby."

Keisha stood there listening to everything he was saying. There were certain rules she had to follow; like put on her seatbelts, drive doing the speed limit, not smoke weed in the car, and take specific highways. But still, Crook had to remind her every trip just to make sure she didn't slip up. The last thing he needed was a glitch in his plan. Keisha was Smooth's down as chick too, and if Smooth told her to do anything, she'd do it.

"Give me a call once you get rid of everything, amigo. Be safe out there traveling on that highway, Crook."

"I sure nuff will. Diablo, thanks fo' everything . . . ."

Crook and Smooth shook hands with their connect before parting from the apartment. They had nothing but respect and love for Diablo. When Crook initially got acquainted with Diablo, it was all business between both of them. But as time progressed, they became very good friends. Diablo was the sole individual that Crook would not betray, he knew if he ever crossed Diablo—it would be crucial; he might lose his whole family.

Diablo nodded his head at them and they out the door. Keisha and Erica stood there in the living room waiting for five minutes to go by before they left. That was how Crook had everything setup whenever he went to see Diablo. Keisha stood there looking at her cell phone waiting for one more minute to go by. Keisha went and picked up the Gucci Bag off the floor, it was about that time.

"Bye Diablo . . . ." Keisha and Erica said unsion.

"Y'all ladies have a nice day," Diablo replied.

Diablo nodded his head at Tony and he escorted the ladies out the door. Diablo's other soldier stood there in the corner never saying a word. He was a certified killer for Diablo; that was what he got paid to do. Diablo was fifty-seven and been in the game since '67. He was still going hard selling coke and heroin all throughout Harlem. Even after Diablo did a ten-year prison stint in Clinton Max, he still came home and sold drugs. He made one phone call and he had coke. His Uncle Alberto fronted him fifty kilos on consignment. Diablo been up and running ever since.

Diablo's name rung bells in five different states besides New York.

Crook watched closely as both girls came walking out the building. To the public's eye they looked like two college girls that were about to take a trip. But little did anyone know, they were mules who transported coke back and forth to different cities. Crook watched his rearview mirror as Keisha put the bag inside the trunk, and then she got inside her car. Crook turned the key on the ignition and followed behind Keisha.

Chapter 12

Crook was pushing his Range Rover to the limit down interstate 95 north. He was switching in and out of lanes trying to keep up with Keisha. She was driving so fast and erratically in front of him and that made him nervous. They were both doing almost a 100mph like it was nothing. Crook was right behind her tailgating not trying to let her get out his sight. He grabbed his Nextel off his lap that was charging in the adapter and alerted Keisha.

"What you want, Crook?" Keisha asked.

"Churp! Churp! Keisha, slow ya stankin ass down some would ya! Ya gonna fuck around and get pulled over if you keep drivin' reckless."

"Aight, I got you—I'm 'bout to slow down some now."

"Please do . . . . I don't need no fucks ups!"

Crook flipped his phone shut and dropped it on his lap. Smooth reached in the astray and sparked up a half of blunt of dro he put out earlier. Crook peered to his right and a Caucasian woman in minivan was smiling at him, he waved at her, and was rising and they were almost back in Massachusetts.

The last three hours Crook been on the highway following behind Keisha the entire time. He didn't mind taking trips to the Big Apple every two weeks. It was just something about Harlem that had him so infatuated with the city. He didn't know if it was all the exclusive clothing and sneaker stores—or Diablo's cheap prices on the coke. Crook put on his right blinker signal and turned off I-95 onto exit 9. They drove down and around the sharp two lanes and they emerged onto route 128. They drove in the slow lane for about two miles and then they got off exit 7.

Keisha drove down route 138 through Canton abiding by all the laws of the road. She knew the State Police were always in the vicinity waiting to snare someone that just got off the highway, hoping they caught someone with vast amounts of drugs. Crook rolled down the driver's side window and with his thumb and forefinger, he flicked out the last of the blunt. Keisha stayed alert watching for speed traps the State Police be having all through Canton and Milton. She knew this road all too well. They were always on the prowl waiting to pull someone over, so whenever she drove through those towns—she was extra careful.

Keisha was a ride or die chic that was down for Crook. She was always down to get paid by any means. She was a certified hood chic that was gutter, she didn't care about nobody but her family and her closest friends; and that was a selective few. Keisha was tall, dark-skinned, with big breast and thick thighs that made her look enticing. Her hair came down to her shoulders and the front was in a bang. Keisha was a bad bitch, every nigga in her hood wanted a piece of her. But Keisha didn't fuck any nigga in the street, you had to be getting some serious money.

Crook and Smooth put them under their wing and molded them to the street life. They turned those girls out even more, they were fucking the shit out them young girls and schooling them to the game. Even though they were both eighteen and still living at their mother's house—they was about making moves and trying to get paid; and that was what Crook loved about them. Crook played them close and only let them see so much. Crook knew he couldn't trust them 'cause if he slipped up they'd probably set him up or run off with a hefty package. Crook believed in karma and knew that what you do can come back to haunt you. That was why he moved so strategic and never trusted nobody.

Crook made sure he hit Keisha with money and took her shopping, he tried to keep a smile on her face all the time 'cause he needed her to make those trips. Smooth always hit Erica off with money and fucked the shit out of her occasionally to always keep her around. That was the main reason Keisha felt so comfortable making the trips, she always had her home-girl accompanying her for the ride. The last thing they needed was some other hustlers scooping Keisha and Erica up and putting them on their team. Erica was a pretty looking light-skinned girl with short red hair. She kept her hair short in finger waves. Erica was short and thick in all the right places and she could suck the skin off a dick and that was a plus in Smooth's eyes.

Since the day they started hitting the highway for Crook, they haven't tried running off once. But still, Crook and Smooth didn't trust either one of them. So that's why they always took precautions and followed Keisha and Erica every time from New York. When Crook used to ride those highways by himself for all those hours, he used to get an eerie feeling in his gut, he didn't trust highways. So that was why he had mules who brought it back for him. Crook couldn't take all those long commutes no more, riding with all those drugs made him paranoid.

Crook glanced up ahead to his left and saw "Welcome to Boston" sign in the middle of the island on Blue Hill Ave in Mattapan Square. He pulled up behind Keisha and stopped at the red-light. The streets were flooded with people on their way to work and school. Crook shook his head in disbelief watching people wait around at bus stops and the green-line trolley stop. He couldn't fathom how people could wake up so early in the morning and go to work for minimum wages. He never wanted that life; he never worked a hard day in his life. The light turned green snapping him out his reverie. Keisha drove straight up the Ave until she got to Walk Hill street and then turned left. Keisha pulled over on her right near Fottler street and parked.

"Smooth, hop in the rental and I'ma follow you to the spot. Tell them hood-rats will get 'em later or somethin."

"Yeah, we definitley gonna get up wit 'em 'cause Erica lookin' right my nig. I'ma have to fuck the shit out that lil bitch toaday!" Smooth smirked at the thought of fucking her.

"Aight, but right now we got dis paper to get bruh, it's M.O.B till the day I die."

"I can dig it, lemme go tell these breezies we got shit to do. That nigga Backs still need dem two things, he been blowin' my jack up lookin' fo' work.

"Word, so that's a hunnit stacks we gotta go collect from these niggas, I needs that! C'mon let's get goin' playboy . . . ." Crook said, ready to get to the money

Smooth stepped out the Range Rover and walked over to the Maxima. "Erica, I'ma see you later on baby-girl, make sure you be around I'm tryna get some of that . . . ." Smooth said, snickering.

"I'll be around Smooth, jus' holla at me ok. Don't bullshit either 'cause I need some of that dick daddy . . . ." Erica replied, with a seductive look on her face.

Smooth liked the way she was licking her lips at him, his dick was starting to get hard. "I sure nuff will sexy. Make sure you wear somethin' erotic."

"Tell that nigga Crook to get at me, Smooth."

"I got you, Keisha, I'm holla at y'all . . . ."

Keisha and Erica walked up the stairs and went inside the apartment. Smooth hopped in the Maxima and drove off. Crook followed behind him all the way to Oakley street where they both unloaded the bricks at. Smooth pulled into the driveway and parked, while Smooth parked across the street. Smooth retrieved the duffle bag out the trunk and went inside the first floor apartment.

"I'm 'bout to call these niggas up and see what's good now, then after I go serve 'em I'm gonna go see wifey, dis bitch been trippin' . . . ."

"Do that Crook, I'll be handlin' business while you on punishment." Smooth joked.

"Nigga fuck you, ain't nah bitch got me on lock."

Smooth twisted his face up at Crook and said, "Stop frontin' Crook—you know Gina got that ass on lock fool, you and I both know that. But it's all gravy though, I'ma be takin' care of all these niggas who need work, go spend some time wit ya family," Smooth insisted.

Crook took out his cell phone and placed a call. The phone rang a few times and a familiar voice answered.

"Yo, what's poppin' doggy dog?"

"Backs, you still tryna get right? Everything is all good big homey," Crook assured him.

"Foshow, bring me two gallons of Ice cream my nigga."

"Where you at, Backs?"

"I'm 'round my way right now, come by the crib. Yo, you got smoke too?"

"Nah, jus' a lil somethin to smoke. But I'm 'bout to be on my way, one!"

Crook hung up the phone and made on more call. Smooth took three kilos out the duffle bag and set them on the kitchen table. Then Smooth put the duffle bag back inside the bedroom closet and locked the door. Smooth came back into the kitchen and saw that Crook was engaged in deep conversation.

"Dee, what's poppin' fam? How's everything out there in Southie?"

"Man . . . . it's dry is fuck out here—nah nigga got work out here I the streets cuz, when you—" Crook cut him off.

"I'm good now Dee, you still needed those two gallons of ice cream, right?"

"Yeah, when you coming? I got my peoples on standby waitin', and dem fizzos iz goin' crazy blowin up my jack lookin' fo' some butter . . . ."

"Gimme like a half, Dee, I'll call you when I'm out front. You in hot ass Old Colony Projects, right?"

"Yep, I'm at 409 Mercer street. It's cool over here where I'm at, Crook."

"I got you Dee, see you in a minute, one!" Crook shook his head at the last words that came out Dee's mouth. Crook already knew about those racist projects where it was predominately Irish people.

Crook got off the phone satisfied that he had two sales lined up. Selling four kilos at 27 thousand a wop, he about to clear over 100 thousand. He put four kilos on the kitchen table inside two separate Save-A-Lot bags and left out the backdoor. Smooth locked the backdoor and unlocked the doors on the Maxima. Crook got in the passenger seat while Smooth drove.

"Smooth, go to Southie first, then we could go see Backs after."

Smooth nodded his head and backed out the driveway, drove forward and took a right turn down Geneva avenue. Crook looked out the passenger window watching all the up and coming gangbangers stand around on corners. Things were changing and it was a whole new era of dudes on the streets trying to make a name for themselves. Crook sat there in silence while Smooth drove through the streets of Dorchester.

Smooth pulled into the Old Colony Projects and drove down Mercer street. He parked in front of building 409. Crook grabbed the Save-A-Lot bag and stepped out the car with Smooth. They walked passed two white ladies sitting on the stoop and walked inside the building. Crook could not comprehend how Dee could hustle in South Boston around all those white folks. The town was predominately white and Crook didn't feel comfortable in the area, but still, he would go through there and deliver whatever Dee wanted.

They ascended three flights of stairs to third floor, and Crook knoocked on the first apartment on the right. The door came open and they went inside the apartment.

"What's good in the hood, 'bout time you got right Crook. A nigga been dry for a while now dog," Dee stated.

Crook gave him dap and said, "Well I'm right now so that's all that matters. You got that fifty-four stacks fo' me? I need strait paper—I ain't takin' no shorts, I'm hurtin' right now, Dee."

"My paper's good pimpin', it's on the kitchen table."

Crook walked in the kitchen and saw stacks of hundred dollar bills laid out on the kitchen table. Crook sat down and started counting all the money. Crook never took nobody's word, he always counted his money himself to be sure. Crook counted the money twice and then put it inside his pocket. He gave Dee three's and headed to the door.

"Y'all niggas be easy out there," Dee said, while clasping hands with them.

"Holla at us soon as you get right, Dee, niggas is in a rush make dis gotta move," Smooth replied, and then walked out the door following behind Crook.

Smooth started the car and drove off. He turned left on East Eight street and drove another block over and then turned left on Patterson Way. He drove through Old Colony Projects and turned left at the end of the road and merged onto Columbia road. Smooth stopped at the stop sign at the rotary, looked both ways, and proceeded doing the speed limit. Smooth took a left onto route 93 south and went down the expressway. Crook rolled down the passenger window a spat out the window.

"Some, slow down some, I think dem fuckin' staties iz behind us. Jus' keep drivin' and don't look in ya fuckin' rearview . . . ."

Smooth did as told and maintained doing the speed limit. A State Trooper hopped in the fast lane and zoomed by them. Smooth sighed out relief and grinned.

"I'm getting' off dis highway, I hate dem staties . . . ." Smooth said, and put on his right blinker signal.

"Stop being so fuckin' paranoid! They ain't worrying 'bout us, all they really want is donuts," Crook said, snickering.

"Yeah, whatever you say biggie . . . ."

Smooth turned off exit 12 and then merged on Galivan Boulevard. He drove straight to Mattapan taking a few side streets to avoid the traffic and the law. Crook pulled out his cell phone and placed a call.

"Backs, I'm comin' through the square right now. I'll be there in a minute."

"Aight, I'ma see you when you get here my nig."

Crook hung up the phone and placed it on his hip. "Take this left down the Harmon street cominu' up," Crook said.

Smooth turned left down the one-way street and then took a left at the end of the street onto Greenfield road. Smooth pulled up in front of a brown double-decker and turned off the car. They both stepped out the car and was greeted by a tall man wearing a Greenbay Packers Jersey and matching cap. The big man smiled showing a mouth full of gold teeth once he saw Crook and Smooth.

"What's the verdict dog . . . . what y'all niggas been up too?" Backs gave them three's.

"Same ole shit jus' another day, Backs, I can't call it." Crook had to look up at the big man who was towering over him by six inches.

"Backs, I see you out here doin' ya thing. That's what I like to see . . . ." Smooth continued, "You got shit locked 'round the "G" I see, it's gwop like that 'round here?"

"Getting' money iz all I know my nigga, it's good paper 'round here, but my niggas won't shop wit anyone . . . . they fucks wit me hard. Come y'all let's go in the crib, the block hot right now. One of dem fuck boys jus got they shit pushed back the other day. Nigga came through tryna stunt and got that ass touched!" Backs said, with a grin. Crook and Smooth followed behind him up the stairs to the second floor.

Backs controlled his block on Greenfield road. He had it flooded with guns and drugs. He had a slew of youngsters who would let their pistols go off he gave them the word. Backs was all about getting his money and trying to stay under the radar from the law. Backs and Crook been knowing each other for years and had love for each other. They were real close. Smooth was also close to Backs too. The trio sat down in the living room and started conversing.

"I hate to be in a rush my nigga, but I gotta make these moves, Backs. I ain't see wifey in coupla days, my bitch been trippin'."

"Do you 'cause I gotta do some serious whippin' in a minute," Backs replied.

Crook gave him the Save-a-Lot bag and Backs took both squares out and sat them on the table. Backs nodded his head and started snickering.

"Hol' up real quick, Crook, lemme go get dis change fo' you in my room." Backs walked out the living room and went to his bedroom.

Backs came back into the living room with a stack of money in a brown paper bag. He passed it to Crook and Smooth sat there watching his partner counting the money. Crook counted fifty-four thousand and it all was in hundreds. He placed the rubber band back around the money and placed it in the brown paper bag.

"Yo, I'ma holla at you Backs, be safe my nigga." Crook gave him three's.

"Aight, y'all niggas be easy mane . . . . I'ma get wit y'all." Backs let them out the house.

Crook jumped in the driver's seat and drove off. Smooth lit up a cigarette and blew rings of smoke out his mouth. Crook honked the horn at a couple of dudes who was chilling on the corner of Radcliff road.

"Smooth, I'm goin' to my crib, go put the money up and take care of everyone who needs some work. I'll be falling back for a few days."

"I got you Crook, jus' go home and be wit ya family, I got dis . . . ."

Chapter 13

Angel spent his entire day collecting money from all his main customers. His empire had now expanded there wasn't a corner in the city that Angel's product wasn't being sold. Diablo's coke was so good that it had the same effects as Frank Lucas Blue Magic. He seen major results from his customers needing a package sooner than he used to serving them. The money kept piling in his duffle bags he kept stashed away.

The South End stay flooded with his product, Angel was almost certain he owned the neighborhood, when it came to getting this money selling drugs. He always wondered but never asked Crook where he'd get this product from, he didn't want to get accustomed to Crook even though they've been dealing with each other nearly a decade. One of the reasons Angel still hadn't attempted to take Crook's life was 'cause of his connects.

Meanwhile, everything with Montana Bags, his cousin Gee, and his regular customers were going up in sales. The money was always on point and never a dollar short. He was proud of his team. Life couldn't get any better. As Angel drove around the city trying to sneak up on his workers—he received a phone call from Crook.

"What it iz, partna!" Angel answered.

"I jus' came back to the bean, you know I got dem mixtapes fo' you," Crook said, referring to drugs.

"Word! Well, I gotta collect first, you know how I do, Crook."

"Aight, Angel . . . . oh yeah, man I need to holla at you bout some real shit, and I ain t tryna do dis ova the jack, you know what I mean?" Asked Crook.

"Yeah, I hear what you sayin'. Meet me at Carlo's bar on Hancock, at like three."

"Nah, fam . . . ." Crook laughed and continued, "I'm tired as shit, I need some sleep. You know how it is comin' from the city. That shits a long as drive." Crook stated. "How 'bout six pm that's enough time fo' me, plus Gina's on my ass about spending time wit her and my daughter. Is that cool?" he added.

"Yeah, ain't nothin' to a boss." Angel confirmed.

Angel hung up the cell phone and headed towards Washington Park on Martin Luther King Blvd where he played men's league for the last five years every Saturday. He played a couple pickup games then he departed so he could prepare for the rendezvous with Crook. He knew Crook was all about money. That's the only thing he liked about Crook, other than that he was just a grimy nigga.

Angel spent the last hour showering and getting prepared. He always kept himself well groomed. He shaved and put on a shower cap so his tight braids would not come loose. If so Carolina would be furious. She was a hair cosmetologists but due to Angel's lavish lifestyle, she never felt the need to go to school for it. On her own time she always did her mother hair. She was the ideal hair stylist.

As Angel was getting ready to the house he began wondering if he should bring his gun, then the thought occurred to him: "I always got it so why wouldn't I bring it now," he laughed. He walked down the corridor and grabbed four duffle bags and them inside his four foot wall safe then left out the house.

It was about 6:17, Angel had a few drinks then he recognized Crook who was flooded with jewelry walk in. As Crook approached him, Angel stood up as the two greeted each other in a hand shake and hug. Crook also admired Angel's jewelry as they spoke a few minutes about fashion. Crook then immediately cut all the small talk and jumped into business.

"Angel we been dealing fo' a minute," Crook started.

Angel immediately thought to himself, *"I know dis nigga ain't 'bout to boost his prices up on me . . . ."*

Crook continued, "I'm thinkin' it's time to expand crazy! Go hard or go home. I own dis city, Angel. But with Smooth, and your help we can own dis fuckin' world! I know you don't know the connect, but I think it's time you meet him." Crook requested.

"Yes! Just what I wanted," Angel thought to himself. "Well I'ma sleep on dis Crook. I like to plan my next step," Angel replied.

"But Angel there isn't nothin' to think about, dis iz big bucks we could make but I have a problem. So there is a twist to dis, but in ya favor." Crook explained.

"I'm listening . . . ." Angel complied.

"I think the feds are watching me for some reason and tryna build a case against me, but I have no idea who is snitching on me," Crook stated.

"Snitching about what?" Asked Angel.

"Drugs, my kingdom nigga." Crook lied.

"Go on I'm listenin . . . ."

"I want you to meet my connect. Smooth already knows him, and I want you to control my work and possibly manage my money and in reward I'll pay you $100,000 a year for ya services and you can get ya own supply through him fo' 19 a key my nigga," Crook explained.

Angel sat in his chair and slouched back, he knew he couldn't refuse the deal it was too good to be true, now he had to play his cards right. He didn't want to seem desperate. He remained silent he was in deep thought. Crook sat back and continued to persuade Angel as if he was a sales person trying to sell merchandise.

"Angel come on man, it's not a bad deal at all. You can't refuse dis, I need you dog I can't afford to lose dis. If I do down, no connect, no good work, plus you got Smooth to back you up. Smooth would kill forty cops in front of the Boston Police Headquarters if he had too," Crook proclaimed.

"Let me sleep on it, Crook, I'll have my paper ready too. I'll give you my answer.

"Aight, Angel, you need to make up ya mind . . . ." Crook replied, still unsatisfied.

Crook left two hundred dollars on the bar desk and left Carlo's bar. Angel continued to sit back and drink as he was in deep thought, now he wondered, what investigation was Crook under and who was snitching on him? Every possible thought came to an end with a block. Crook was silent killer, it had to be with the murder of Troy and Karen. But who would be brave enough to testify against Crook?

Angel also knew the connect was in New York City. His mind was made up soon as Crook mentioned it, but he didn't want to seem desperate, he definitely played a good role trying to hide his excitement. He really didn't want to make that decision without confronting Money Bags about it. Angel had envisioned this day for a long time. The new millennium was on its way he had big goals. Carolina and him had also discussed having kids together. She was definite that Angel would be her children's father. He couldn't get any younger so he thought why not. First he made it his goal to get rid of Crook.

Angel drove down Hancock street running a red-light in the intersection of Columbia road and Hancock at the Strand Theater. He then took a left and merged onto Dudley street, Upham's Corner. As he drove up Dudley street he started realizing how time was flying by. Everything seemed like it was moving so fast around him lately.

"This iz what life has to offer . . . . there's gotta be more," he thought.

When he got to Backwoods Pizza he was directed by patrolman to follow the traffic cones. There had been a shooting and yellow tapes were everywhere. Two bodies were covered with white sheets and shell cases were identified by yellow mini cones, while Homicide detectives took photographs. Boston was becoming the worst, every street were feuding with the next street over frivolous things. Project buildings were warring with other projects. Angel knew after the hit it was time to go. Miami, Atlanta, Los Angeles, anywhere but Boston was fine with him.

Angel drove through Roxbury until he reached his destination, Money Bags apartment. Money Bags lived in

Ruggles street projects even though he was getting money. It wasn't the principles of life that he chased, he loved the hood. Despite the money he was making, he couldn't leave the project life. He was a legend in the hood that's how he got his name "Money Bags". Angel walked into the apartment with his own set of keys that Money Bags had made him. All though Money Bags mother lived with him, Angel was the only dude he trusted with their lives.

"Hey ma, how you doin?" Angel greeted Money's mother.

"I'm still breathing my child . . . ." Grace replied.

"Where's my brother? Is he home?"

"You know that lazy bum still sleeping. I wish he was more like you." Grace embraced Angel.

"He's fine ma, chill out. Here, next time you go out buy yourself something," Angel gave Grace five-hundred dollars.

"oh god! Bless you child I'll pay for every night," Grace promised.

"Thanks ma, I might really need it, oh yeah don't tell Eric about the money.

"Ok, I won't say a word," Grace winked.

Angel walked through the apartment to find Money's bedroom door. Before he entered the room he could smell of marijuana coming from inside. He shook his head in disbelief then smiled as he turned the doorknob. "What's good cuz," Angel greeted him.

"Ain't shit, you right on time I was about to start dis smoking session. Rap City's on too," Money Bags replied.

"Seems like you been started dis session," Angel laughed. "Yo man, me and Crook had a nice real talk today, but I need ya honest opinion," Angel asked.

"Big Pun's a beast lyrically, Angel, I gotta listen to dis freestyle hol' on."

Money Bags was so into the show he looked like a 5-year old watching cartoons. Angel had felt really upset for being cut off, he walked to the televison and turned it off as he grabbed the blunt out Money's hand.

"Come on dog, you know I fucks wit Pun!" Money Bags sniped.

"Well dis iz more important, it's 'bout the connect!" Angel began to explain. "Crook want's me to go to N.Y. wit him and meet his connect Diablo, but you there's a twist. I gotta get his work to our city from N.Y. and I get my bricks for the same price he does," Angel proclaimed.

"Why would you do that?" Asked Money Bags.

"What you mean . . . ." Angel was puzzled.

"I thought you hate Crook, now you want to move and deliver his work?"

"It's 'bout the connect, bruh, are you ridin' wit me on dis one or not? After I meet him I want you to get dis goin' wit me," Angel requested.

"Nigga if it's 'bout money you know I'm down, but be careful my nigga."

"You already know . . . ."

The two of them hung out for an hour or more smoking purple haze. The blunt literally had them dazed sitting there watching Rap City re-runs. Money Bags loved watching Rap videos when he was high 'cause everything seemed more slow to him. He would catch on to what rappers were rapping about. He was always alert even though he was high. The weed calmed his nerves and made him feel good.

"What the fuck was that?!" Angel asked.

"What the fuck you tallkin' 'bout? Lemme find out you tweekin'."

"Nah! Somethin' fell down, it looked like a body." Angel walked to the window, "Oh shit! Look Money . . . ." Angel pointed down.

"Damn, that's Lou. I knew they was gonna get him . . . ."

Money Bags looked over his head to see who was on the roof and he was met with a familiar face, Buttah. Buttah and Lou was going to court for second substance on gun charges, Lou's second and Buttah's second.

"Man, Buttah told Lou he'd bail him out in time to see his son's birth if Lou took the raps for the guns and he still hasn't done that. He bailed him out for $100,000 that's a lot of money, plus they would have hit Lou wit 18-months. He didn't keep his side of the deal," Money Bags looked down at Lou.

Lou's lifeless body stood there clashed into the back windshield of a Mustang. Neighbors all surrounded the car looking up for suspects. It was too late Buttah was long gone. He was about to get hit with 5-7 years, therefore he was feeling remorseful.

"Damn, Lou should've have took that . . . . I can understand where Buttah's comin' from that's crazy. Never make deals you can't comply wit," Angel said and continued, "I'm out cuz. I ain't tryna be 'round all these cops when they get here, plus you know they right 'round the corner. I'm jus' glad that wasn't my whip," Angel shook his head and walked away from the window.

"Aight, Angel, lemme know what you decide on doin'."

"Aight one . . . ." Angel left.

Angel left the apartments on Ruggles street and could hear sirens wailing really close by. The police headquarters were less than two minutes away. He had a decision to make and money to count up. If he was going to go to New York he wanted to make sure his money was right to get enough work to last long enough until he killed Crook. He always dreamed of the day, but he knew the longer he rocked Crook to sleep, the more comfortable he got around Angel.

Angel had a few drinks earlier and he was still high off the purple haze. He had four bags of money to organize. He had $228,000 to put aside. He thought to himself, *"I'm going to just get 12 bricks and I might be done with this game, who knows . . . I member when I started with 2bricks, now I got enough for twenty."* Angel thought to himself and laughed.

Chapter 14

After a couple of years of high school Jerome was now on his way to college and his relationship with Mercedes had blossomed. Jerome had now also entered the drug game and he was really growing up, it's been over a decade since his parents were murdered. His anger was taken out on the streets and people who owed him money. After a tremendous hustle throughout his high school years, Jerome was now an upcoming name in the game. He was in his prime, a senior in high school and a marijuana dealer. He was so deep in the game that he was purchasing twenty-six pounds of mid-grade weed for nine-hundred and fifty a pound. At his pace he was doing well for someone in high school.

Jerome had most of his success that year in '02 without the help of Angel. He purchased a fresh off the lot, late model Acura TL with a custom installed street pilot navigation system. Angel was furious when he found out that Jerome started hustling, but Carolina convinced him to show Jerome the ropes instead of allowing him to get tangled in the game. Angel hated to admit it but he was wrong also 'cause Jerome had been accustomed to seeing Angel moving weight. Some nights Angel would sit with Jerome and let him hit a blunt of weed and tell him how much of a street legend his father was. Now how could he stop the son of a legend from getting money—it was in his blood. He showed

Jerome how to move in the streets. Carolina began teaching him how to cut coke and he was a quick learner.

With the help of Carolina and Angel at his side, Jerome began expressing his relationship with Mercedes, who he been in a four relationship with. Carolina of course had met Angel the same way and she told Jerome as long as he treated her correctly, she would stay by his side no matter what. Jerome took the advice and secured it. He wanted Mercedes to be the same down ass chick that Carolina was.

Jerome was the man at high school, all the drug dealers at Charlestown High bought ounces and half pounds off him. He sold work to guys who had each high schools on lock; Madison Park, East Boston high, Dorchester high, and even High Park high. He was making a great deal of money. For the senior prom, Jerome rented an all white Hummer limousine for him, Mercedes, an picked up some classmates to takeout. They all got picked up and had a ball at Lombardo's in Randolph, where most of the city's high school go.

Jerome was learning from the best how to keep his woman happy. Him and Angel would take trips to Copley Presidential Center and ball out in Neiman Marcus blowing stacks like it was nothing. Then they would stop at Tiffany's for their woman. Angel began telling Jerome he has to watch his surrounding and really find out who Mercedes is involved with, but Jerome had fallen in love with her. Angel was cracking jokes when Jerome had told him that he and Mercedes had lost their virginities to each other on prom night. As they walked through the mall they continued to talk about his special night.

Time was running out until school let out, then it was off to college. Mercedes had received a four-year Scholarship to Umass Boston and she decided to study medicine. Jerome on the other hand decided he would pass. He became so involved with money that he felt no need in pursuing further education. He had a safe full of cash and jewelry, so school was the last thing on his mind. On the last week of school Jerome started collecting all his money from dudes he dealt with at school. Attendance on the last week were usually poor but somehow he felt dudes were trying to dodge him.

While standing in the hallways of unit C, he was anxious for one of his clients to come pick his gown up for graduation which he had no choice but to come in school and pick it up, or he wouldn't be able to participate. Joe had been dodging his phone calls for the last three days. He owed Jerome close to three thousand for four pounds. Joe had a surprised look on his face when he saw Jerome standing in the dead hallways by himself. Joe knew immediately that Jerome meant business.

"Ayo, Joe, what's good bro, what's been the holdup wit my mula?"

"Man, listen I was—" Joe started.

"Nah, you listen! Bitch ass nigga you thought since school was out you was gonna beat me, right?"

"Rome, cut it out, I get money. Plus, you ain't even built like that so all that raw shit needs to stop," Joe insulted him.

"What you sayin' nigga?!" Jerome stood there mean mugging him.

"You heard me so stop actin' tuff," Joe replied.

Joe sucked his teeth and turned his back as Jerome took out his .38 revolver in the empty camera less hallway. Jerome walked up on him from behind and began beating him over the head with the pistol and then dragged him into the bathroom. Once in the bathroom, Jerome put his gun on his waist and started stomping Joe out with his Nike ACG boots leaving prints on Joe's face.

"Stupid muthafucka! You know who I am?!" Jerome requested, "I'm a fuckin' boss, you fuckin wit!" He added.

As Jerome continued his assault, a student walked into the severe beating that Joe was receiving, as he seen what was happening he turned around and exited the restroom without any words. He knew not to snitch or he'd be next. Jerome took his rings, a wad of money, which was more than Joe owed him. Then he took Joe's cuban links chain.

"Have a good summer bitch!" Jerome spat on him and left.

Joe was left for dead in the bathroom bleeding profusely. Jerome had seriously injured him with that pistol. But Jerome was taught by Angel to never take shorts and never let another man sport his money. He exited the building and headed to the projects where he paid a fiend for residential parking, due to no parking. He got into his Acura TL, threw his revolver into the stash box, cracked the sunroof, and sped off never returning to school again. Graduation was two days away and he had all his money, his girlfriend, life couldn't get any better.

Graduation was held at Northeastern Campus. Gloria, Carolina, Angel, Money Bags, and a couple of Mercedes relatives attended. Jerome's two cousins Tyrell and Tyrone was also there to support their little cousin, it was a happy moment in their lives. They had accomplished something that many teens in the city don't. Mercedes was at her best, going to Umass Boston on a four year Scholarship. Jerome was at his prime. Joe didn't attend the graduation and wasn't surprise.

After the graduation, Mercedes mother took pictures of her daughter and Jerome. Mercedes had told her mother all about her boyfriend. Mercedes and her mother kept everything a secret about her boyfriend, while her father was over protective. Mercedes father didn't attend the graduation 'cause he was buying her a new car for her accomplishments. Tyrone invited Mercedes and Jerome to dinner at Friday's restaurant down the street in Brigham's Circle. Angel and Gloria had been proud of Jerome and was happy to meet Mercedes. Carolina offered to hangout with Mercedes and go shopping sometime and the group all agreed.

Tyrone and Tyrell were inner city kids accustomed to the street life. They also played roles in the drug game and they were natural born killers. They loved the fact that they were Troy Jenkins nephews 'cause their uncles legacy played a big role, motivating them to live larger than life. They had their own apartments and they had Mattapan booming with coke and weed.

Jerome and Mercedes had a good time at Friday's with his cousins. They ate and celebrated with lots of food and desert. Tyrone started kicking it with his little cousin, who was being named on the streets as the new comer coming up. Jerome was unaware that his status was changing and his name was ringing bells. But if his older cousin knew, there was no sense in lying.

"Yo cuz, I heard you been on the scene in these streets," Tyrell said.

"Yeah, lil somethin' here, somethin' there," Jerome replied.

"Word on the street iz ya movin' lots of weight and ya man's, Angel . . . . man listen, that nigga get money cuz," Tyrone added.

"Yeah, Angel do his thing, he fuck wit da best ya know, me!" Jerome joked.

"Man you need to start fuckin' wit us, plus we family man! And we can start fuckin' wit Angel." Tyrell explained.

"I'll see what he says cuz, plus I'll put in word for y'all."

"Well what about you, Mercedes, where do you stay?" asked Tyrone.

"I stay in Medford with my mom and dad. I kind of have a feeling my dad got me a car today, but I don't know yet. I hope he did." She replied.

"Who's ya dad?" asked Tyrone.

"My father's name is Christopher Walker, many people know him as "Crook".

Jerome continued to drink strawberry lemonade slush as his cousins continued to get to know his pretty girlfriend. When Mercedes said "Crook", the two brothers looked at each other in disbelief; they nor Jerome had no idea that Crook murdered Jerome's parents. Crook had become a legend on the streets, his name always buzzed and Jerome stood dumbfounded that his cousins recognized Mercedes father who was a notorious drug kingpin.

"OG Crook?" the brothers chimed.

"Uh yah . . . ." She replied with no street knowledge.

"Ya father iz a legend on the streets—you jus' don't know it girl!" Tyrone said.

"I guess . . . ." She replied.

The two brothers did not know that Crook was Troy's right hand man and neither did Mercedes nor Jerome. They continued talking about Crook and Jerome learned a lot. They even convinced him to meet Mercedes Father, but Jerome always avoided it. Plus, he just met Gina for the first time.

"I'll think about it baby," Jerome said.

"You always say that . . . . pleaaasssee . . . ?"

"I really will. I swear Mercedes I am," Jerome lied.

Tyrone paid the bill and left the waitress a hundred dollar tip. The waitress was ecstatic after receiving the enormous tip. The brothers had enough money to blow; therefore, it wasn't nothing to them 'cause they were high rollers. As they exited the restaurants, they took flight right out to the parking lot. Tyrell had a black BMW 745 and Jerome was excited to see his family getting money.

"Damn cuz that's how you doin' it?" That's clean right there!"

"Yeah lil daddy only the best. Oh yeah, before I forget, I'ma need to see you later on, strictly business cutty . . . ." Tyrell winked.

"Aight cuz I got you."

"Aye Mercedes, ya boy needs a friend ASAP," Tyrone added.

"I'll see what I can do," Mercedes lied.

Jerome waved to his cousins as they pulled off in the BMW. The whole time on the highway, Jerome kept wondering what his cousin wanted to talk to him about. After Jerome dropped Mercedes off, he called his cousin back to see what the business was all about.

"What's good cuz? What you wanna holla at me for?"

"We going to the club at midnight and you goin' too, we ain't done celebrating."

"Club! Nigga you forgettin' I'm only eighteen."

"Rome, we get into every club now 'cause we twenty-one, but we been hitting the club since sixteen, off the strength of uncle Troy," Tyrell stated.

"My father?"

"Rome, ya pop's was a don he owned the city. We get so much bein' his nephews, even bitches throw pussy at us . . . ."

"Well what do I wear? Is there a code?"

"Man, you can wear anything you want . . . . ya Troy Jenkins Jr, you better start acting like it cuz. Oh yeah, bring a pistol jus' in case these fuck boys wanna act stupid."

"Man what about security, dog?"

"Rome! For the las' time don't worry man, we got dis cuz," Tyrell hung up.

<hr />

Jerome went home and got dressed. He put on some wheat Timberlands, Evisu jeans, and a black eight ball leather jacket. On his way out the house he called his cousin back. It was about 11:15pm, every student from Charlestown high was partying in the city. Jerome was ready he had five stacks in his pocket and he was feeling good.

"Where you want me to meet you cuz?" Jerome asked.

"Tremont street, club Aria, in the theater district downtown."

"Aight, I'ma hit you up when I get down there."

Jerome drove downtown and the night was beautiful. He loved the city at night time. As he continued driving he sparked a blunt and got high to start his night. He parked his car on Tremont street in the handicap section and put Gloria's handicap sticker on his windshield. He was greeted by his cousins.

"Ok cuz I see you fresh and all," Tyrone said.

"I try man, you know how I do . . . ."

As they got the door, the bouncer automatically knew the familiar face of Jerome who resembled his father. He had a face expression like he'd seen a ghost, Jerome became nervous.

"Damn! You look like ya father lil man. He was a great friend of mine. God bless his soul and same fo' ya mama. Never hesitated to ask fo' anything, ya hear me?" the bouncer told him.

"Aight, I wont homie . . ." Jerome nodded his head.

"I tol' you cuz uncle Troy was the man!" Tyrone added

"I see . . . ." Jerome said.

"You boys are all set go 'head in and stay safe, and lil man what's ya name again?"

"Rome." He answered coldly.

The trio entered the club flossing, the first thing they did was hit the bar. This was Jerome's first time in the club he wasn't familiar, they immediately shut the bar down and bought it out. All the females in the club started mugging them. Jerome had no time for hoes, he was about cash and the only girl he loved besides his mother, was Mercedes and Gloria of course.

While Jerome had his back to the bar, he observed Joe in VIP section. He immediately told his cousins that Joe was a problem. To make matters worse, he was sporting Joe's chain he robbed him for. Jerome was dazed off the Hennessey, he excused himself and went to the bathroom. As he cut through the dance floor, Joe spotted him and followed. After Joe the twins also followed.

Jerome took a nice long piss and felt untouchable like what can Joe possibly do. He didn't want no parts of the Jenkins. Jerome was nice and wavy off the liquor. He didn't even feel like he could drive. Once in the stall he heard a door squeak open thinking nothing of it.

"What up fuck boy! You thought you'd get away wit dat shit, bitch!" Joe walked up behind him.

"Yeah bitch nigga! I'ma dog you know me," Jerome replied.

"I think you got somethin' that belongs to me, right?" Joe asked, raising his gun to Jerome's head.

"Yeah! Dis bitch!" Tyrell interrupted with his pistol out. Bang! Bang! Bang! Bang! Bang! Shots rang out from Tyrell's pistol.

Blood went all over Jerome's face and he was now aware of his surroundings. All three cousins ran out the restroom with their pistol in hand. The club was already being evacuated after the first couple of shots. Tyrone drove his own C-class Benz and Tyrell left Jerome's TL. Jerome thanked his cousin for saving his life.

"Yo cuz good looks back there, I was sleepin'."

"Rome, you gotta keep ya eyes open, I does dis foreal," Tyrell replied.

Joe was left for dead in the club shot seven times; three times behind the head, once in the cheekbone, once in the jaw, and twice in his left shoulder blades piercing his heart. Jerome laid low at his cousin's crib until the next day. It was too hot to leave the spot. So much for a graduation celebration!

Chapter 15

Jerome woke up in a unknown apartment and he noticed blood all over his clothes and boots, he quickly grabbed his gun off his waist. He completely forgot about his cousins, and the night at the club. He opened the door to a bedroom and seen Tyrell knocked out asleep. At that point he put the gun down and quickly changed into some of Tyrone's clothes which fit perfect. As he left the house he told his cousins to get rid of the dirty gun used in Joe's murder. He definitely didn't want his cousins going down for a body he was responsible for. After that night Jerome took big perspectives about his cousins. He never seen his cousins in action. Now he understood that blood is thicker than water, 'cause if it wasn't for his cousins, Joe would have him killed.

On the drive home Jerome started thinking about meeting Mercedes family, especially her father who he'd never heard of. How could he not know about Crook who was a street legend. His cousins knew who Crook was. He started wondering if Angel knew him, besides Angel was a street legend already. There was only one way to find out, he never met her father so he would leave that suggestion to Angel. He could always go to Angel for advice on just about anything.

Jerome walked into the apartment and noticed Angel counting money on the table. He smiled at Angel and commented, "That's what I like to see, money!"

"What's good lil homie?" Angel asked. "How was your right?" he added.

"Ah man, Angel! We had to cook dis fool las' night. He almost murked the kid."

"You talkin' 'bout that nigga that got hit up at club Aria?"

"Yeah! How you know bruh?"

"That shit's all over the news and Boston Herald . . . ."

"Angel, that was scram ass dude who owed me three stacks . . . . he tried to act tough at the club and Tyrell slumped the nigga and left him stankin'!" Jerome told him.

"Rome, you gotta be careful man, I get worried bro I ain't tryna lose you too. The streets is crazy," Angel pleaded.

"Angel, I understand but I can't let another man disrespect my pockets 'cause when he does that, I jus' ain't a man." Jerome explained.

Jerome went to the kitchen and greeted Carolina with a kiss on her cheeks. After he grabbed a bottle of Corona to balance his hangover from the night before.

"Eeeww! Don't kiss me I don't know where ya lips been last night you whore!" Carolina smiled as she joked.

"Stop it lina, you know there's only one girl for me and that's Mercedes-Benz," he laughed.

As Jerome walked back to the living room where Angel had been counting money, he sat on the couch and grabbed stacks to help Angel put his money in piles of ten thousands preparing for New York.

"Yo, Angel, what you think 'bout me meeting Mercedes peoples? She been stressin' the fact that schools out and I should meet her family if I want to have her around all the time," Jerome said.

"Well that's a good step but you gotta watch how you present yourself. The first time they meet you, you will tell 'em exactly ya intentions, so I see why not."

"Yeah, but its jus' her pops. He's supposed to be some type of street legend, Tyrone and Tyrell knows of him. But if he's a street nigga, I don't think he's gonna feel me," Jerome said, while wrapping a rubber band around another stack.

"Well if you like Mercedes and you in love you gotta face the music lil daddy, but who's her pops I gotta know him if he's a street nigga?"

"Damn, um, oh I remember his name is Chris, but everyone call him "Crook".

Angel completely froze up and lost count of where he left off in his money. He never expected this day to come until he had put Crook down in the dirt himself. Now he stood before Jerome who had no idea that Crook was Troy's partner. Time was up Crook had to die. Angel could not live with Crook taking Jerome out too. It was written in a book Crook had to go.

"Crook?" Angel asked.

"Yeah, you know him?" Jerome asked.

"Yeah we do business sometimes . . . ." Angel confirmed. "I don't think he would approve of you dating Mercedes, Rome he's a hood nigga give it a month or two and try," Angel said, disgusted.

"Aight whoadie!" Jerome answered.

Angel only told Jerome to fall back from the meeting fearing Crook would kill him, but only wanted time to kill Crook. He could not take that chance to let Jerome meet Crook. He had to put in a big order then kill Crook, who was in New York copping more work. Angel's day had been destroyed. He was tired from collecting money from his local hustlers, but to actually find and meet the day Crook would meet Jerome made him sick to his stomach.

As Angel laid on his bed, he started planning Crook's death and his mind was racing with thoughts. Carolina was also in the room cleaning up like she would on a regular basis. Angel knew what he was facing, Crook was a handful and a problem. If he got Troy then it wouldn't be hard to take him down knowing Troy was a silent killer who watched his surroundings.

"Baby what's wrong? It looks like something is bothering you," Carolina asked.

"Remember how I told you that I had an idea 'bout who killed Rome's parents?"

"Yeah, baby, but you said you needed time."

"Well, I jus' ran out of time, I'm pretty sure it was him, but guess who he really is?" Angel asked. "Mercedes, father!" he continued.

"Oh—my—god!" Carolina said, as had a shocked look on her face. "Does, Rome, know this?" Carolina asked.

"No, baby, and he doesn't need to know. I rather him know after I deal wit him for the sake and safety and Mercedes wants him to meet her father. We can't let that happen."

"Ya right, but baby you got to be careful. I don't know what I'd do if I lost you," Carolina said, with a somber look.

"I hear ya baby, I'm smarter than that." Angel ran his hands thru her hair. "I gotta meet Money Bags, baby dis too much, everything is gonna be ok, I promise . . . ."

Angel grabbed his keys and stormed out the house dialing Money Bags cell phone. As he dialed the number to Money Bags he jumped in his car. Angel kept switching up cars every time his money jumped; therefore, he can change up his disguise. Now he had sold the Trailblazer and one of his favorites, the Chevy Nova. Now he was driving a BMW X-5, times were changing and people were too. After attempting three times, Money Bags finally answered the phone.

"Damn, Angel, a nigga iz tied up right now what's wrong?"

"Dis ain't the time Bags, something really important came up and Rome's life might be in danger. I need you to meet me at Packy's right now."

"Aight, well that's enough said cuz, I'ma jump in the rain and I'll see you in forty five minutes."

"Aight homie, I'll see you there."

At this point Angel had a mental block. He knew he could trust Money Bags since the two had already departed Wally from this world. Angel always turned to Money Bags when it was time to put someone down. Money Bags always knew a strategy. As Angel walked into Packy's, it wasn't as crowded at this time of the day, but still he kept his eyes open. Packy's had a reputation and violent history. It was just a center of attention period. After a few drinks, Angel observed Money Bags walk in, he was very popular, everybody greeted him with handshakes and head nods.

"What it do mane?" Money Bags asked, as he greeted him with three fingers.

"Not good, sit down," Angel replied, as he ordered drinks. "Remember when Troy and Karen got killed?" Angel asked.

"Yeah! That was a decade ago, Angel, let it go . . . ."

"I can't Bags, I put these pieces together all these years, but I jus' been getting right tryna get dis money," Angel continued. "At the scene the suspect wore size ten and a half, and guess who wasn't at Troy's funeral?"

Money Bags started thinking real hard 'cause it's been ten-years, he couldn't refresh his memory, but coincidently he remembered. "Crook, so what?" Money Bags was confused and didn't know where Angel was going with the conversation.

"Man, Crook wears size ten and a half and all of sudden he gets work."

"You got work all of a sudden . . . ." Money Bags snickered."

"Seriously, I played Crook for those bricks, he went for the story and when we murked Wally, guess who he was 'bout to rat out for to get off on a case?"

"Who nigga . . . ?"

"Crook! Who else you thought I was tralkin' 'bout?"

"Hell if I knew, Angel! How'd you find all dis out?"

"My man told me he's fuckin Wally's Cape Verdean bitch. Man I put two and two together and plus the streets talk."

"You shoulda been a cop," Money Bags joked some more.

"Money dis isn't even why I brought you down here.

139

"Well get to the point, 'cause time iz money."

"You know Rome got his lil young thing on his side and to make things worse, she wants him to meet her pops."

"So the fuck what! What that gotta do wit dis?"

"Her pops iz Crook!"

"Oh shit . . . ." Money Bags started laughting. "Good shit now he's fuckin' her daughter."

"Man stop playing . . . . Crook gotta go dog!" Angel said seriously.

"Aight, I'm down for whatever dog you know me, stay wit heat."

"Well I need some strategies you know that's where you come in Money!"

"I got dis lil daddy . . ."

They sat Packy's for nearly two hours and they had brainstormed all possible ways to get Crook. They knew Crook had a few soldiers to die for him. Smooth was one of them. Smooth had a mean reputation, it was once rumored that he had ten or more bodies under his belt. After a basketball game at Almont Park one night, Smooth shot the whole park up nearly killing five people 'cause the team he betted on didn't win. He had ten thousand on that game. Money Bags had simply laid the blueprint plan down. Crook's deathbed was marked.

"Yo my nigga ya a genius," Angel complimented.

"Remember Angel we gotta get dis work from N.Y. first or it'll be a drought."

"Aight, well that's what's poppin' fuck that nigga, I'ma go meet dis connect and it's a rap!" Angel said, then threw back the last of his Heineken.

They left Packy's and headed their own ways. Angel had Money to finish counting and he had a plan to stick to. He had enough money saved up to get enough work that would simply allow him to step out the game. He jumped into his BMW and flew down the mean streets of Boston with his sunroof open. He then inserted the Lox album we are the streets, he skipped to his favorite track "Fuck You". "You heard L-O-X came through in a yellow Lex and hopped out wit the air force one's wit the yellow checks, and you liable to see me dolo, ice in the rolo, burna under the polo, a lot of you niggaz is homo's, funny style niggaz ain't down wit me, type of nigga that go to the barthroom to sitdown and pee . . . ."

That was how Angel was feeling at the moment, he was a big Jadakiss fan. When Angel got home he parked the car and turned off the ignition leaving the system on. He dialed Crook's number as he reclined his seat and turned the music down.

"Hey Angel! My nigga . . . . what's poppin' daddy."

"Crook, man I need somethin' big I'm movin' these cd's too fast. I'm tryna expand like you, plus we been dealin' wit each other for years, my money's right."

"I already know that Angel, I been tellin' you to make dis NY move. The city is tight, my man Diablo movin' some really good mixtapes you have to meet him." Crook assured him. "Plus his flow is one of a kind, best in the city." Crook spoke in codes meaning quality of the drug

"Well you already know! I got my Cape Verdeans on Camron and Homes Ave, plus my cousin been tellin' me to hit him off wit some cd's, you know G?" Angel asked.

"Yeah, I know him he jus' came home from doin' a nickel." Crook confirmed.

"Aight Crook, well I'll be waitin' to go get them mixtapes, hit me asap . . . ."

"I got you, one!" Crook hung up.

". . . . *Bitch ass nigga,*" Angel said after the line disconnected. Angel began thinking to himself, *"I'ma go to N.Y. to get dis work and then I'm gonna murk him with Money Bags or maybe even do it myself."* The plans were all into play Angel knew what he had to do. The plan was in motion. He took the key out the ignition and clicked the alarm button as he exited the car. He walked into the apartment and was quickly greeted by Jerome.

"Angel, I'm off dis I'm 'bout to swing by Rell's crib, then I might slide off with Mercedes later on tonight."

"Rome, be safe and don't forget I'ma get the scoop on Crook before you meet him so fall back on meeting him," Angel demanded.

"Aight, Angel, you got that I'm out . . . ."

As Jerome stepped into his car he looked for a CD to pop in his system. He then inserted Jay-Z's the Dynasty. "The Dynasty niggaz as promised." Jerome turned the music up loud then sped off. Jerome thought about his parents as he was driving. *"Would they approve of my living? Damn pops how'd you do dis all those years,"* he thought to himself. As he arrived to Tyrell's house he sounded the horn to alert his cousin of his presence.

It was a beautiful day and Jerome was not in the mood. Mercedes was trying to cheer him up and offered him Dinner at 'Fire and Ice", he requested a couple of hours to think about it, truth is he didn't want to bothered. The brothers entered his car with flowers and they were ready to leave. Every July for the last nine years they would visit Troy and Karen's grave site in memory of their birthdays which was a week apart. Jerome was down at his parents gravesite every Sunday faithfully.

Jerome stopped at a flower shop and purchased a dozen of roses for his deceased parents. After he purchased his roses, they drove to Mount Hope Cemetery. While Jerome drove down the stipulated streets inside the cemetery, he noticed his aunt Vanessa, his cousins mother sitting on the grass with balloons. They exited the car and greeted Vanessa who's eyes were puffy from crying.

"Hey, ma, we missed you!" The brothers greeted their mom with kisses.

"Hi auntie V . . . ." Jerome hugged and kissed her on the cheek.

"Hey, Rome, how you been? Look at you now growing up! And that facial hair looking just like your dad . . . ."

"I'm ok." Jerome replied. "I jus' graduated from Charlestown," he added.

"I heard I'm really proud of you baby! And if you mother and father were here they would be too," Vanessa replied, while wiping a tear away.

Jerome knelt down and said a prayer as he placed his flowers on the gravesite which people had visited already. Jerome also noticed that Angel and Carolina visited the site previously. Jerome grabbed the guest book and signed it with a message that read:

"I'm missing you two so much mommy and daddy. Keep watching over me like I pray for y'all every night, I love you mommy and daddy . . . ."

After an hour visit they all hugged and said goodbye to Troy and Karen. Jerome kissed the headstone that were joined together. *"I love you mom and dad,"* he said to himself.

Vanessa left and right after she left Jerome released thirty-nine balloons in the sky celebrating thirty-nine years his father life and 38 years of his mother's life. Although they were not physically alive they lived on in his heart. As Jerome and his cousins got back into Jerome's Acura TL, Jerome's favorite song in the album was on and he turned it up knowing he could relate to it. "This can't be life, this can't be love, this can't be right, there's gotta be more, this can't be us . . . ." He drove down the cemetery and back to his cousins house. "I could've rapped about my hard time in this song, but heaven knows I would've been wrong . . . ."

Chapter 16

Angel stood on the balcony at his two bedroom condo overlooking the Charles River and Memorial Drive. He stared down from the eleventh floor watching the city of Cambridge, the panoramic view was amazing at night. He could see people jogging around pathways clearly on the Charles River. Whenever he wanted to get a piece of mind he'd walk to the balcony and stare out into the water, sometimes he would stand there for hours on out and just think. Angel would isolate himself from the world and stand on the balcony contemplating on his next move. He always put great thought into his plans before he out them in motion, he made sure he stayed a few steps ahead of his enemies and the law. He had a lot of things on his mind lately, he was constantly dealing with the day to day drama on the streets.

He bought the lavish condo to accommodate Jerome and his girl Carolina. Jerome was older now and needed his own privacy and space. Angel didn't want to keep him on West Dedham street no more, it was too many bad memories for Jerome. Angel put plasma TV's in every room and furnished his place with top of the appliances. Carolina helped designed the inside of their condo too, she played a major part in picking out everything. Angel kept in contact with his mother by phone every other day and he'd go by to visit her occasionally. Gloria was shocked when she saw how lavish her son was living. Gloria always knew he was doing something illegal to get his money, but she never expected him to be living this large. Angel even suggested that Gloria move out the South End and move to the outskirts, but she refused to leave, she was comfortable right where she was at.

Angel put the Backwood cigar to his mouth that filled with purple haze and lit the blunt. He inhaled the potent weed and then blew it out through his nose. Angel coughed lightly and choked a little bit from the deep pulls of smoke he was inhaling. The weed instantly started to effect him and put his mind at ease. Angel had to have his blunts daily, he was a heavy weed smoker, he only smoked the best. Angel had a high tolerance for it and could smoke seven grams a day easily. Carolina would sit in the house and smoke all day by herself. Angel didn't mind spending money daily on weed, it was pocket change to what he was pulling in every day. He was hustling in the streets hard, he was stacking up for a rainy day.

When Troy was alive he always explained to Angel that you have to save money no matter what. Troy used to tell him that you couldn't sell drugs forever. Angel took heed to everything that was told to him. Angel had it all planned out; another year or two he'd be retiring from the game. By the time he is thirty-one he wanted to be out. Ten years in the game selling weight had him financially strait, but Angel still wanted more money, the game became addictive to him.

The wind was blowing lightly making the night feel cooler than most June nights. Angel had on a white tank top, stonewash polo jean-shorts, and a pair of white air

Jordan's. Angel had six corn rolls in his hair that came to his shoulders with a rubber band around his tips to keep it in a ponytail. Angel heard the glass sliding door open and shut bringing him out his train of thought. He turned around to see Carolina standing behind him in her Channel silk bathrobe with two glass cups in her hand.

Carolina's hair was still damp from getting out the shower and her curly hair hung down her back. Carolina handed him a cup and he started sipping the Hennessey. It left a burning sensation in his chest and he made a sour facial expression, Carolina looked at him and started chuckling.

"What's da matter papi . . . . the henny too strong for you? There's wine coolers in the fridge," Carolina said, then sipped from her glass.

"You know I'm not no lush like you, next time throw some coke inside my shit, would ya . . . ." Angel stated.

"Yeah you got that baby, I'll make sure I water it down too." She smiled.

"I see someone got jokes tanite, looks like I'll jus' be smokin' dis haze by myself too," Angel said, then exhaled smoke right into her face.

"Gimme some of that purple, papi . . . . and I need some while ya gone in the city."

"You got that bay, I'ma leave you somethin' before I make moves," Angel passed her the blunt. "It's beautiful out her tanite, it's not too hot or too chilly—it's jus' right out here . . . ."

"Mmm-hmm, it's gorgeous out here, Angel. I feel like goin' to the beach tanite wit you and makin' love to you, 'member when we was kids and we go to Revere Beach and fuck? We would get drunk and fuck all night . . . . those were the days papi," Carolina exclaimed.

"Yeah, I member all that mami, we was young and did a lot of crazy shit together. Youse a lil freak bay, I swear . . . ." Angel said, shaking his head and smiling.

"It's too bad you're goin' to the city tanite, I really wanna spend some time wit you, Angel. Lately all you've doin' iz runnin' the streets and I've been missin' you daddy," Carolina said, sincerely.

"I know ya right Carolina, I've been on my grizzy real hard lately. Don't even wet it though mami—we gonna do some things once I get back in town. What I'm tryna do iz 'bout to be real major—after I make dis power move, a year from now you'll have ya own hair salon somewhere, how that sound?" Angel stated.

The thought alone of Carolina having her own hair salon made her blush. Ever since she was a kid she envisioned herself with a hair salon. But now hearing Angel say he was going to purchase her one was a dream come true. Carolina was ecstatic after hearing the good news, she couldn't stop smiling.

"Oh, baby, I'd love to have my own salon . . . . Angel, I love you so much! You don't even know daddy," Carolina cooed.

"I love you more my lil princess . . . ."

Angel sipped his liquor while Carolina ran her fingers through his braids. He admired her features and loved everything about her, Carolina was his best friend and lover. Angel was quiet and in deep thought as he swallowed the last of his drink.

"Papi, what's the matter? Is everyting alright . . . ?"

Angel kept his eyes on the city never turning around and said, "Bay everything iz alright, jus' got a lot of shit on my mind that's all."

"If you wanna talk papi I'm here for you," Carolina assure him.

Angel felt his Nextel on his waist vibrating and took it off the clip, he looked at the caller ID and then answered it.

"Talk to me Money Bags . . . ." Angel answered.

"I'm out front now, Angel, I'll be upstairs after I park the wheels."

"I ain't goin' nowhere my nigga, see you in a minute cuzzo," Angel hung up. "Come on bay lets go inside the crib. Put some clothes on, I got company comin' upstairs any minute now," Angel told her calmly.

Carolina flicked the last of the blunt off the balcony and went inside their bedroom. Angel walked in behind her and shut the door. She dropped her bathrobe to the floor and underneath she was naked. Angel took a glimpse of his girl and smiled. Carolina slipped on a pair of sweatpants and put on white t-shirt while Angel walked over to his safe. He started taking money out and stacking it inside his backpack. Each stack of money was $10,000 he took out, and each stack had rubber bands wrapped around it to keep the money in place. Angel filled the backpack up with $230,000 and zipped it close. He heard a light knock at the door and went to go answer it. Angel looked through the peephole and afterwards let Money Bags inside.

"What's the word homie," Money Bags said, greeting him with three finger dap.

"Dog who let you in downstairs?" Angel asked.

"Some lil' blond head bitch was comin' out as I was 'bout to ring the bell, so I jus' figured I come upstairs instead of makin' you come down."

"Oh, come in the crib and take a seat in the living room," Angel shut the door and locked it behind him. "It's goin' down tanite, after dis power move we make we'll be aight, then all we have to do iz take care of that las' lil' problem . . . ." Angel said, with a solemn look on his face.

"I'm already hipped fam—I can't wait 'til that day comes, ever since you 'tol me 'bout Crook—"

"Shhhh . . . ." Angel had his forefinger on his lips telling him to be quiet. "Be easy my dude I don't want wifey hearing us, that's the last thing I need."

"My fault doggy, I forgot she was in the spot. You got all the gwop together?"

"Yes, lemme go in my room and grab that so we can make moves."

Money Bags flicked the TV on while Angel went to his bedroom. Money Bags put it on HBO and King of New York was on. *"What a coincidence,"* he uttered to himself. Carolina was sitting on the king size bed unraveling a Backwood when Angel entered the room. She had the purple finely broken up on a twenty-dollar bill waiting to go inside the blunt. Carolina ripped the leaf carefully taking off the right amount. She didn't like a lot of paper 'cause it made her blunt taste harsh. Angel looked at her and started shaking his head.

"You better make them trees las, Carolina. I ain't comin' back home 'til tomorrow."

"If worse comes to worse I'll jus' have Rome go get me some more," Carolina put the blunt to her mouth and lit it.

Angel went to his nightstand beside the bed and retrieved his .45 semiautomatic from inside the draw. He pulled out the clip to make sure it was fully loaded, and then inserted the back inside. He cocked it back and put one in the head, clicked the safety button, then tucked it in his waist.

"Be safe out there papi, call me soon as you get back so I can know ya alright," Carolina said, with deep concern.

"I sure will baby-girl, stop stressin' me out please . . . ."

"Sorry if I am papi, I jus' love you so much and I don't wanna lose you," Carolina exclaimed.

Angel could see the somber look on her face and knew she was a little distraught. For the past few months Carolina been trying to slow him down from hanging in the streets. Angel always told her that he couldn't take no breaks from the block, he had to always keep his ears to the streets and watch his workers. Angel came too far in the game now to start slacking. Carolina understood that he had money to earn and appreciated everything he did for her, but lately she has been feeling as though she was going to lose him to the streets. Angel put on his black polo rugby shirt with white stripes to conceal his pistol. He picked up the backpack off the floor, adjusted the straps, and then put it on over his shoulder.

"I love you bay," Angel gave her a peck on the lips. "Tell Rome I said be at the house tomorrow 'round six o'clock in the evening," Angel said, while caressing her face.

"I will tell him what you said. Don't forget to call me when you get back in the city, baby. Please don't have me worried over ya ass, Angel."

"I'ma call you bay, don't even wet that. Come lock dis door behind me."

Carolina said hello to Money Bags before they left and locked the door. Lately Carolina haven't been too fond for Angel running the streets. Especially ever since she got pregnant two months ago, she been very emotional. She was still waiting for the perfect time to tell Angel she was pregnant. Carolina was a little timid 'cause she didn't know how he'd take the surprising news.

Angel stepped in the elevator and the garage button to take them to where his car was at. Angel and Money Bags got off the elevator and walked through the parking garage where all the tenants kept their vehicles. Angel hit the alarm button and his Honda Odyssey doors unlocked. Nowadays he was constantly switching up vehicles to stay under the radar. Angel had two other vehicles parked beside his van; a BMW X-5, and a Lexus IS 300 on chrome Ashanti's. he put the key in the ignition, rolled down the driver's side window all the way, put the radio on 88.9, and hit the hazard lights. He walked around to the back of the van and put the backpack into the secret compartment in the trunk area. Angel was glad he bought the stash spot for $8,000, 'cause he knew it was well worth it. Angel jumped in the driver's seat and drove off.

Angel pushed the button on top of the visor and the garage door automatically opened up. He took a right turn and drove to end to his street and took a left. He drove for a couple of minutes and hopped on Storrow Drive. He felt his phone vibrating and glanced at the caller ID, it was a private call. He debated whether he was going to answer the phone or not. After letting his phone vibrate five times, he answered.

"Yo who dis callin' me private . . . ? Angel inquired.

"My nigga . . . dis Crook on the jack, meet me down at the South Street Diner. Change of plans, I had to stop off and get some grub before I hit the highway."

"Yep, I'll be there in minute, Crook, I'm en route now."

Click! The phone call ended and Angel shut his phone. He plugged his phone into the charger and sat it on the console.

"What that fuck nigga was sayin'?" Money Bags asked.

"He talkin' 'bout meet him downtown at the Diner, man I can't wait 'til I meet the connect and these bricks, 'cause dis nigga gotta go!" Angel emphasized. "I'm tellin' you Money—we murk dis fuck nigga, then Smooth has to go. Once we take care of 'em, then dis all could be off my mind. I been waitin' patiently for ten-years, now iz the time my dude," Angel said, with a solemn look on his face.

"What 'bout his soldiers, Angel? You know Crook's lil' gunners gonna try and get back at niggas once they find out," Money Bags stated.

"Fuck 'em, we'll bury 'em right along wit Crook and Smooth," Angel said, sternly.

"Let's do dis shit right and put these niggas in the dirt. After we twist these niggas caps back—Troy can rest in peace."

"I feel you, let's make dis happen, Money. Every dog has his day, homie."

Angel pulled up in front of the South Street Diner on Kneeland street and double parked behind Crook's Range Rover. He high beamed his headlights on the Range Rover to let Crook know he was behind him. Angel picked up his phone and called Crook. The phone went straight to the voicemail, he sat the phone back down on the console.

Crook came walking out the restaurant with a bag in his hand and walked right over to Angel in the van. Angel rolled his window down halfway.

"You ready to hit dis highway boy? Nigga ya better keep up, I'm doin' a buck all the way there," Crook stated.

"Nigga I'm waitin' on you . . . . lemme know when you ready to ride out."

"We 'bout to bounce in a minute, I'm waitin' on Smooth to come outside wit these two bitches we got," Crook said, then took out his sandwich. Crook took a bite of his cheeseburger and started looking around observing his surroundings.

"My nigga, I ain't tryna have no bitches in my BI that I don't even know. Dog for all I know, these hoes could be tryna set me up in N.Y.!" Angel retorted.

"Chill out, Angel, it ain't even that type of muthafuckin' party! Dem hoes gonna be in the telly chillin' wit Money Bags while we handle our business."

"Aight, make sure of that, Crook, I would hate to put dem hoes in the dirt . . . ."

Crook devoured the rest of his sandwich and then opened his apple juice and took a swig. Smooth came walking out the South Street Diner with two females by his side. One female hopped in the passenger's seat, and Smooth hopped in the backseat with the other female.

"We gonna hit up club 40/40 and see what's all the hype 'bout. What's good Money Bags . . . . what you too good to speak to a nigga?! Lemme find out you on some other shit," Crook said, with a grin.

"Nah, ain't nothin' like that dog—a nigga jus' tired right now. All dis purple got me tired as fuck," Money Bags lied.

"Well I suggest you wake ya ass up, 'cause it's goin' down tanite! Don't nothin' come to a sleep but a dream! Angel, I'm 'bout to get sucked off all the way to the city, when we get to the telly we gonna run a train on dem hoes," Crook grinned, and looked around checking his surroundings. "Dem two Hazleton street hoes could suck the skin off a niggas dick," Crook ranted.

"I'm definitely tryna get some dome," Money Bags added.

"I'm off dis fellas. Angel, make sure you keep up . . ." Crook walked off to his truck and drove off. He made a left turn onto Albany street and drove up the ramp going towards 93 on the Southeast expressway. Angel followed behind him doing 35mph abiding by the speed limit. Crook turned right onto route 90 west and accelerated down the Mass Pike increasing his speed to 70mph. Crook hit the cruise control, sparked up a blunt of wet, and unbuckled his pants.

"Shawnda, lemme feel that tongue ring sweetheart, take care of me and when we get back tomorrow I might take you shoppin'," Crook said, with a smirk.

"Dis my las' time doin' dis shit for you, Crook!" Shawnda sucked her teeth and leaned over.

"Chill out honey, you been sayin' dat for weeks, go on and take care of big daddy."

Shawnda grabbed his swollen penis and wrapped her lips around it. Crook put his right hand on her head and guided her through while he kept his left hand on the steering wheel. Crook reclined his seat just a notch and sat back getting oral sex while smoking his wet. Shawnda was making him feel good the way she put it on Crook, he had to keep his eyes on the road to keep from swerving.

"Yeah . . . . jus' like dat ma . . . . damn dat shit feels good," Crook moaned.

They arrived in New York City at quarter to midnight. Angel followed behind Crook all the way to club 40/40. The club was packed to the capacity, Crook gave the bouncer an extra hundred dollars to let them all inside. Crook bought six VIP passes and they all went to the VIP section to the lounge. Crook told the bartender to keep the bottles of Don Perion and Grey Goose coming to their table. The bartender kept the champagne on ice, and brought cranberry and cups to mix the grey goose. Money Bags twisted up a few blunts of some white widow weed while listening to Beanie Siegel blaring through the speakers. "You know I don't do much, you know Mac stay sucka free, so please don't fuck wit me . . . ." Angel was slouched back on the leather couch nodding his head to the tunes. Money Bags had three blunts rotating while they were having drinks.

Crook was on the dance floor with a bottle of champagne in his hand, and trying to dance with a female while he was drunk. He was grooving to the beat and had rhythm on the dance floor. Smooth played the VIP section, along with Money Bags, Angel, and both females they came with. Angel had two cups of cranberry with grey goose and chose not drink no more, he wanted to stay aware of his surroundings. Angel was in town for one thing only, and that was for business. Crook blew through three thousand in the club like it was nothing. They all left the club around 2:00am, and went straight to the Marriott.

Angel went and got his own room next door to where Crook and them were staying. Angel was exhausted and was in need of a good sleep. Money Bags and Crook took turns having sexual intercourse with Shawnda and Crystal. Smooth fell asleep on the couch after getting his dick sucked. Money Bags and Crook went to sleep around four in the morning after their orgy with Crystal and Shawnda.

The next day Crook woke up at 10:45 in the morning with a migraine headache. He rolled up a blunt of wet and lit it to deal with his hangover. Over the years Crook became addicted to the drug, the embalm in the weed would make him blackout sometimes and do crazy things. Crook woke everybody up in the room and then went next door to wake up Angel.

"Get ready, Angel, we gotta go see my connect. He's waitin' for us my nigga. We gonna leave Money Bags and dem hoes here," Crook informed him.

"Aight, gimme 'bout fifteen minutes, I wanna wash my face and brush my teeth," Angel said, groggily at the door.

"Hurry up then I'ma be next door waitin' on ya playboy."

Angel shut the door and went in the bathroom to freshen up. He checked his phoine and noticed he had fifteen missed calls and four voicemails. He didn't even bother checking his messages. He put on his sneakers and walked out the door. The corridor was reeking from weed smoke when he stepped out his room, he rapped twice on the door and Crook let him inside.

"You ready to make moves, Angel? I jus' got off the horn wit the man, I tol' him we on our way."

"Let's ride out then, I'm waitin' on you doggy."

"We finna breeze outta here now—Money Bags, you stay here and fall back wit the hoes, we'll be back later on."

The girls looked at Crook with rage in their eyes after hearing him disrespect them. "Nigga who the fuck you callin' hoes?!" Shawnda inquired, with her hands on her hips. "You better start respectin' us!" Crystal added.

"Come on bitch you know what it iz, Shawnda. Don't act brand new!"

"Watch ya mouth, pussy! I'm tired of ya bitch ass disrespecting me and my girl," Crystal retorted.

'Crook raised his arm and backhanded Crystal across the face. Angel intervened and stopped Crook from hitting her again. Angel stared at Crystal kneeling on the floor holding her hand over her bloody lip.

"Crook, we got things to do dog, leave her alone my nig and lets get up outta here," Angel stated. "You gonna fuck 'round and get a 209A hittin' dis broad."

"Yeah you right on that one, Angel. Come on let's get outta here."

Shawnda mumbled some words behinds Crook's back as he left out the hotel room. Crook got off the floor crying after being humiliated and abused. Crook paid the lady at the desk to keep the room for another night, just so Money Bags and the females could have somewhere to wait until they came back.

Angel stared in amazement looking around at Diablo's mansion that sat on 20,000 square feet of property. Crook pulled up at the front entrance and parked. Diablo's henchmen were standing around the premises with high powered automatic machine guns glaring at Crook's Range Rover. Angel felt a little awkward noticing a bunch of guys with machine guns all around him. Diablo opened up the front entrance door and stood with a cigar in his mouth.

"Crook, dis dude is a boss for real! He ain't no joke I see," Angel stated.

"Yeah, Diablo is that dude foreal! Cross that nigga he'll bury ya whole family," Crook replied. "But on the real he's a good dude, A, you'll see . . ." Crook advised.

Diablo beckoned for them to come inside. Crook turned the truck off and departed with Angel and Smooth. Two of Diablo's henchmen escorted them inside the mansion. Angel looked around admiring Diablo's style and extravagant living. The mansion had marble floors in the corridors and chandeliers hanging from the ceiling. Diablo took a seat at the dining room table and then gestured everyone else to sit. Diablo sat there stoically smoking on his cigar. Angel was feeling uneasy the way Diablo was glaring at him. Diablo sat his Cuban cigar down in the ashtray and broke the silence. "Crook, how's everything goin' with you and Smooth?" Diablo inquired.

"Same ole shit papi, jus' tryna expand my hustle and fall back from the scene for a lil bit. I'ma let Smooth and my buddy Angel make all the trips to see you, that's why I wanted you to meet him," Crook stated.

"So this ya friend, Angel?" Diablo pointed with his finger. "You know I really don't like meeting new people, Crook, but for you I might make an exception."

"Yep, that's my good friend I was tellin' you 'bout."

"So tell me somethin', Crook—what makes you think I wanna do business with him? What if he ain't the person he claims to be, then what? You know I don't like dealing with new customers," Diablo blew smoke out his mouth.

"I've been dealing wit him for the past ten-years, Diablo. Not once has he ever crossed me or dealt wit anyone else on the biness aspect, he's one of the loyalist dudes I know. He has heart and he's a good earner, you got my word on that, Diablo. If he wasn't who I said he was—trust me, I would not be vouching for him," Crook stated, while looking Diablo in the eyes.

Diablo sat there and listened intently to everything Crook was telling him. He trusted Crook to certain extent and knew he wouldn't introduce someone to him that was no good. But still, Diablo had to be cautious on doing business with people he did not know. Diablo been in business too long and was not about to start slipping. "Angel, nice to meet you amigo," Diablo got out his seat and shook his hand. "Take a walk with me, Angel, I wanna talk to you." Angel got out his seat and stood next to Diablo who was slightly taller than him. "Excuse us fellas . . . . we'll be back in a few minutes," Diablo said, then walked off with Angel.

Diablo and Angel walked off from the dining room. Diablo had on a Armani short sleeve shirt, and a pair of matching pant with some gator shoes. Angel admired his style and the way he conducted business. Diablo walked into the backyard and stood by his massive pool with a waterfall.

"So tell me Angel—what makes you think I can do business with you? How I don't know you ain't no informer for the feds?" Diablo said, sternly.

"Where I'm from we cut the tail off a rat, I despise snitches and stick-up kids! I ain't no muthafuckin' informant, and I ain't no stick-up kid . . . ." Angel said, coldly while looking him in the eyes. "I came out here to do business and hopefully meet a new plug. I'm a man of morals and principles, Diablo. I don't burn my bridges—and I don't bite the hand that feeds me," Angel exclaimed.

"So you think you can handle this back and forth on the highway? You fillin' in Crook's shoes right now, those are some big shoes to fill in."

"I sure can, Diablo. Crook already gave me the run down on how everything iz done. We still got them two broads who'll transport the bricks back and forth to Boston," Angel reassured him. "And I'll only do biness wit you no matter what."

"I like you, Angel, I see the truth in you. For now on out, you could come see me with Smooth. So what you got in the bag for me, amigo?"

"I got $230,000 in the bag," Angel replied. "Let's go back inside so we could go do business then . . . ." Diablo said, with a snicker.

Angel passed him the backpack and Diablo dumped all the money on the table. Diablo had a grin on his face when he saw the stacks of money. "Toney, gimme the money counter, and go get the twelve keys," Diablo demanded. "Crook, I like this kid right here, he got heart. For now on out, he could come see me with Smooth, you need to lay low and stay in Boston. The last thing I need is the feds watching me . . . ."

A smile crept across Crook's face. Everything was starting to fall into place for him. Now he could be the man behind the scene making money without being seen. But little did Crook know he was never going to be able to fall back.

Angel was excited deep down inside after finally meeting Diablo. He felt relieved that he got another connect and some cheaper prices. Angel refused to let Crook know how ecstatic he was about meeting Diablo. Angel kept his poker face on and remained humble. Now that he met the plug, and everything was squared away—Angel was finally ready to put Crook in the dirt and take over all his blocks.

Diablo ran all the money through money counter and Angel counted all the bricks. After Diablo counted all the money, he gave Angel his cell number and vowed to do business again with him. Crook was glad now he didn't have to take the rides to New York every two weeks no more. Now Crook was content, he could sit back and collect money while everyone else got their hands dirty for him. The trio left out of Diablo's mansion.

"Crook, when we get back in town I need to buy a couple of hammers off you."

"I got you, Angel, gimme a couple of days and I'll have it for you."

"Aight good looks my nigga . . . . I appreciate it Crook."

Chapter 17

Jerome waited impatiently for Mercedes to come outside of her parents Medford home. Jerome knew her father wasn't home so because his Range Rover wasn't parked in the driveway; therefore, he parked right behind Mercedes new A-4 Audi that Crook had got her for graduation in surprise. Jerome hated when he came to pick Mercedes up. She always took hours to prepare herself and that he didn't like.

Jerome had just came from shopping at the Galleria Mall in Cambridge. He loved shopping, especially for jewelry. Before leaving the shopping center he had some panda express Chinese food for lunch at the food court. Now that he had no access to the restroom he needed to take a leak really bad. He already met Gina so he didn't have a problem meeting her again. Jerome called Mercedes for the fifth time embracing her to come out.

"Yo, come out ya takin' forever I ain't got all day baby and I need to pee bad," Jerome complained.

"Ok, big head calm down, and why don't you jus' come inside and pee?"

"Girl you crazy or somethin' . . . ."

"No! But my father ain't here so why can't we jus' chill here?"

"Nah I'm straight, but I'll come in to use the bathroom." Jerome agreed.

"Ok!" Mercedes said, then hung up.

Jerome was amused at the luxury bathroom. Whatever Mercedes father was doing, he was doing very good, Jerome thought. The bathroom had a walk-in shower space and Jacuzzi tub. As Jerome took a leak he observed the bathroom. The sink had bright light bulbs going across the top of the mirror. The colors were coordinated well, Jerome quickly washed his hands and exited the bathroom when he was interrupted at the door. "Hi Jerome! How are you?" Gina hugged him.

"Hello, Ms. Alexander, it's a pleasure to meet you again!" Jerome replied, feeling a little awkward around her mother.

"Boy you can call ma! If you gon marry my daughter," Gina said, with a sense of humor. "Jerome you better quit being shy around me too," Gina smiled at him.

"I plan on marrying ya daughter one day, but right now we too young."

"I'm glad you're thinking that way," Gina said. "Finish school too Jerome 'cause it's important," She added, referring to college.

"I am Ms. Alexander," Jerome lied.

Gina told Jerome to have a seat then she began to question him. Jerome felt a little awkward because he never dealt with a situation like this before. Jerome had spent an hour talking to Gina, he was ready to leave but she was convincing. Gina wanted to know exactly who her daughter was dating, besides she always wondered what Jerome's parents do for a living that's got her daughter in the latest clothing. Not that she couldn't afford it, but Jerome spoiled Mercedes, so Gina wanted to know as the trio sat in the living room.

"So Jerome what is it that your parents do?" Gina asked.

"I'm adopted by Gloria Sanchez, the Spanish decent lady you seen at my graduation," Jerome replied.

"What happened to your biological parents?" Gloria asked.

"They were murdered on Christmas Eve in 1992," Jerome explained.

"Oh Jesus, I'm so sorry Jerome . . . . I didn't mean too . . . ." Gina uttered.

"It's ok ma," Jerome smiled. "Anytime son," Gina welcomed.

Gina sat in her loveseat feeling guilty because she remembered the incident on Fox 25 news, but she did not want to get into details. A mother and father was lost at an early age for Jerome. Gina couldn't possibly imagine what he was feeling so she changed the subject. "Well are you hungry? I can make you y'all something to eat."

"No thank you. We were gonna grab some Kentucky Fried Chicken. Maybe next time you can cook somthin' for us," Jerome replied.

As Jerome began saying goodbye, high beam lights flashed through the living room on the first floor of the house. Seeing through the window Jerome thought to himself. *"Now this cannot be happening."* Gina immediately looked at Mercedes and laughed as she looked at Jerome.

"Take a seat Jerome. You might as well meet the whole family," Gina requested.

'Uh—oh ok I guess so," Jerome began sweating.

Crook had just got home and he was curious about the Acura parked on his private property. Crook remained calm as he killed the ignition leaving his Range Rover parked behind the Acura, while his Range Rover blocked the sidewalk. Crook prayed this day would never come. He always believed someone would try to hold his family for ransom. As he stepped on the porch he looked into the door window and his heart dropped completely. Crook had a killers intuition. The face of Troy's was now sitting on his couch. Thoughts from that night replayed in his head. Now he was prepared for the worse. He reached into his holster inside his mink jacket and pulled out his 9mm and reached for the doorknob.

". . . . Daddy! Put the gun down it's Jerome my boyfriend!" Mercedes explained.

Gina got up, took the pistol from Crook, and slapped him in rage. "What you want wit my family?!" Crook asked confused.

Jerome stared at Crook coldly, he recognized this face and the same tattoo somewhere. This was too crazy to be true. The only place he recognized this face was in the nightmare, but not the person he wanted Crook to be. Jerome was confused, he recognized Crook but he wasn't sure if it was who he thought it was. Every time he stared into Crook's eyes he got goose bumps.

"Nothin' I'm dating ya daughter sir," Jerome replied.

"Do you know who I am?" Crook asked, still unconvinced.

"No, but I heard good things about you," Jerome complimented.

"Oh yeah from who lil' nigga?!" Crook aksed rudely.

"From me daddy! Be nice to my boyfriend . . . ." Mercedes interrupted.

Crook finally calmed down and took a seat as he gave Jerome a handshake. *"Maybe he doesn't remember me after all,"* he thought. "My names Crook lil' man. My fault for pulling the burna out on you. I thought you probably was robbing my family, feel me?" Crook apologized. "Gina, get me some Henny, dis iz too much me to handle . . . . my lil' princess got a boyfriend fuck that," Crook stated, then sat down on the couch staring at Jerome who was standing up next to Mercedes.

"I'm kinda in a rush I should get goin'," Jerome said.

"Nah, sit down homie if you takin' my daughter out, I wanna know who she dealin' wit. Gurls please excuse us for a couple of minutes," Crook requested.

Mercedes and Gina went upstairs and stood by the ledge as Crook and Jerome had their one on one conversation. They sneaked to the stairs and listened quietly.

"What's ya name?

"Jerome . . . ."

"My mother and father are dead. It's Jerome Jenkins."

Crook's worse thought came to mind. *"If we was on the streets I'd kill you right now. I should have done it 11 years ago."* Crook knew who Jerome was, but he was surprised Jerome didn't recognize him. Now his old best friend's son was dating his daughter. It couldn't get any better. Crook felt bad because he immediately regretted the murders after he committed them. The Christmas gift for Mercedes definitely messed his mind frame up.

"You fuckin' my daughter?" Crook asked.

"No—no sir, I'm not trying—" Jerome got cut off.

"Don't lie! I know how lil' niggas think, I was once y age. You love her?"

"Yes I love ya daughter . . . ." Jerome said proudly.

"Who do you live with?" Crook inquired.

"I live wit my foster brother, Angel." Jerome answered.

Jerome was getting interrogated, this was harder than he thought. When Jerome mentioned Angel, Crook became paranoid. *"Dis might be a setup,"* Crook thought. Now Angel had to go. His whole personality was exposed.

"Angel works construction on the streets," Jerome added.

"Where were y'all goin' tanite?" Crook asked.

"Movies and Dinner," Jerome lied.

"Aight lil' homie, don't break her heart or I'll take yours, on dead dogs," Crook stated, meaning every word.

"Aight, I won't . . . ." Jerome promised.

"No fuckin' either!" Crook requested, knowing it's impossible. "Mercedes! Come down here . . . ." Crook yelled. "Don't be home late or it'll be las' date!"

"Ok, daddy, damn! . . ." Mercedes replied, with an attitude.

Jerome left Mercedes house and Crook moved his Range Rover out the way because it was blocking Jerome's exit. Crook stared at the Acura which seemed to flashy for a foster child to have for his age. Angel definitely had to go before the truth was revealed. Little did he know, Angel was feeling the same way.

Mercedes discussed the situation all the way to Jerome's house, which was the original plan. They wanted to be alone, and it was impossible at Mercedes house. Now that Jerome met Crook he would have to confirm it with Angel who had also just came back from New York with Crook, but he didn't know. As they entered the house Carolina and

Angel were already on the job chopping up coke. Mercedes was now accustomed to this life. Like Carolina she done seen it all, so to her this was nothing new.

"Hey gurl!" Carolina yelled.

"Hey mama, look at my nails, Rome paid for them to get done. Ain't they pretty, Carolina?" Mercedes asked.

"Yeah, but I'm kinda busy right now we'll kick it later . . . ."

"Hi Mercedes!" Angel chimed in.

Carolina got back to work, she had a lot of separating to do. *Two hands are better than one,"* Carolina thought. Angel was tired but money came first so he had to get it together. Meanwhile, Jerome and Mercedes were in his room. Soon as the door was shut and locked, Jerome and Mercedes were at it.

Jerome started kissing Mercedes while his hand palmed her head, leaving her long beautiful, jet black hair over his forearm. Throughout the years his sexuality had advanced. Thanks to Angel he was no longer an amateur. Mercedes quickly removed her sweatpants and sweatshirt off until she was in her Victoria Secret booty shorts and bra. Jerome became hard soon as he stared down her flawless body. Mercedes loved to role play, acting was also something she wanted to do. At the moment Jerome would have given her an Oscar.

Mercedes grabbed him on the edge of his own bed. Jerome was completely dazed from her beauty. Mercedes always put on a show before they had sex. She got on her knees and began crawling like a cat to Jerome. She went straight for his pride. Mercedes began taking his Louie belt off then pulled out his manhood through his boxers.

Mercedes began licking his penis up and down in a vertical direction. She had Jerome in a fairytale world. She stroked his penis nice and slow directing her head side to side. Jerome thought he was about to climax. She was giving him the best oral sex of his life. She almost made him climax and he pulled her off his rod, because he wanted it to last as long as possible. Her head game was proper.

"Ohhh shit . . . . fuck!" Jerome was loving the moment.

Mercedes was also wet and Jerome knew it so he picked her up and put her on the bed, and began to please her rotating his tongue around her clitoris. Mercedes could not handle it. Jerome had placed her at the bottom of his king size bed, now she had her hands around the sheets yelling out the top of lungs trying to keep silent.

"Ssshhh . . . . be quiet Angel, listen . . . ." Carolina said.

Mercedes could be heard down the hall moaning out the top of her lungs. Angel stared at the door while he smiled. He then turned to Carolina who had a seductive look on her face. "So we gonna be doin' this all night or do you have something in mind?" Carolina smiled.

"Nah, I think dis can wait 'til tomorrow," Angel replied, as he got up and grabbed Carolina.

Angel and Carolina had went to their rooms and began having sex also. They admired Jerome's passion for Mercedes, because it reminded them of how they used to sneak around just to have sex, trying to find a good place to do it at. Jerome and Mercedes had been going at it close to twenty five minutes now having sex.

"Rome, don't stop . . . . I love you so much! Ooohhh I'm about to cum!" Mercedes reached her climax clawing her nails in his back.

Jerome had her legs over his arms and she now was kissing him in the forehead. She looked Jerome in the eyes and recited the words again. "I love you, bighead . . . ." She said, while gazing into his eyes.

"I love you too, bay." Jerome said, with a grin.

Jerome set his alarm clock for 9:45, he wanted to bring Mercedes home early like her father requested. They both laid down and fell asleep. Jerome was tired, as him and Mercedes were awaken when the alarm went off. They were lazy after all the fucking they did. As Jerome walked down the hallway, he started smiling at Mercedes. He loved her innocent look, and how she always hated leaving him. Before Jerome got to the door, he was intrigued by yells coming from Angel's room and started smiling.

"Hey they gotta do they damn thing too," Mercedes said.

"My man Angel . . . ." Jerome replied, complimenting Angel. "Try living here," he added, as they both laughed.

Jerome had wanted to embrace the meeting he had with Crook to Angel. But Angel was occupied so he left the issue alone for now, but was happy he met Mercedes father although it was contemptuous. Mercedes did not want to leave but she was forced too. As long as she was under her father's roof, she had to follow by his rules. She spoke fond of living with Carolina, Angel, and Jerome. But Jerome wasn't ready for all that yet. He dropped her off then headed back home.

Chapter 18

"Say word that nigga pulled the toast out on you, Rome?" Angel aske, with a twisted face. "I'ma have to put some holes in that bitch!" Angel was vexed.

"On everything I love—dis nigga really pulled the hammer out on me! Soon as he came in the crib he had the hammer out, talkin' 'bout what the fuck I want wit his family! Dog for some reason that nigga was noided, he looked like he saw a ghost," Jerome explained. "Then on top of that, Angel—he looks mad familiar, and then that tattoo on his neck," Jerome added.

"Rome, don't even worry 'bout that shit that happened the other day. Crook's jus' a street nigga and was jus' stayin' on point. Everything should be cool between y'all now. But still, I don't want you goin' by his crib no more." Angel demanded.

"Why you sayin' that for, Angel? Me and the nigga started choppin' it up after that he's cool," Jerome was puzzled.

"Yeah, ya right Rome, I can't stop you from seeing Mercedes," Angel replied. "So what you and Crook was talkin' 'bout?"

"The nigga was askin' me mad questions 'bout his daughter and if I was fuckin' her, that old head iz crazy. Then the nigga was askin' me who I stay wit."

"And what you tell the nigga?!"

"I tol' him I stay wit you, Angel."

"Damn! Why the fuck was he askin' you questions for?" Angel was confused.

"I don't know dog, the nigga jus' concerned 'bout his daughter. Of course he wanna know who his daughter iz fuckin'! You aight, Angel? You look like somethin' iz bothering you, bro."

"Nah, a nigga jus' chillin' Rome, I'm good jus' got some shit on my mind. You didn't tell Crook where you stay at did you? 'Cause he's cool and all—but I stop fuckin' wit that dude and I don't buy work from him no more," Angel told him.

"What I look stupid to you? Fucks no I ain't tell that nigga where we stay! The nigga didn't even ask all that anyways.'

"Well that's good, Rome, what you doin' for the night?"

"Probably take Mercedes to the movies, I don't know yet. Why what you 'bout to get into?" Jerome asked, then walked into to the kitchen.

Angel sat there on the living room couch and was thinking about everything he just heard from Jerome. Hearing about Crook pulling out his pistol on Jerome confirmed his theory. Why else would Crook pull out a pistol on Jerome? A part of Angel wanted to tell Jerome that Crook was the one who murdered his parents, but instead he opted to say nothing about it. Jerome came walking back into the living room with a cup of apple juice in his hand.

"Listen, I'm 'bout to run to the hood real quick. I'ma get wit you later, Rome." Angel clasped hands with Jerome and left out his condo. He still couldn't believe the news about Crook pulling out a pistol on Jerome. Angel hopped in his Lexus IS 300 and started the ignition. He pulled out his .45 semiautomatic, cocked it back, and then sat it on his lap. Angel pulled out his cell phone and tried calling Money Bags but it went straight to the voicemail, he left a message on the phone.

"Dis is Angel my nig . . . . I'm 'bout to go meet up wit Crook. I gotta handle dis shit tanite it's goin down. I know you probably in some puss right now, so do you cuzzo. I'ma hit you back as soon as I handle dis, one!"

Angel ended the phone call and sat his phone on the passenger seat. He turned off Storrow Drive and turned right onto 93 south. In a way Angel didn't make move without his right hand man, but he was running out of patience and wanted to handle the situation as soon as possible. He was not trying to prolong it any further. Crook knew too much about him and that was not a good sign. Plus, Crook knew Jerome was Troy's son and the only reason he didn't kill him was because his daughter was home. Angel came up with all these conclusions as he pushed his Lexus down the highway. Angel turned off exit 11 and drove through Lower Mills. Angel drove down River street all the way until he got to Cummins highway and turned right. He pulled into the Burger King parking lot and backed into a parking space and called Crook.

"Angel . . . . my nigga what's up, playboy?! Where you at?"

"I'm at Burger King in the parking lot."

"What you in? I'm in the parking lot right now."

"I'm in the blue Lexus . . . ."

"Ok, I see you now . . . . you in that IS 300 over there wit the shoes on it?'

"Yeah, want you in, Crook?"

"I'm in the black Pontiac, the one across from you." Crook was on the other side of the parking lot looking at Angel. "Follow me up the street, I ain't finna do nothin' in dis hot ass parking lot." Crook stated.

Angel hung up the phone and circled the parking lot and pulled up behind Crook. He tried looking inside the Pontiac Grand AM but the windows had dark tints. Crook turned left up Cummins Highway doing as Angel followed behind him. Crook bypassed Fairlawn Estates on his left and jumped in the left lane. Crook put on his left blinker and turned down Rugby road down the street until he came to the stop sign at the four way intersection. He proceeded straight across driving down Blake street and then turned right up Taunton avenue. Crook cut his headlights off once he turned on Oakwood street. The street was a private street and too many cars drove down it. Angel pulled up in back of Crook and cut his car off.

Angel concealed his forearm inside the small of his back and stepped out the car. Crook stepped out his car by himself with a grin on his face. "What's the word my nigga," Crook gave him three finger dap. "I got some brand new .40's fresh out the box, Angel. What you tryna do? I'm lettin' 'em go for nine hunnit each and I got two boxes of shells for 'em," Crook stated.

"I'll fuck wit 'em dog, where they at? Let's hurry up and do dis 'cause I don't feel right doin' biness outside 'round here," Angel said, while checking his surroundings.

"No need to be all noided baby-boy—it's all gravy 'round here . . . . I fucks wit niggas 'round here, they my peoples." Crook assured him.

Angel peered around observing his surroundings on the gloomy dirt road. Angel glanced up at the house they were in front of and noticed that all the lights were off. A couple of houses on the street had their lights off. Angel felt like this was the perfect place to leave Crook dead at. Crook opened his trunk and unveiled three .40 caliber firearms that were under a blanket. Crook picked one .40 caliber up out the trunk and let Angel see it.

"Yeah I like dis right here, Crook. I can definitely fuck wit these .40's my nig . . . ." Angel said, while examining the pistol closely. Angel cocked it back to see if any shells were in the magazine. Next he took out the magazine to double check and see if there was any shells inside.

"Where the shells at playboy?" Angel asked.

"They inside the trunk, you want the hammers or not?! I got things to do and I ain't finna be out here bullshittin' round," Crook retorted.

"Yep, I want all three of 'em, gimme all the shells for 'em too."

Crook turned around and looked inside the trunk for the box of shells. Smooth rolled his window down just a touch to hear what was going on, and kept his eyes in the rearview mirror watching his partner like he was told. Angel whipped out his chrome .45 and released the safety button. Smooth couldn't believe what was transpiring before his eyes. Crook turned around and was staring down the barrow of Angel's gun. Out of shock Crook dropped both boxes of shells out his hand. The shells fell out the boxes and spilled all over the ground from the impact. Crook had to think fast and try talking Angel out of pulling the trigger.

"What's dis all about, Angel? I thought we was dogs . . . why you pulling out on me for?" Crook asked, pleading for his life with his hands in the air.

"Nigga shut the fuck up! Why the fuck you kill Troy for?! Huh nigga?! Youse a grimy ass nigga, you thought I was never gonna find out! I been had the drop on you bitch!" Angel snarled.

"Come on dog, put the gun down my nigga I ain't kill Troy . . . . that was my right hand, I would never do no shit like that," Crook exclaimed.

Crook was scared to death and was not trying to lose his life. He knew Angel was a silent killer like himself. Angel saw the fear all in him and loved the power he had over him.

"Walk ya bitch ass into the woods! Hurry the fuck up befo' I blow ya top off!" Angel said, gritting his teeth.

"Aight jus' don't shoot me dog, I got nothin' to do wit Troy—" he got cut off.

"Shut ya bitch ass up and walk! I'm tellin' you don't make me pop you!" Angel grabbed him by the shirt and walked him into the woods. Crook walked backwards and kept the gun trained on him. Angel had his back towards the dirt road and never saw Smooth creep out the car with his pistol in his hand. Smooth was kneeling down as he snuck into the woods quietly.

"Jus' tell me why you have to kill Troy and Karen for?! You got the money and the bricks and you still had to kill him," Angel asked, with a deranged look.

Crook saw his partner creeping up behind Angel and was relieved. He was glad Smooth decided to roll with him to meet Angel. He smiled once he saw Smooth coming to his aid.

"Nigga you think dis shit iz funny?! I should peel ya cap right now!" Angel sniped, with rage in his eyes.

"You pussy ass nigga, you should've killed me when you had the chance . . . ." Crook laughed in his face.

"I'll show you a pussy, bitch!" Angel pulled the trigger but his pistol jammed. Smooth walked up behind Angel and put the pistol to his head. When Angel felt that cold steel up against his head he knew it was about to be over.

"When you fuck wit my nigga Crook . . . . you get took out the game!" Bang! Angel's life flashed before his eyes. Smooth shot him in the back of his head killing him instantly. Blood got spattered all over Smooth's face and clothes. Crook ripped the platinum chain off Angel's neck, then took his bracelet and pinky ring. Crook went through all Angel's pockets and retrieved a big bankroll and put it inside his pocket.

"Good looks on comin' through for me dog, now let's get up outta here." Crook walked off to his Pontiac. Smooth walked over to Angel's lifeless body and stood over top him. Smooth emptied his clip on Angel's body riddling him with slugs.

A week later Angel's funeral was held at the J.B Johnson Funeral Home in Roxbury. Angel had a massive funeral, every hustler in the South End stopped by to pay their respects. It was about five hundred people who showed up for the funeral; Angel was loved by many. Half of Warren street was lined up with cars trying to find parking places so they could come inside the funeral. Jerome mad the funeral arrangements and decided where Angel was going to get buried. Carolina and Gloria were both devastated so neither one of them could make funeral arrangements. Jerome stood by Carolina and Gloria's side when they went to look at Angel lying in the casket full of embalm. Angel went out in style; he was buried in street clothes inside a custom made Mercedes Benz casket with wheels on it. Carolina broke down and started breaking down and bawling when she stood over the casket looking at Angel.

". . . . Noooooooo! Why me god?! Why did he have to leave me for?! Angel why did you have to leave me?! Baby I can't live without you!" Carolina collapsed to her knees crying her eyes out.

Money got up out his seat and rushed to Carolina's aid. Jerome helped her to her feet and Money Bags helped escort her to sit-down. Gloria broke down crying and walked back to her seat next to Carolina. Jerome sat there with his black shades on trying to conceal his tears from coming down his face. Jerome wore his black t-shirt with a picture of Angel at the club on his shirt. All Angel's boys and cousins wore all black with RIP t-shirts. Jerome sat by Carolina and Gloria's side consoling the both of them. This was the day of Gloria's life; she had to bury her only child.

On the other hand Money Bags was not holding up too good, he was bawling and yelling in the funeral home. He kept on blaming himself for not being there with Angel. Ever since Angel's death, Money Bags kept beating up himself for not being there. Jerome tried telling him that it was not his fault. Money Bags was not trying to hear it he was furious. Money Bags knew who was responsible for Angel's death and vowed to get revenge.

After the ceremony was over, Jerome and Money Bags with four other people carried the casket to the hearse. A convoy of Boston Police Officers lead them all the way down Warren street clearing the way making sure it was no traffic. Angel was buried at the Mount Hope cemetery a couple of rows down from Troy and Karen. Jerome put the flowers on top of the casket and watched Angel get lowered six feet deep into the ground. Jerome said a silent prayer to himself and everyone left the cemetery.

Chapter 19

Angel's death was a blow to Detective Barros and Jerome was the last person he had standing on the positive side of his conscience. Crook on the other had was out of hand, but he had no strong evidence to put him away forever. All his leads were gone. Wally dead, Troy dead, and Angel was gone now. Detective Barros sat more comfortable in his office knowing he had Sarah on his back and they had the perfect relationship. She understood what his duties were, so she did not stress him out, which made him more aggressive towards the case.

Barros sat at his desk and drank his venti, mocha latte from Starbucks coffee. He ran through Crook's criminal files and wrote down every co-defendant he had in numerous cases even the victims. Some cases even had Troy linked to them. As he checked the address from one of Crook's files he came across a resident he never knew Crook lived at.

"Motherfucker, I'm get you!" Barros said, out loud as he placed attack in the middle of Crook's forehead between his eyes, on a mug shot hanging on his bulletin board.

Barros wrote the address down on a post it note, and he grabbed his jacket. He locked his office door and left the headquarters so he could stake the address out. He immediately thought, *"Hey, I'm going to check out the address, ask a few questions, what can possibly go wrong."*

Barros got into his '05 Jeep Wrangler. He loved his new Jeep; he debated whether he should've gotten into his into unmarked vehicle. But he figured everybody could possibly identify the cruisers because of its antennas.

As Roy pulled onto the street, the Oakley street sign was hanging down. He called city officials to have it fixed, but little did he know Crook was the mastermind behind the plan to take it down. Crook took it down so the street would be hard to find, in case of a run down with the police. That was until everybody started purchasing street pilot navigation systems.

The street was full of dope addicts and crack heads. Roy took his GPS system off the window view so it wouldn't get stolen. If a dope fiend got a hold of any electronics they would trade it for some drugs just to get a fix. Roy was smarter than that he didn't become the cop he was for was for no reason. For ten minutes he observed the house and no activities were going on.

"I guess I'm just gonna have to make the first move." Roy stepped out his jeep. He rang the doorbell and he received no answer. After a few more attempts, his pride forced him to try own entry and amazed the doors were all unlocked.

"Hello? Boston Police, I just got a few questions." Roy questioned anybody's presence wondering if anyone was home. He locked the door behind him and proceeded to evaluate the house. The safe spot looked completely a mess. Roy automatically knew the home was a Crook house, where fiends got high not worrying about law enforcement. Surprisingly nobody was in the apartment. As Roy entered the kitchen, he observed nearly five scales on the kitchen table. On the stove there were pots filled with boiled water, and on the floor by the stove, rested a huge box of baking soda.

"Bingo! This is what I like to see," Roy expressed happiness as he pulled out his Sony digital camera to take photographs. Roy photographed the scales, the pots on the stove, and boxes of baking soda. Now he needed drugs, but there wasn't any in the kitchen as he went through the cabinets with his latex gloves on.

"Fuck! Where could it be? I got you by the balls now Crook!" Roy thought.

Roy walked down the hallway then came to stop. He grabbed the doorknob and tried turning it, but the door was locked. He had came too far to just turn away with nothing. He wanted to present enough evidence to judge so he could issue a search warrant. His mind was at ease. He reached for his gun and pulled it out. He stepped back, took a deep breath, and kicked down the bedroom door as he brandished the pistol to each corner of the room.

"Oh yeah! Now we're getting somewhere," Roy felt like a soothsayer as he observed a half quarter of coke in ziploc bag on the mirror stand.

He took a picture of the coke and left it like it was. Barros continued to briefly search the bedroom. Everything he was seeing was too good to be true. Barros didn't find anything in the drawers, so he proceeded to the nightstand, where he now found $7,000 tied into a rubber band with a Rolex next to the cash in the drawer.

"This is unbelievable, I know you're watching me now Moses," he thought about his partner as he placed his hands on his waist.

Roy stood there shocked at what he was seeing. He stared at the mattress as he was lost in a deep train of thought. He quickly snapped out of it and continued to work. He had now gone through everything he could think of. He completed his search by lifting the queen size mattress to find a collection of five firearms.

"Jesus Christ! Today is my lucky day, stay wit me!" Roy cheered. He supported the mattress with one hand as he took photographs of the weapons, with the camera in one hand. Crook had a huge collection of weapons; two .40 cal's, one Smith and Wesson .38 snub nose, three nine millimeters Berettas, a tek-9, an AK 47 Assault rifle, and an AR 15.

"What the fuck! Is he going to war or something?" Roy questioned himself.

When Roy put the mattress back into its place he located some more jewelry on the nightstand opposite to the opposing one. He walked over to the nightstand and observed a heavy looking chain with an "A" medallion, and ring covered in blood stains. *"I hope this isn't what I think it is,"* Roy questioned himself.

Roy took the jewelry and put it in a plastic evidence bag for DNA sampling. His first reaction to the chain was connections to Angel since it was a letter "A" medallion. Roy felt like he had more than enough to get a search warrant. Due to Roy's past experience, he was certain that it was blood he was seeing on the medallion.

Roy Barros also felt like his pursue on catching Crook was coming to an end since he had all this evidence. Drugs, weapons, and now DNA that could possibly lead to an arrest for Angel's death, life could not be sweater. *"Crook you're so gone, you don't even know it . . . ."* Roy Barros spoke to himself.

Roy heard the first door to the house being slammed and he grabbed his gun immediately, then looked for a way out the apartment before he could be caught in a crossfire with whomever was coming into the apartment. He looked at the window and had no choice, he was lucky it was a first floor apartment and not the second. Roy quickly exited out the window as he heard two voices have a conversation.

"Man u done tol' these niggas to stay out the bedroom, now I'ma have to handle that . . . . and they kicked down my door!" Crook was mad at the heist he believed was a feind.

"Damn they didn't even take the work?" Smooth asked.

"I guess not! I'm gonna jus' throw dis work in a bag, and you jus' grab Tina." Crook told Smooth referring to the tek-9.

Barros remained silent by the window hearing the full conversation. He was paranoid, but this was his biggest shot at taking Crook down.

"Aight, Smooth, let make these moves . . ." Crook stated.

Roy Barros ran to the edge of the house and observed his surroundings before making a run to his jeep. This was good investigating. Now all he had to do was follow Crook. He waited patiently until they walked out the safe house.

"Who the fuck is that?!" Money Bags asked Jerome.

"I don't know but if he's down wit the set he could get laid down too," Jerome said, referring to Barros, who from a distance looked different.

After Angel's death Jerome had been vicious. He couldn't wait until he killed Crook, who now took away his family. Detective Barros was in a different jeep and from a distance Jerome could not recognize him. Jerome sat in his car watching the whole scene. Money Bags sat in the passenger side with his .40 caliber on his lap.

"Here they come, pay attention cuz." Money Bags advised.

Roy sat in the jeep and waited patiently to follow behind his two suspects. Crook and Smooth got into the Range Rover not aware of their surroundings. Roy knew Crook and Smooth were armed and dangerous, but this was too good to be left alone. As the Range Rover pulled off, Roy gave it a few seconds and he pursued to follow Crook.

"Stay with them, don't lose them . . . ." Money Bags told Jerome as he cocked the .40 caliber back putting one bullet in the chamber.

"I ain't! Trust me, I want dis nigga as bad as you do," Jerome replied.

The three cars followed each other up Geneva avenue and took a right onto Bowdoin street as they continued to drive up the busy street.

"Ayo, call dis fool and tell him be outside wit da cake so we won't be waitin' wit all dis work!" Smooth told Crook with package on his lap.

"I got you my duke!" Crook replied, as he called the customer. "Ya Ya, I'm takin' a right on ya street right now so come outside wit da gwop." Crook informed her as he took a right onto Draper street.

"Aight, Crook, I'm comin' downstairs right now . . . ." Ya'Ya disconnected.

Smooth was real militant he always kept his eyes open to any misplacement around him. He was smart and a coldblooded killer. As Smooth exchanged the package he observed the black jeep behind him.

"There you go! Now get the fuck away from the car!" Smooth advised Ya'Ya.

"Damn, Smooth, that's my customer you can't be like that," Crook reasoned.

"Nigga! We got the tek under my seat! If we get caught that's my second substance for me! I ain't havin' that my dude!" Smooth was furious.

"Yes! Yes! Yes!" Barros spoke in excitement as he took photographs of the transaction that just occurred.

This was not enough for one day, Barros wanted more so he continued to follow the Rover, and behind him, Jerome and Money Bags continued to follow also, assuming the second car was with Crook too. The two cars followed Crook down Arcadia road and Adams street.

"Crook hurry up and catch that light so I can see somthin'," Smooth requested out of suspicion.

Crook sped through the intersection of Dorchester avenue and Adams street baring right onto Dorchester avenue, barely making a pass at the traffic light. Barros could not afford to lose pursuit so he ran through the red-light. Jerome ran the red-light just like Barros did. At this point Smooth was aware that they were being followed.

"Crook, take dis right on Charles street, we got company." Smooth told Crook as he reached under his passenger seat retrieving the tek-9 holding thirty shots.

Detective Barros followed Crook as they were taking a left onto Geneva avenue and then a sharp right onto Tonawanda street. Barros did not lose sight of them as Jerome did the same. Smooth the told Crook to lose him.

"Crook, you already know what it iz! Jus' keep drivin' I'ma take care of dis."

Crook started speeding up long Tonawanda street picking up speed close to 60 miles per hour. On a main street that was too much. Detective Barros and Jerome kept up with him.

"Damn this guy is reckless," Barros expressed as he seen the Range Rover take a sharp left onto Greenbrier street.

"Don't lose them Rome, I can't afford dis." Money Bags said, with a serious face expression.

"I'm drivin' man fall back!" Jerome shot back.

"Yo cross over the park street to Alpha road and park on the left side of the road as soon as you turn down the hill," Smooth demanded.

Barros kept up to paw as he seen the Range Rover turn left down Alpha road. He stopped at the stop sign on the corner of Greenbrier and Park street, then he followed through onto Alpha road.

Smooth rolled down the passenger side window and stuck the tek-9 out, waiting for the appearance of the black jeep. "Yeah! Follow dis bitch!" Smooth aimed with a smirk on his face.

As Barros turned left down the road he drove into rounds of shells. Smooth fired the tek-9 at the jeep immediately shattering the windshield of the jeep wrangler. He continued to fire at the jeep until the tek-9 was empty "Die!" he yelled as he put the tek-9 back on his lap. The tek-9 had smoke coming out the chamber as he put it on his lap. They followed the jeep as it swerved down Alpha road hitting a light pole. The front end of the jeep was hugging the pole as smoke released from the engine.

"Hurry up man! I know you heard them shots I'm tryna let dis forty blow too. Your losin' them," Money Bags expressed.

As they turned down Alpha road they noticed the jeep crashed into light pole. "Oh shit, what the fuck jus' went down," Jerome questioned.

"If you had kept up I would've knew," Money Bags replied sarcastically.

At the end of the road they witnessed Crook's Range Rover take a left on Waldeck street. They continued to drive pulling up behind the smashed jeep wrangler. Detective Barros laid on the air bag with wounds. He was inches from reaching his death. Thinking nothing of it, Jerome knew the person driving the jeep was anonymous and he was going to find out who it was.

"Come on lets see who dis nigga iz and smoke dis fool. Grab the heat Rome!" Money Bags yelled, as he walked to the passenger side of the jeep.

Jerome walked to the driver seat with a .32 revolver in his hand. As he approached the jeep, the engine smoke was blowing in his direction. This made it hard for Jerome to identify who the victim was. As he got closer to the door he brandished his pistol at the driver's side door and recognized a familiar face.

"Officer Barros . . . ?" Jerome asked, trying to confirm his identity.

"You finally talked to me," Barros smiled in pain, half out of breath.

"Why you following Crook?" Jerome asked, believing he knew the purpose.

"Jerome, he killed your parents and I think Angel. I just never got the chance to prove it." Barros handed Jerome the chain and ring inside a plastic bag.

"Ayo, lets get out of here before them blue and whites get here bro!" Money Bags ran back to the car.

"Barros hold on! Your tellin' me Crook killed my parents and Angel?" Jerome asked, not wanting to believe the words he was hearing while staring at Angel's jewelry which he recognized.

"Crook—" Barros died before finishing his sentence.

Jerome jumped into his car and drove around the city in deep thoughts. He knew he recognized Crook from somewhere. His mind became stressful at this point. The love of his life was caught in the middle of a war between Jerome and her father. Mercedes, was still not aware of the whole drama, and Jerome wanted to keep it that way.

"Rome . . . . I got somethin' to tell you . . . ." Money Bags looked over at Jerome was silent. "Anything you decide to do I'm rollin' wit you. I know dis iz more personal to you but I'm ridin' lil homie. Everyday since Angel got murked I couldn't live wit myself for missin' that phone call." Money Bags addressed him, sounding hurt.

"Money, it's not ya fault. I witnessed him kill my mom and dad, he shot them like they were dogs . . ." Jerome explained.

"It ain't gonna be that easy, Rome." Money Bags exclaimed.

"I know, but I'm gonna make sure he's gone before I leave dis earth. And I can't believe my girl's father killed my peoples, my dude." Jerome said, in confusion.

"It's a small world, Rome, she ain't got nothin' to do wit dis so don't push her away my nigga."

"Ya right my dude, I'm gonna jus' keep rockin' Crook to sleep, we gon get dis cake and plan his funeral out, bitch!" Jerome told Money Bags referring to Crook.

———◆———

Detective Barros funeral was attended by many friends. Jerome attended just to a man who fought deeply to take down the murderers in the city of Boston, including his parents. Sarah on the other hand was crushed by Roy's death. She noticed Jerome at the funeral services and respected him for it. The funeral services were being held at Saint Patrick's church on Dudley street. Every time a Capeverdean victim passed away, their funerals were held there. Every Sunday the church was packed with the Capeverdean culture people. A few of Roy's friends spoke out for his service and Sarah felt the need to let Jerome know how important he was to Roy.

"Jerome, can I speak to you?" Sarah asked.

"I know Roy was an important man to all of you, but I don't speak to cops."

"Well can I get two minutes, I bet I'll change your mind," Sarah pleaded.

"Make it fast!" Jerome replied. "I'm finna get out of here I got things to do . . . ."

"Roy was your grandfather's partner back in the day when he started his career. When your father, Troy died, he took this case really personal. For years Roy has tried to take down the killers in the city and that's why it doesn't surprise me someone killed him . . . . all I'm saying is . . . . you respect that man, because believe it or not he cared about you and never gave up trying to solve the Christmas eve murders of your parents," Sarah ended in tears.

"Thank you," Jerome replied, feeling sorry. "I know who did dis!" Jerome added.

"Who, motherfucker tell me?!" Sarah asked, barely giving Jerome room to breathe. "Jerome, I want the bastards who did this to Roy!"

"I'm sorry, but it's personal to me and I already told you . . . I'm from the streets and we don't snitch." Jerome said sternly.

"It's Crook isn't it?" Sarah asked desperately.

"That's why you became a cop, do ya job," Jerome began to walk away. "Oh yeah, Ms. Cop lady . . . . find ya man, before I find him." Jerome added referring to Crook.

Jerome had a totally different look at Roy Barros. He hated all cops, but now he knew Barros lost his life trying to close a case over a decade ago. Sarah knew Crook was behind the whole death of Barros, but she had no proof. She had the pictures in Roy's digital camera developed, but where the pictures came from was the big question in her mind.

As the year passed by, Jerome became more sufficient with all the rumors, and he just sat back and observed the situation. Mercedes and him had now been dating for seven years, and Carolina was now a single parent with Angel's son, Angel Jr. named after his father. He was only one years old, but Jerome treated him the same way Angel treated him when he lost Troy and Karen. Everything Carolina needed, Jerome had gotten for her. Jerome was stuck with all the work Angel had left before passing away. Carolina was so accustomed to the streets that she began showing Jerome the rules to the drug game. It was close to a new year and Jerome had his New Year resolution; get money, make sure his family was set, and the most important was kill Crook.

"Dis is my year, I can feel it!" He thought to himself, as he stared at the Boston skyline. *"I need you watch over me, Angel."* He thought about Angel, as he stared at the stars in the sky.

Chapter 20

For the past three weeks Jerome's life been in a turmoil. Everything in his life was falling apart drastically. Jerome lost the three things he held dear; his father, his mother, and his best friend Angel. After hearing the shocking news from Homicide detective Roy Barros about who killed his parents—he was fed up and on the edge.

Jerome sat back plotting on how everything was going to be handled. He knew it had to be at the right time and place or it could be a possibility he'd get caught. On the strength of Mercedes and her mother, Gina—he chose not to bring no gunplay to their home. He had the uppermost respect for the both of them. The day it was time to his ultimate vengeance, he was going to do it right and make Crook pay for killing his parents and Angel. He had Crook right where he wanted him.

There was so much pain built up inside of Jerome that he was on the verge of going off anybody. The way he was feeling was like fuck the world! In his eyes everyone was a snake, so he had to keep the grass cut. The only people he had love for was family and a selective few people, he kept his circle tight. Everyone else was a potential enemy in his eyes.

Its been thirteen years since the gruesome murders he witnessed when both his parents were killed execution style.

Every so often he would have flashbacks of that horrific day. He lived in agony since he was a youngster and learned how to cope with it. Now he was so close to bringing everything to a closure. Jerome was well aware that Crook was a coldblooded killer who would kill for the slightest reason. So killing Crook was not going to be an easy task. It had to be well planned out and done right.

Money Bags explained on a daily to Jerome how they were going to touch Crook. Money Bags suggested that they play Crook close and befriend him until the time was right. Therefore, Crook would be more vulnerable and easier to touch. Initially, Jerome did not concur with the plan, but after doing some serious elaborating he came to a conclusion. Jerome realized that everything Money Bags was saying was right. Jerome knew he could capitalize on it due to the fact he was with Mercedes.

Money Bags took the demise of Angel hard, he vowed to get vengeance. It was painful for him trying to cope with everything without his right hand man. Now he felt as though he was carrying the world on his shoulders. Running the enterprise without Angel was becoming a burden on Money Bags. Angel was the one who always kept him grounded and motivated. Money Bags was comfortable with being Angel's enforcer when he was alive. He caught himself slipping but then reality struck, he had to pick himself up. He knew that Angel would not like the fact he was sitting around mourning and being depressed. So it was back to handling business and controlling their blocks.

Everyone in the streets and underworld knew Money Bags was known gunslinger, who handled his business when it was time to put someone in the dirt. The streets were talking for weeks about Angel's death, but nobody knew who was responsible. Money Bags wanted to keep it that way; the less people knew the better, he didn't want nobody knowing so they could have an idea he did it. Money Bags was known for making his enemies perish, so it was vital nobody knew he had something to do with it when Crook got killed.

It was time for Jerome to put everything behind him momentarily and focus back on getting money. After flipping the twelve bricks he got from Carolina, he went and bought twelve more and fifty pounds of weed. He had Angel's old connection on the coke and Crook knew nothing about it. All Crook knew was that Jerome was making lots of money in the city. Jerome's name was buzzing out in the hood, he was the man to see with descent prices. His whole intuition was to flood the streets with product and rise to the top. The timing for everything couldn't been any better—it was a drought in the city and he was taxing.

Money Bags suggested to him that they should sell half of the bricks for $30,000 a piece due to the drought, and then break the other half down into ounces so the workers could distribute the coke. Therefore, every worker that got a package could break it down into grams and see a vast profit. That way the workers were always happy, and they'll keep making the money for them. That's what it was all about; giving dudes packs and letting them make money so they could feed their family.

Money Bags explained everything about selling coke to Jerome on a day to day basis. For years Jerome shunned from the drug game due to the fact he saw too many fall victim to the streets. Jerome knew off top that coming into the coke game he had some big shoes to fill, and he was calm and collective about the situation. Jerome prided himself in being an excellent listener but not a very good follower. He wasn't trying to slip up like his father or Angel. He was prepared to take the good with the bad and deal with whatever god had in store. Jerome was now full-fledged in the streets and it was no turning back.

Jerome watched intently as Money Bags stood over the stove cooking coke in his tank top and jeans on. It was hot inside the small kitchen from all the moisturizer rising from on top of the stove. Money Bags wiped the sweat off his forehead with the back of his hand and proceeded to working his wrist. The coke was emitting a vile odor into the air. The entire apartment smelled like coke. This was the stash house where Money Bags and Jerome kept all the drugs and guns at. Living inside the projects in the city everyone knew each other and minded their own business. Especially living inside Ruggles street projects, nobody fucked with Money Bags and they looked the other way when he did something in their presence.

"Yeah . . . that bitch 'bout done now, lemme give it a lil more stirring. Looka here Rome, dis here that butter! Stop playin' . . . . call me chef boyee Money," he ranted.

"Yeah, that shit look like some butter Money, you ain't lying . . . ." Jerome said, looking into the Pyrex pot.

Money Bags turned the heat on the stove and stirred the fork around slowly inside the Pyrex pot that was boiling on the gas stove. He didn't want to burn the coke, so he turned the heat down on low. Money Bags filled a bowl up with ice so he could stick the Pyrex inside and cool it down. Jerome made sure he got all the details down packed so he would know how to do it himself.

"Rome, go fill me up another bowl wit ice cubes in it, I gotta cool dis shit down . . . ." Money Bags said.

Jerome went over to the freezer and started emptying ice trays into the bowl. He emptied three ice trays into the bowl and then walked over to the sink where Money Bags was at and watched him. Money Bags put the Pyrex pot underneath and let just a dab of cold water go inside. Afterwards, Money Bags went and sat down at the table.

"Rome, put twenty grams of soda on the scale for me."

"I got you, gemme a second I gotta find it."

"Dog it's right on the countertop next to the microwave, Rome."

Jerome went and retrieved the baking soda and commenced to weighing twenty grams on the scale. Jerome ripped a piece of cardboard from off the Glad sandwich bag box and scooped the baking soda up. Jerome took a pinch at a time and dropped it inside the Pyrex pot while Money Bags whipped it slowly with a fork.

"That's how you whip right there boy . . . . watch how dis bitch rock up and come back my nigga," Money Bags said, while sitting the Pyrex inside a bowl of ice.

That was the first step on a three step progress. Money Bags had let it cool off, harden up, and then air dry by the fan. He made sure it was always completely dry before he bagged it up. Money Bags didn't believe in giving anybody wet product. Some hustlers would do that to get over a couple of grams on somebody, but Money Bags, he didn't do none of that petty stuff.

"Let that shit cool off for 'bout fifteen minutes inside the bowl. Then you can dump it on a plate so it could dry from the fan, Rome. After watching me doin' dis all day, dog you'll be a beast in the game. You should be able to do dis on ya own now," Money Bags declared.

"Dog I got it down packed, I know I can cook on my own bro. You put twenty grizzes of soda on each hunnit grizzes, right?" Jerome inquired.

"Yep, somethin' like that homey. It all depends on how much you tryna stretch or how good you want ya work. The more soda you add to the yola . . . . the more ya gonna stretch it. I like to have it good so niggas will keep shopping wit up. If the workers got garbage, then they'll wanna go somewhere else and get the work. But if we always supply them wit butter, they'll always wanna work for us 'cause they'll be eating. You gotta always remember, none of these pollies wanna be copping garbage! It's a competitive biness my nigga, everyone's hustling crack, so our shit gotta be different and the best . . ." Money Bags emphasized.

Jerome sat there nodding his head listening while Money Bags dropped jewels on him about the game. The more he hung around Money Bags, the more of a liking he started taking in him. Jerome like how Money Bags always told the truth and kept it real at all times.

"Damn that shit look like some strait drop dere," Jerome said, as he picked up a piece of crack. "You ain't lying playboy ya cheffing skills iz ill! You can do ya one-two on the stove. After that shit dry we should go break Paula off wit a piece so she could tell us how it iz. You know she good peeps and she gonna keep it trill and tell us how it taste," Jerome stated, while looking at the product in his hand.

Money Bags nodded his head to what Jerome told him. Paula was one of their loyalist customers that spent money. Paula was a friend of Angel's mother who ended up getting high after losing her son to the penal system. Every package that ever go cooked, they would have her sample it to make sure it was good product.

"You already know Rome, off top we gonna tear Paula off so she could tell us how the shit iz. I can't hit none of my peeps off wit no garbage ass yola . . . . that's bad for biness lil homey," Money Bags proclaimed.

"Foshow I can dig it, Money, do whatever you gotta do to shake these bricks. I'ma go hit my cousin Ty wit ten pee's of dis green in a minute. You rollin' wit me after we go see Paula?" Jerome asked.

"Yeah, I'ma ride wit you, Rome, but first lets finish baggin' up . . . . all that other shit could wait. Ty ain't goin' nowhere iz he? Plus, it's only a weed play anyways . . . ." Money Bags said, unconcerned about what Jerome wanted to do.

"So here you go wit that he could wait shit . . . . that got things to do jus' like us. I don't care if it iz only a weed play, dog that's money I need! A nigga want it all!" Jerome said, looking him in his eyes and meaning.

"I feel you my dude, a nigga should've seen the big picture. Rome, you right, that's money to get and we need it all . . . ." Money Bags touched the four and a half ounces he had on the plate drying. "Word, that's all so we can break that down wit the rest. Rome, go grab me more sandwich bags out the cabinet. Lemme bag the rest of dis up before we make moves, and then we could drop dis big 8 off to Gee, and then hit Montana wit a six dooby," Money Bags stated.

Jerome went over to the countertop and grabbed the box of sandwich bags and the razor from inside the draw. Jerome passed the Money Bags the utensils and he went to work chopping it into individuals ounces for later on.

"Word, everything iz all bagged up for niggas . . . I'm still waitin' on Shizz to call me, I know he need more work over there in Lenox street." Money Bags glanced down at his Panda Bear Cartier covered in diamonds and sapphires. "Damn it's two o'clock already, I coulda swore we jus' came up in here at eight dis mornin'."

"Dog we did, ya goin' nutz Money!" Jerome started laughing. "We done put it down today, we cooked everything quick as fuck. We made two extra bricks off those six we cooked, right? 'Cause if worst comes to worst and niggas ain't tryna pay thirty a wop, we could jus' chef the rest of dem up," Jerome suggested.

"Hol' up lets get dis shit right, nigga I jus' cooked everything up . . . . all you did was watch and learn from a vet! I hope you getting the game down packed, 'cause I might not always be here to walk you through dis. And we made an extra two keys off those six I cooked, so that's jewel money after we flip that," Money Bags said, grinning from ear to ear.

Jerome looked at him and just shook his head. Money Bags was a lot older than him and was stuck in his ways. Jerome couldn't tell him that he had enough jewelry . . . . because Money Bags was too stubborn. So Jerome opt to keep his mouth quiet and let Money Bags do him.

"Whatever big homey, a nigga iz good now on cooking. I know how to work my wrist now, might not be as nice iz you yet, but the kid can cook. Believe that Money, I've been observing." Jerome reassured him.

"That's what I like to hear, a nigga been doin' dis shit for a long time my nigga. Sometimes dis shit get's tiring, feel me my G?"

"Yeah, I feel you aight . . . . I feel you full of shit! Money, all you know how to do iz sell drugs and cook, that's all you love doin'. It ain't in you to go work a job . . . ."

They both busted out laughing at the remark Jerome said. Money Bags knew he was absolutely right about what he said. Money Bags been in the streets for ten years selling drugs and busting heads. Money Bags was infatuated with the game and liked the vast profits he got from hustling.

"Damn bro you look jus' like ya pops, you a splitting image of Troy." Money Bags looked at Jerome who now had a solemn look on his face. "My fault Rome, I should've never brought up ya pops name," Money Bags said sincerely.

Money Bags knew the mere thought of his father made Jerome feel down. Jerome sat there staring off at nothing. Jerome was in a reverie thinking about his parents. Jerome sat there reminiscing about his childhood years and wondered how his life would've turned out his parents were alive. Money Bags noticed he was in deep thought and decided to break the silence.

'Rome, ya pops was a dog my nigga, I know you probably done heard stories . . . . but I'ma state the facts," Money Bags voice trailed off and his eyes started to get watery, but he couldn't let it out he had to hold his composure. "Ya pops iz the one who taught me the game; Troy showed me how to get money, and how to be a man first. That man showed me how to take care of my family and provide food in my refrigerator. When I met ya pops, Rome, I was 'bout thirteen at the time and homeless on the streets. My mom dukes was a strait dope fiend, we lived from shelter to shelter in the bean." Money Bags wiped the tears away from his eyes.

Everything Jerome was hearing from Money Bags was all new to him. Jerome didn't know Money Bags had a rough childhood too. Now he kind of understood why Money Bags did the things he did. They both grew up without their parents in different circumstances. Jerome wanted to really know how is father really was so respected in the city. Even until this day people still talked highly of his father.

"Yo, my pops used to be a goon back in the days, huh? He used to clap mad niggas I bet?" Jerome asked, inquisitively.

Money Bags began to smirk a little bit, "Rome, ya pops was far from a goon, ya pops was a gangster! He had goons who'll go put in work for him if he gave the word. Troy, was all about getting money, everything else came with the territory. You know how the saying goes: the more money you see, the more problems you get. Ya pops had blocks on smash, beat a body and a bunch of conspiracy charges, ya pops was a soldier," Money Bags told him.

"Come on lets roll out, I gotta go see Ty. Grab that work for Gee and Montana, I got that for Paula," Jerome said, while picking up his backpack with ten pounds of weed inside it. "Lets get dis fuckin' paper my nigga til the death of us. *It ain't no turning back now,"* Jerome thought.

They grabbed their pistols and left out the apartment. Jerome hoppede in his SL 500 with the 20inch Ashanti rims. Money Bags put in a Gucci Mane CD and gave it some volume. "Money kinda short, but we can work it out . . . . Made a hunnit thousand, out my trap house . . . ."

Riding down Columbus avenue Jerome was getting looks from various females that were outside. He caught one Puerto Rican female at the bus stop smiling at him and staring as he sat at the red-light. If he wasn't in such a rush and didn't have so much drugs on him, he probably would've stopped and got her number. She was definitely something to fuck in his eyes. The light turned green and Jerome turned left on Dudley street bypassing the Reggie Lewis Center on his left.

"Call Paula and tell her open the door," Jerome said.

Money Bags pulled out his prepaid T-Mobile cell phone and hit her on speed dial. Money Bags hustled smart in the streets that's why he never been arrested. He switched up phones every three weeks because he always thought they were tapped, and he seldom used any other phones besides prepaid. After the phone rang three times a lady answered the phone.

"Hello, what's good Paula? Oh you don't know who it is . . . ? It's Money Bags, yeah . . . . well, me and lil' Rome out front. Open the door, we got somethin' for you. We out front now, bye . . . ." Money Bags disconnected the call and put his phone in his pocket. "Pull over and park behind that raggedy ass Integra on ya left, Rome. She said for us to come upstairs."

Jerome parked behind the car and killed the ignition. The both departed from the Benz and walked into the apartment building where an elderly lady with salt and pepper hair was standing in the doorway holding the door open. The lady smiled when she saw both of them walking over towards her.

"Look at y'all . . . . I can't believe how big your getting Rome, and Money Bags you looking sharper than ever. Y'all come on inside . . . . it's cold out here, the last thing I need is for my arthritis start acting up." Paula walked over to the elevator and they all went inside.

They got off at the fourth floor and walked straight across to her apartment. Even though Paula got high, she kept her apartment looking descent. Her place was well furnished and immaculate. "Y'all boys take a seat if y'all want in the living room, go on and make yourselves at home." Paula gestured for them to sit down.

"Now what you got for me, Money Bags? You know I'm going to give it to you funky . . . . if that shit some garbage I'll tell you, and if it's that butter you'll know." Paula said, cutting the small talk and getting strait to the point.

Money Bags pulled out the garbage and handed it to her. "Paula that's three eightballs right there, so you go on and smoke up in front of us," Money Bags stated.

Paula pulled out her straight shooter form inside her robe pocket. She took a seat on the couch directly across from Jerome and Money Bags and started breaking up the crack on the coffee table. Paula picked up a nice size rock, placed it on the end of her straight shooter, and put the flame to a glass vial. Paula took a long hard blast and instantly her ears started ringing. She was high as a kite.

"M-M-Money Bags this is some good shiiitttt . . . ." Paula stammered.

Money Bags looked at Jerome who had a smirk on his face because he was glad they had watched Paula get geeked out her mind. Now it was time to get the work on the streets to all the workers and customers.

"Paula, we getting' ready to get up outta here . . . . I'll talk to you," Money Bags said.

Paula was so high she couldn't even talk at the moment. Paula kept walking to her window and looking out thinking she heard someone outside. Money Bags just shook his head in disbelief 'cause he knew she was high. Every time Paula would smoke she would get paranoid thinking the police is coming for her. Money Bags and Jerome left out the apartment.

"I tol' you baby-boy dis iz some butter, Rome, you seen how she was in there geeking. We 'bout to make a killin' wit dis fire lil daddy . . . . watch and see my nigga," Money Bags was excited as he walked to the car.

Jerome nodded his head to all the ranting Money Bags was doing and hit the alarm button to unlock the doors. Jerome drove to Mattapan next to go meet his cousin Tyrell inside Morton Street Projects.

"Turn left down Mildred ave my nig," Money Bags said, while staring in the passenger side rearview mirror.

Jerome put on his left blinker and turned off Norfolk street onto Mildred avenue. Now Jerome glanced in his rearview mirror and noticed a gray Crown Vic was behind him driving slow.

"That look like dem boys behind me dog, if they put on those lights I'm gone . . . ." Jerome stated, while keeping his eyes in the rearview.

The Crown Vic turned right down Maxwell street and Jerome was relieved. Jerome proceeded straight all the way until he got to Gallivan Blvd and turned right. Jerome pulled into the projects and it looked deserted as he was cruising through. A few buildings were boarded up with no trespassing signs posted on the building. Jerome turned down Woodbole street and then parked behind a 745 BMW. Jerome pulled out his cell phone and turned his ignition off.

"Ty, open the door, I'm out front," Jerome said, then hung up.

Tyrell came to the door with his tank top and boxers on. "What's good fool, how you doin' cuz? What's good Money Bags, I see you shinning wit the Cartier on . . . ." Tyrell said, with a smile on his face while dapping his people up.

"Man I ain't no where I'm jus' tryna keep up wit you playboy," Money Bags replied.

"Ty, I need the whole eight stacks cuz, I need all my gwop 'cause I gotta go to the store." Jerome handed the backpack over to Tyrell.

"You got that Rome. Lemme go upstairs and go grab that for you fam." Tyrell walked upstairs with backpack in his hand.

The first thing Tyrell did was weigh each individual pound on the scale. He did this to make sure the weight was right. Even though him and Jerome was family—this was business and nothing personal. After weighing all eight pounds and seeing that they were correct, Tyrell went inside his safe in the closet and counted out $8,000.

"Here you go cuz . . . . it's all there too, the whole wop. Count it out if you wanna," Tyrell handed Jerome a knot with a rubber band around it.

"You already know I'ma count it, Ty, it's biness dog nothin' personal!" Jerome tore the rubber band off and commenced counting the hundred dollar bills. "Everything all good Ty, yo hit me up after you shake all dat. What you getting' into dis weekend?"

"Shit . . . . I'm fallin' back I gotta get dis paper, I jus' lost ten stacks at Foxwoods. So I'ma chill for probably a month before I go out. Matter of fact, I'll probably jus' fall back 'til New Year's eve, then I'll do it big." Tyrell said, with a grin.

"Aight. I'm out Ty, I gotta go make these runs. Get wit me doggy," Jerome dapped him up.

"I'ma get at you definitley, be easy Money Bags." Tyrell dapped Money Bags up. "I still got my eye on dat fuck boy Crook, so when the time iz right, he gotta go bro!" Tyrell said, looking Jerome dead in his eyes.

Jerome felt what he was saying but wanted him to stay out of it. This was a one man mission, this was personal. Jerome wanted to handle this on his own.

"I feel you dog, but dis something I gotta do on my own. If I need help on dis one, trust me you and Money would be the first ones I call," Jerome assured them.

"Be easy lil' cuz, I love you my nigga. Real talk fam, if you need me for anything . . . . I mean anyhting1 Jus' call me up and I'll be there . . . ." Tyrell said sincerely.

Jerome looked his older cousin Tyrell in the eyes and nodded his head. Tyrell was a standup dude who was down to die for his peoples. Jerome had nothing but love for him.

"I'll be in touch . . . ." Jerome turned his back and walked out the door.

Chapter 21

Jerome's mind was rambling as he was driving through the backstreets of Mattapan. He was trying so hard to understand life and cope with all the pain he endured. Things in his life were dramatic and changing daily whether it was for the good or bad. Jerome made his moves wisely and never let his right hand know what the left was doing. He kept his friends close and his enemies even closer. Angel instilled them values in him as an adolescent. After figuring out all the pieces to the puzzle it took everything in him no to react, instead he sat back and devised a plan, a plan so organized that if he pulled it off he'd be able to lift the burden off his chest that he carried for over a decade.

He reached down in the ashtray and grabbed the dutch he had lying there neatly rolled ready to be lit. Jerome put the blunt to his lips and lit it up while he kept his eyes on the road. He wasn't an avid weed smoker, but whenever he had stress on his mind he smoked. After turning right off Itasca street, Jerome emerged on Cummins Hwy. He drove another five blocks until he got to Mount Hope Cemetery and then pulled inside the largest cemetery in Boston. It was like a world inside another world driving down all the different streets inside the cemetery. Many men have been laid to rest there for either gangbanging or drug dealing. Plus, there was your Vietnam Vets and War heroes who were laid to rest also. Jerome drove slowly peering to his right until he found his destination. It was a beautiful night outside and the wind-chill made it feel like a fall day instead of it being a winter day on New Year's Eve. Jerome killed the ignition, retrieved the 5th of Remy Martin off the backseat, and then departed from the vehicle with a blunt dangling from his lips.

"I miss y'all so much . . . ." Jerome said in a low monotone. In front of him were the three people he loved dearly: Troy, Karen, and Angel. He could feel the tears welling up and he couldn't hold them back anymore, so he let them flow freely as he drank from the bottle of cognac. Jerome stood in front of his mother's headstone first and began talking.

"Momma, I know ya lookin' down on me right now and ya probably sayin' that a lot of things I'm doin' out here ain't right, but God knows ain't nobody perfect, momma. I mus say I did grow up fast and even though I'm not in college or trade school—I finished high school. Momma, goin' to college isn't for me, I never really believed in getting' a higher education. It hasn't been the same for me ever since I witnessed that nigga kill y'all . . . ." Jerome wiped his tears away with the back of his hand. "I swear on everything I love momma, I'm not gonna rest 'til I make dis problem go away. After I handle this one last sin I vow to leave the streets alone for good. Momma, I love you so much and miss you daily, I'll see you someday up above and we'll reunite and catch up on old times. But 'til that day comes, I'll be out here living my life to the fullest so please watch over me . . . ." Jerome paused for a moment and then kissed her headstone.

Jerome walked a few feet to his right to the headstone of his father who was juxtaposed to his mothers. He put the dutch to his mouth and lit the blunt up again after letting it go out. He took three deep pulls of the haze and held the smoke in for a few seconds as he sat there contemplating. Life was like chess and Jerome played the game inside his head daily just to stay a few moves ahead. No matter how bad he wanted to murder Crook there was no bringing his parents or Angel back. Even though he understood that theory quite clear, vengeance was on his mind for over a decade; so he was going to play the judge and jury, and Crook was guilty which meant death by any means.

"Pops, whassup man . . . I miss you and momma like crazy down here. I'm just tryna maintain out here without losing my mind. Shit is a mess out here in these streets, pops! The game ain't the same no more and tellin' is at an all time high. Sometimes I wonder what life would've been like if y'all were still alive. I know you probably thinking to yourself up above and sayin' that I'm following in your footsteps, pops, but I'm really not. I know a lot of things I'm doin' right now you wouldn't approve of it if you were still alive—" Jerome's voice trailed off and he took another swig of cognac. "Well the truth iz, the streets iz in my bloodline, pops, and at times it feels as though dis iz the only thing I know." Jerome inhaled the blunt three more times then blew it out through his nose. "But on the real pops I gotta make a change, I plan on goin' legit soon. I know I can't hustle forever. 'Cause I know the game can't be lived, it's only to be played . . . ." Jerome knelt down in front of his father's headstone and kissed it.

Jerome took one last pull off the dutch and then chucked it on the ground once it became a roach. He walked over to his right a couple of feet to Angel's headstone and dug into his jacket pocket, he pulled out a dutch filled with purplehaze and sat it on the headstone. Every other Sunday was a ritual for Jerome to go visit his family at the cemetery. Whenever he went to visit Angel's gravesite, he'd pour out liquor and leave a blunt behind for his best friend. He was loyal to his family so showing up every other week was a must; Angel was more like a brother from a different mother.

"Whassup big homie . . . . I know you watching over me right now and can see my every move I make. I miss you like cooked food my nigga. I gotta keep it one hunnit witcha; Angel, you taught me everything I know out here in these streets. If it wasn't for you bro, I don't even think I would've lasted dis long out here getting' money. As far as business, dawg shit iz boomin' and everything iz lovely. Me and the nigga Money Bags iz holding it down out here. That nigga iz a good dude foreal, A. Your son iz getting' so big, and the more I look at him, the more he reminds me of you." Jerome let the tears fall freely down the side of his face. "Carolina iz doin' a hell of a job raisin' ya lil boy, you picked the right woman to bear ya child bro. She's a good woman and excellent mother. I'm still wit Mercedes and we still going strong. That's my heart bro no bullshit. I don't want no other lady in my life but her, she's my better half. But the fucked up thing iz she's gonna lose her pops . . . ." Jerome shook his head from side to side 'cause he hated to put his girl through what he endured. "Even though it's gonna hurt my bitch, I can't show no remorse or let it ride, it has to be done . . ." Jerome was crying as he poured out the rest of the Remy Martin for Angel who was resting in peace. Jerome climbed inside his Benz and sped into the night. He had work to do on the other side of town.

Chapter 22

"I tol' em strait drop dis and Ziploc that . . . . right on my waistline iz where I kept that strap . . . . I remember nights, I didn't remember nights, where I damn near went crazy I had to get it right . . . ." Crook let Young Jeezy's CD play as he sat in the driver's seat of his Money Green Aston Martin Vantage driving it through the city. Crook got his lean on while smoking on the purple and nodding his head to the music. It was like the music was soundtrack to his life. Crook really didn't really rock with too many rappers but something about Jeezy's style he could feel—it was like he could feel dude really was living the life or lived it at one point in time. Crook looked down at his lap where his phone was vibrating and hit the ignore button after seeing it was Gina. Crook wasn't trying to argue with her or hear her complain about him going out to the club.

Crook had the luxury coupe zooming down 93 south in the carpool lane. Going over the Zakim Bridge at nighttime you could see the bright lights illuminating the ground. The V-12 engine had the coupe purring like a cat on quiet night in heat, but the power and speed was like a cheetah in the jungle. The HID lights gleaming from the Aston Martin lit up the bridge like Times Square at night. Crook was flaunting his opulence tonight. Not too many minorities coming from the slums like Crook were able to beat to odds and be successful. There were a lot of good dudes who laid to rest before their time or were doing natural life; Crook happened to be lucky and make it to the next level in the game. Crook prevailed from being a street corner to becoming the man with bricks. Crook took the good with the bad and played the hand he was dealt.

Smooth was sitting low in the passenger seat with a blunt dangling from his lips as he was listening to Thug Motivation 101 and staring out the window through the tints. Smooth peered to his right and got a glimpse of the TD BankNorth Garden as Crook switched from the fast lane and was getting ready to get off at exit 26. Tonight Crook and Smooth had plans on bringing in the New Year with a bang. They intended on partying to the extreme and spending lavishly at club Aria. Crook passed the blunt back over to Smooth who was in a reverie staring out the window and peering in the rearview. Smooth stayed vigilant and that's one of the main reasons Crook brought him to the club tonight. Smooth was a enforcer and Crook was the mastermind. He liked to bust heads and really wasn't too fond for selling coke. Smooth lived for the moment and was all about fucking mad bitches and shooting dudes for his right hand man. They were loyal amongst each other. Smooth's motto was anybody could get touched. There wasn't no bullshit or half assing about Smooth—his name rang bells in the streets and prisons for laying down his gun game. It was always about getting respect in Smooth's eyes—he solidified his position as a gunner.

Crook and Smooth were ciphering the blunt back and forth to each other as there were a few words between the two. They were feeling like a million bucks with fresh haircuts and new apparel. Crook was clad in so much diamonds it looked as though he was on his way to do a video shoot. Smooth on the other hand kept it simple with just a pinky ring and iced out bracelet. When Crook pulled up out front of club Aria, he shut it down out front. He was turning heads everywhere out front the club as females were breaking their necks trying to peer through the twenty percent black tints. Crook was loving the attention he was receiving from the groupies out front the club. Even though he knew it was the car they really was lusting over—he still got a kick out of it. Seeing hood-rats flocking over him boosted his ego. Crook was feeling himself at this moment. He was ready to go blow some stacks and show off. Crook was well known in all the clubs Downtown for his lavish spending. Just about every bouncer knew who he was and Crook got in everywhere with his pistol. Crook reached down underneath his seat and retrieved a P89 Ruger and placed it on his lap.

"Let's go party hard and ball outta control my nigga," Crook took the last pull off the haze and chucked it out the window.

"You already know doggy . . . . now let's go bring in the New Year right."

"Smooth, you got the blick on you, right? Niggaz got too much smoke out here and we can't be caught slippin', feel me dawg?"

"Dawg I'm already hipped about these bustas hating . . . . I stay wit my joint everywhere I go. Even when I go takes a shit my bulldog iz watchin' my back," Smooth flashed him the chrome .44 snub-nosed and grinned. "Now let's go pop a few bottles and do our thing. I got bitches to see holmes . . . ."

Crook couldn't help but smirk at his partner. True in deed Smooth never went anywhere without a pistol on him. For all the bodies that Smooth had under his belt it was rational that he stayed equipped. Smooth wasn't paranoid of any sort like that—he was just prepared. Smooth was a firm believer of the old adage; live by the gun, you die by the gun. Better safe than sorry.

They stepped out the vehicle and all eyes were on them from the patrons in the line that snakes halfway down the block. Crook had a cheese eating grin on his face 'cause he was never going to be one of them waiting in line. Crook gave the valet a ceenote and the keys to his whip. When Crook and Smooth walked up on the bouncers they were embraced. Crook slid the three hefty bouncers hundred dollar bills and they parted out the way of the two hood legends in the making.

❦

Jerome sat in the lab watching naked women break down bricks of cocaine. All the workers wore rubber gloves, goggles, and surgical mask. Their task was to break apart each brick of coke and remove 125grams (an eight). The weight was then replaced, or cut with a filler, or comeback. Both the cocaine and the filler, typically a liquid addictive called proscent, were thrown into a food processor and thoroughly blended. The workers then used spatulas to spoon the mixture into a mold. Finally, a five-ton jack would be used to press each kilo back together. For every seven kilos that were cut, blended, and pressed, a new kilo would be formed out of the grams that had been removed. The females were paid crumbs for the task and they didn't complain. Jerome had fourteen kilos that were in the process of being cut, and after the workers were finished, there would be sixteen kilos. Not to mention if he decided to cook them all up into crack, he would probably produce an extra five kilos tallying about twenty-one bricks—best believe Jerome was good with math.

The labs were set up in inconspicuous locations: a house on Rosemont street, a house in the upscale suburb of Canton, a nondescript apartment on Fairmount street, and another swanky home across town. The room used for the lab would be outfitted with air-filtration system, to make sure the workers didn't get too much of a contact high. The last thing Jerome needed was one of his workers getting high. Becoming a drug abuser would be out the picture, he wouldn't be able to put up with a larcenous crackhead. He knew crackheads and dopefiends were desperate individuals, and in other words they were far from trustworthy. But still, Jerome had trust issues and that is why he kept the females naked so they couldn't steal nothing.

Money Bags stood at the far corner of the room opposite of where Jerome was standing. He watched intently as their workers worked diligently getting the task complete. Money Bags gave his partner a head nod and then Jerome walked back into the other room. Jerome sat down at the table and resumed to counting money. Every penny and every dollar, Jerome counted it himself. In the life he was living you had to be extra cautious or else people would steal from you. But for the most part he kept a small circle and didn't allow people outside his circle to know too much. Everything was done on the sly. It had to be done this way in order to stay two steps ahead of the wolves and the law.

Jerome sat there running bills after bills through the money machine. Every thousand dollars he tied a rubber band around it and pushed the stack to the side. The process was done meticulously at least once a week to keep up with the earnings. Jerome knew that if he wasn't on the job keeping an eye on his peso's, there could be a possibility someone would be skimming. Dudes in the streets knew Jerome wasn't no joke so he got respect. Last dude who tried running off with a package got put in the hospital. Money Bags made it a point to lay his gun game down on anybody out of line. If you owed money and didn't pay you got dealt with accordingly. So after that episode nobody else tried Jerome. Just off his father's name alone OG's in the game bought coke off him. He was the man that made it snow in the hood.

The past four hours Jerome been in the stash house counting money and breaking bricks down. He had stash houses all throughout the city but this specific one he liked the most; this house was located on Rosemont street in Hyde Park, the area was not too quiet and not too wild—it was just right, the ideal location to store drugs at. All the neighbors minded their business and that's what he like. It was nights like these where he thought about having a normal life. Granted, he was getting serious money in the streets, but his heart longed a different life. It was like his hand was forced to be who he became, sometimes he wondered if his parents didn't get killed would his life still be in shambles? Well that's what his mind kept telling him. Jerome's thoughts were interrupted by the sound of his phone ringing. He pulled the phone from inside his jeans and looked at the caller ID before answering.

"What's good witcha, Rell . . . . scream at me my, G."

"Dawg . . . . you ain't even gonna believe who right here at the club wit me right now." Tyrell said, barely above a whisper.

"I'm listening." Jerome sat there and remained silent while listening to everything that was being said right at the moment. He couldn't believe his luck. Now was the chance to settle an old score that he been desperately wanting to do. The pieces to the puzzle were now coming together. Jerome quickly formulated a plan in his head while listening to all the details. This had to be done right. The club was the ideal place to handle the situation; but still, sometimes things didn't always go as planned.

"Rell, whatever you don't let that fuckboy leave ya sight. I'm on my way right now as we speak."

"Rome, you know I got ya cuz on some real shit. I'm on it say no more. Jus' hit me on the jack when you get downteezy."

"Bet." Jerome clicked his Nextel shut.

Club Aria was packed to the capacity and everybody there were enjoying themselves tonight. Crook played the back of the club with his cohort. Soon as they entered the club they were immediately ushered to the VIP section by security. The club owner knew Crook well and made it a point to accommodate his services whenever he was in the building. Crook reserved the table a week in advance to ensure himself there would be a table waiting. A bucket of ice with two bottles of Moet Rose' were waiting for Crook and Smooth soon as they were seated. Crook popped a bottle and Smooth followed suit. Weed smoke lingered in the air like clouds outside. Crook snickered to himself as he caught the eyes of a few females staring him down from across the room. The group of females were posted at the bar parlaying and sipping on mixed drinks. From his viewpoint the females looked attractive. Crook beckoned them over to the VIP lounge and all three of them walked over.

"Ayo I got three bad ass bitches comin' over to the table right now." Crook said, getting Smooth's attention. "Throw ya game face on."

"Nigga my game face stays on doggy, you ain't know." Smooth placed a Backwood to his lips, and sparked it. "Hoodrats love me, and they baby daddy's wanna plug me . . . ." Smooth ranted while puffing on the haze.

Crook did a light chuckle at his partners response. Smooth was a fool like that sometimes. It wasn't a chick in the 'hood that didn't know Smooth or done heard about his trifling ways. Smooth done slept with half the town.

"Well, jus' in case these bitches are some squares from Delaware, my nigga please act accordingly. Don't play yourself in front these hoes, lemme feel 'em out first and see where they heads at. You know I stay in a bitch head like a migrane . . . ." Crook sipped the Rose' as the broads walked up to the table.

Crook was in a state of bliss when he saw the three women before his eyes. All three of them were sexy. The swarthy one in the middle of the trio caught his attention. She was built like a stallion and the way her dress accentuated every curve made Crook fantasize about copulation. She had her hair cut short in the front and wore it in a bang while the back hung down to her shoulders. The stiletto's she had on made her stand about six feet and gorgeous. This woman had plenty of sex appeal. Crook stood up to introduce himself to the females.

"Hello, ladies, how y'all doin' tonight? I hope y'all enjoying yourselves, 'cause if you ain't, I'm sure me and my homeboy can brighten up y'all night up. By the way, my name is Cory, and it's a pleasure to meet y'all . . . ." Crook smiled and reached his hand out to shake all three their hands.

"Nice to meet you Cory, and our night is coming along alright. My name is Chauntae, sweetie."

"Hello, ladies, how y'all doing tonight? I hope y'all everything yourselves, 'cause if you ain't, I'm sure me and my homeboy can brighten up all up y'all night up. By the way, my name is Cory, and it's a pleasure to meet y'all . . . ." Crook smiled and reached his hand out to shake all three of their hands.

"Nice to meet you Cory, and our night is coming along alright. My name is Chauntae, sweetie." The dark-skinned one said who Crook had his eyes on. "And this is Jackie." She pointed towards her right. "Is there anything else you would like to know about us, Cory?" Chauntae smiled from ear to ear.

"Boo, I want to know all about you eventually, if you don't mind. But right now let's have some drinks and kick back. And by the way ladies, this is my homeboy—" Crook got cut short.

"Beautiful, ladies, it's pleasure meeting all of you. My name is Shawn, the ladies charm . . . ." Smooth turned and looked Tiffany in the eyes. "Now if you don't mind, love, I'd like to get acquainted with you, have a seat and let's have a toast for the New Year. What type of drinks do y'all ladies want? Get whatever y'all want it's on me." Smooth slid to the side and let the ladies take a seat on the sofa.

Smooth and Crook seldom gave their government name out to females. They never wanted none of their dirt to catch up with them. The way they looked at it was always better to cover you tracks. Plus, if a baby sprung along the way the woman wouldn't nowhere to delve.

"Shawn, you can get me some grey goose with cranberry that'll be fine." Tiffany smiled at him showing her dimples. "A cup or two would be cool with me I'm not too much of a drinker." Tiffany sat her purse on the side of the couch positioning it between her arm.

"Me and my dawg don't buy drinks in the club—we buy everything by the bottle and then pour our own drinks." Smooth placed his left hand on her thigh and let her get a glimpse of his ten karat diamond bracelet glistening.

Tiffany looked at his wrist and pinky finger in awe, she never saw that many diamonds on somebody in her life. She knew both dudes were getting some serious money by the jewelry they wore and how they carried themselves. Tiffany didn't resist the extra touching Smooth was doing to her in VIP. Her nose was open and Smooth could see she was feeling him. If it wasn't a dude like Smooth she would've been pissed that someone was fondling her. But Smooth was a major dude and she knew he had long money so she didn't mind. All she saw was dollar signs in Smooth and was going to let him do whatever he wanted tonight. Smooth had a thing with light-skinned broads and always had to have them. That's why Smooth usually fucked them and ducked them. Tiffany was going to be treated no different from the rest.

Tiffany was beautiful with caramel complexion and hazel eyes. She had soft full lips and wore her hair cut short in a Halle Berry design. Smooth wanted to suck on her juicy lips just sitting there watching her work the lip gloss. Tiffany had knee high leather boots and a fitted BeBe shirt on that hugged her chest. Smooth smiled at her adoring her voluptuous body. She was thick in all the right places. Crook noticed the chemistry between his partner and Tiffany and broke the awkward silence.

"Shawn, get the waitress over here ASAP these pretty young ladies want some drinks. And roll some of that purple up, I'm tryna get high . . . ." Crook downed the last of Rose'.

"Aight, my dude I got you, Cory." Smooth said, with sarcasm. "Yo, shawty and dem wanna drink goose too?" Smooth waited for response.

"Yeah goose is cool with us . . . ." They replied in unsion.

"Here my nigga . . . ." Smooth passed the blunt. "I'ma roll up some more in a minute, but first lemme order some more drinks, I mean bottles . . . . : Smooth beckoned for the blond headed waitress to come over.

"Do what you gotta do doggy dog." Crook replied and then resumed to conversing with Chauntae.

Smooth was playing it cool and willing to do whatever to accommodate the ladies. His main objective was to get some pussy and head from Tiffany and get gone with the wind. Smooth was known for meeting a broad at the club and having his way with her the same night. The blond headed waitress came walking over to their table.

"Damn this snowbunny got the cheeks," Smooth thought to himself. "Miss lemme get two more bottles of Rose' and a bottle of Grey Goose also. Oh yeah, and lemme get some cups with the Cranberry juice too. And make sure it's on ice miss . . . ." Smooth pulled out a knot and peeled off eight ceenotes and handed them to the waitress. "Keep the change boo don't even worry about it." Smooth smiled at her.

The blond headed waitress jotted down everything Smooth asked for. The waitress was turned on by Smooth's swagger. She loved black men and at the moment she fantasized about his big black dick in her mouth. It was something about black men that made her pussy throb. "My name is Britany, and I'll be your waiter tonight, is there anything else you need?" Britany let the words roll off her tongue slowly. "I mean anything . . . ?" Britany winked.

Smooth's dick began to jump and rise when he saw her diamond tongue ring. She looked at Smooth seductively but he didn't want to play himself in front of Tiffany. He had to brush it off and see her another time. "Nah that'll be it."

Smooth dug in his pocket and pulled out a half ounce of haze and some Backwoods. "Ma, you burn?" Smooth took out a ceenote and broke the weed up on it.

"Yeah I smoke but not like that, Shawn."

"Well smoke wit me tonight then and let's bring in the New Year together." Smooth put his left hand on her thigh and started rubbing her pussy through her jeans.

"Mmm-hmmm . . . . let's bring in the New Year together daddy . . . ." Tiffany cooed, her pussy was pulsating.

"That's what I like to hear boo . . . . we gonna live it up tonight shawty. I'ma show you what it's like to come kick it wit a real nigga." Smooth licked the Backwood and folded it over.

"A bitch is wit, Shawn. I'm all yours tonight . . . ." Tiffany licked behind his ear. "That's jus' to show you how my tongue will feel later on.

Smooth was turned on by her freakiness and couldn't wait to get to a motel later on with her. Smooth sat back and rolled five blunts up and continued to have small talk with Tiffany. He looked to his right and saw the other two females laughing with Crook. The blond head waitress walked up with the drinks. Crook started making drinks for everybody and made sure he added more Vodka in the females drinks. Crook looked over at Jackie who was sitting to the right of him with her legs crossed. Jackie wasn't a bad looking woman and was something worth fucking in his eyes. Crook was spitting to both females and was trying to get a ménage a trios.

Crook downed his cranberry and grey goose quickly while everybody else were still sipping. He liked to feel his buzz fast so he always drank excessive amounts of liquor and fast. He popped open another bottle of Rose and stood up and started bobbing his head to the music. Crook's speech was little slur and every time he tried rapping Gucci Mane's lyrics in the club it sounded like he was mumbling. "I'm so icy . . ." Crook blurted out singing along to the chorus. He was two stepping to the music. Females across the room in the other VIP were staring at Crook and Smooth who were buying bottles after bottles. Crook kept his hands on his waist while he diddy bopped making sure his pistol didn't fall. Chicks in the club were thirsty and was curious to know who they were.

Crook noticed all eyes were on him so now he was really feeling himself. His ego was huge and it wasn't a soul in the club that was fucking with him. He shut down clubs when he got drunk. Crook was sending drinks to females at different tables even with their dudes there. Before he knew it broads from different tables started coming over to him and Smooth. They were feeling the love everywhere from females while niggas were hating. Crook was there to have a good time and wasn't worried about no nigga flexing 'cause shit could get real ugly in the club.

The DJ came in through the speakers in the middle of the song and started the countdown. In thirty seconds it was about to be a New Year and "2005" was out the way. Crook was on cloud nine two stepping while a thick red bone was grinding up on him. Chauntae sat back sipping her drink watching him and feeling some kind of way. She knew better to bug and make a fool out herself 'cause Crook wasn't her man. So she fell back and enjoyed the scenery taking in everything.

"Dis iz for the New Year my nigga!" Crook held up his Rose. "Let's have a toast and bring in '06 wit a bang!" Crook smiled.

"Foshow my nigga . . . ." Smooth held up his Rose and toasted. "Let's bring in the New Year wit new money and new pussy!" They both busted out laughing.

"Five, four, three, two, one!!! Happy New Year!!!!" The DJ bellowed through the speakers.

Smooth looked to his far left and saw Erica walking with Keisha coming towards their table. He knew it was going to be trouble the moment he saw them coming. He nudged Crook on the arm but that was pointless 'cause Crook was pissy drunk and didn't feel Smooth elbowing him. Smooth smoked his blunt and rocked to the music with a smirk on his face. He could tell by the looks on Keisha and Erica's face that they were angry. The last thing Smooth and Crook needed was them causing a scene in the club. But Smooth already knew what time it was and knew their hood-rat ways, so making a scene was what they were more than likely going to do.

———◆———

Jerome sat back low in the Benz with his seat reclined. He pulled out his cell phone and made a call to his cousin Tyrell to let him know he was downtown. He sat up the street from where Club Aria was and from his viewpoint he could get a good look at who's coming and going from the club. Jerome's palms were sweating from anxiety; he been patiently waiting for so long. Now the day was here and he couldn't' wait to close this chapter in his life. The phone rang and it rang until it went to the voicemail again. Jerome banged on the dashboard and was getting frustrated. *"Dis clown ass nigga needa answer the fuckin' jack,"* Jerome said to himself. He called again and finally he answered on the third ring and Jerome was relieved.

"Rell, why the fuck wasn't you answering the jack? Nigga I'm outside the club now. What kind of whip the nigga drivin' in?"

"My fault cuz, I ain't hear the shit ringing with the music playing. Aight stay where you at, I still got my eye on the nigga too, he pissy drunk right now. The nigga in a money green Aston Martin, you'll know it when you see it. It got tints on the window and it's the only one down here . . ." Tyrell informed him.

"Alright I got you. I'm about to circle the block until I can find the whip, Rell. You jus' keep an eye on the nigga and hit me as soon as he's on the way out the door." Jerome stated.

"Rome, I got you my eyes is on the nigga now . . . ."

"Cool. Hit me back then . . . ." Jerome flipped the phone shut.

Instead of driving around looking for Crook's car, Jerome got out and walked the block. It was too much traffic outside and he didn't want to chance it losing his parking space. After walking around the block and halfway up the street, Jerome spotted the Aston Martin sitting in the parking lot. Jerome walked up to the car and pulled out his shank and commenced to stabbed holes in all four tires.

"Crook! Who the fuck iz these bitches?!" Keisha walked right up in front of the trio with her hands in their face. "Nigga I know you ain't fuckin' play me like that! Crook I'll bust these bitches ass! Nigga you fuckin' hear me?!" Keisha was so loud people in the club looked at the commotion.

"Bitch! You better go sit yo fuckin' drunk ass down somewhere, befo I beat dat ass! Don't fuckin' worrry 'bout who da fuck at my table! You ain't my girl, so fall da fuck back and play ya position!" Crook was all in her face.

"Nah, nigga, fuck you and these bum ass bitches right here! Crook, I should smack the shit outta these bitches!" Kesiha retorted.

"Smooth, I don't know why the fuck you laughing for?! Ain't shit funny you dirty-dick-ass-nigga!" Erica chimed in.

"Y'all birds better calm the fuck down befo I bat a bitch! Erica you better watch ya mouth how you talk to me! Bitches can get it hoe . . . ." Smooth shot her a cold look.

Chauntae sat up quick out her seat and was quick to say something to Keisha. Her two girls got up out their seats and was ready to throw down if shit got ugly. Chauntae and her home girls were ready if it had to go down. Smooth played the mediator and walked off with the three other girls leaving Crook alone with Keisha and Erica.

"I can't even believe this nigga Smooth gonna play me like that, Crook." Erica was vexed watching Smooth walk off.

"I'm 'bout to get up outta here, Keisha come on . . . ."

"Take the car home Erica and I'll call you tomorrow."

"Alright bitch, call me tomorrow after you get dick down all night."

"Don't get jealous 'cause you going home to play with yourself," Keisha quipped, while walking off with Crook.

"Whatever hoe, bye!" Erica stormed off.

Tyrell kept his distance as he watched Crook staggering to the main entrance getting ready to leave the club. He picked up his phone and placed a call Jerome and to let him get into position.

Crook was beyond drunk leaving Club Aria with Keisha by his side. He bumped into a few dudes on his way out the door without saying excuse me and that turned into some evil stares towards him. Keisha didn't like the look of things and knew that it could get volatile quickly. She tried grabbing him by the arm and urging him to keep moving. Crook brushed her off and did what he had in mind. Crook mean mugged them back and flashed his pistol and they threw up their hands in defeat. He kept it moving with Keisha by his side out the front door after realizing they didn't want no drama. When they stepped outside none of the valet workers were nowhere to be found. He was livid that he gave the valet dude such a nice tip and he wasn't on his job. So Crook started walking to the nearest parking lot where they usually parked the cars.

Keisha had to help him walk straight down the street 'cause he was staggering all over the place almost falling into people. Everybody congregated on the streets anticipating the club let out. Music blaring from a host of cars could be heard as they gradually walked through crowds of people. He could feel his head spinning in circles and his stomach was doing flips from all the weed and liquor his body consumed. They walked in a slow pace and his steps became less calculated and eventually they came to a halt. His mind was saying walk some more but his body wouldn't agree with him. The next thing he knew he was vomiting all over the ground. Crook stood there bent over vomiting letting all the liquor freely come out while people close by parted way to let him have his space. The last thing somebody wanted was mucous all on them. Crook let it all out and it splashed off the concrete and then onto his Louis Vuitton shoes. Keisha held onto him tightly making sure he maintained his balance.

"Daddy you good now? Let it all out before we get to the car."

No response. He just shook his head yes and let the last of the vomit out. A long piece of saliva hung from the corner of his mouth as he stood there trying to regain his composure. Crook wiped away the slime with off his mouth with the back of his hand. After letting all that excess grey goose and Rose out his stomach he felt a lot better. All of a sudden he didn't feel so intoxicated now. He got himself back together and kept walking. After hitting the corner, Crook walked up on the man and smacked the dude and took his keys.

"Hey mon . . . . what thee fuck iz yo poblem?! Why yu smack me I de face fo?!" The Haitian man held his cheeks.

"That's for makin' me walk two blocks to come get my wheels! Ya bitch ass should've been outside the club wit and went to get my whip for me! What the fuck you think that hunnit was for?! Now get the fuck outata here befo I whoop ya ass!" Crook pretended as though he was going to hit him again and the man ran off holding his face.

"You need to stop being a bully daddy . . . ." Keisha laughed.

"Somebody gotta keep these hoe ass niggas in check! Come on let's get up outta here ma."

When Crook got to the car he hit the alarm and passed Keisha the keys so she could drive. He didn't feel like driving 'cause he was still wasted. The last thing he wanted to do was wreak his pride and joy. Keisha brought the engine to life and put the car in drive. Something wasn't right 'cause the car didn't drive right; so she threw it in park. Crook was leaned back in the seat half sleep when he was brought back to reality by Keisha nudging him.

"Whassup, Keisha, why the fuck you over here fuckin' up my buzz?!"

"Nigga you might wanna check and make sure ya shit ain't flat . . . . 'cause this muthafucka struggling to get out the lot."

"What the fuck! . . . I hope my shit ain't flat 'cause I'ma whoop somebody's ass . . . ." Crook glared at her.

"Yeah nigga what-the-fuck-ever . . . ." She retorted. "You better worry about how the fuck we getting home. That's what you needa do!" Keisha sucked her teeth and rolled her eyes. "Keisha shut the fuck up! I ain't even tryna hear ya annoying ass voice right now." Crook steeped out the car and left the passenger door wide open.

When he saw that two tires on the passenger's side were flat he was furious. Crook wanted to go upside somebody's head to take out the frustration inside him. Keisha got out on the driver's side, and noticed that it was flat also, she gave him the "I told you so look". Crook was busy hooting and hollering with Keisha about his tires being flat that he never saw what was in the shadows lurking. Crook kicked the side of the car not caring about the dent he put there. His head was throbbing in so much pain all he wanted to do was get to Keisha's house and call it a night. Crook felt as though somebody was behind him just watching him. Crook wasn't the one to caught slipping without his watchdog Smooth by his side, but right at that moment he was being careless.

All the weed and liquor clouded his judgment. Many Men were laid to rest in the streets due to not staying on point. But lately Crook had been slipping and tonight it was going to cost him. When he turned around and saw Jerome staring him down with a nickel plated .45 is his palm, Crook just froze up. It was as if he saw the holy ghost. For a split second he thought he was staring at Troy, but he knew that it couldn't be possible. His mind was playing tricks on him. There was no escaping this one or slithering away like the snake he was. Crook knew the young man before his eyes came to play no games with him. He looked into the eyes of Jerome and all the saw was darkness in them. He didn't even realize that all along Jerome was plotting and scheming on him from the moment they met. It never dawned on Crook that karma was going to come back to haunt him.

"Do what you gotta do lil nigga and get it over wit 'cause I'ma die a legend anyways . . . . I should've killed ya bitch ass wit ya mother and father when I had the chance!" Crook smiled and stared him down.

"Ya so right, you should've murked me when you had the chance, pussy! Checkmate nigga!" Jerome snarled, gritting his teeth and then pulled the trigger.

Crook's whole life flashed before his eyes. From his childhood days all the way up until his adulthood. Jerome let off both guns in unison ripping apart Crook's flesh hitting him in the upper body area. His body jerked in convulsions as he took shots to the chest and stomach sending his body crashing to the cold concrete floor. Keisha stood there in deep shock crying while Crook was lying on the ground bleeding. Jerome walked up on him while he lied there dead with his eyes wide open. They say you deserved it when you die with your eyes open.

Jerome aimed his pistol at Keisha contemplating whether he should kill her or not. Keisha pleaded with him for her life and Jerome let her get a pass. He didn't believe in killing children or females 'cause he had morals. He walked off leaving her with a broken heart. He let the tears fall freely 'cause he could finally be at peace with himself and live peacefully with his girl, Mercedes. That chapter of his life was done.

Chapter 23

"Word on the streetz iz that fuckboy Smooth put twenty five stacks each on our heads," Money Bags, "As of right now I don't know if somebody took the contract or not. But once I find out, I'm bodying whoever the fuck it is and then I'm offing bitch ass Smooth." Money Bags voice was cold.

"Is that so," Jerome sighed, "Well if somebody took the contract it looks like Smooth is gonna have to get his money back. We ain't going nowhere and I be damn if one of his lackey's succeed in getting' at us. I'll touch everything that nigga loves . . . . first startin' wit his ugly ass baby mother." Jerome meant every word he said.

Even though Jerome didn't believe in killing females he was taken aback, if he had to get to Smooth's baby mother to send message so be it. Eventually Smooth would realize he was playing the game for keeps.

"You a could nigga, Rome."

"The streets made me this way."

"Yeah I'm hipped . . . . be like that sometime."

"You got any insight on who you think might wanna take the hit?"

"Nah, no clue, and that's really bothering me. A lot of dudes is pissed off right now in the streets . . . . nobody is eatin' anymore now that Crook is dead. It's a free for all there's more freelance dealers on the streets and more shootings." Money Bags threw up both his hands confused.

"So you know what that means, Bags."

"It means there's more free agents out there waiting to be put on the right team." Jerome continued, "If niggas iz tryna get dis paper then we'll put 'em on, I got work for all these thirsty lil niggas. It's time to divide and conquer. Our team is like the '96 Bulls—we can't be stopped." Jerome chuckled and gave him dap.

"What if these young boys don't wanna re-up off us or ain't tryna pump for niggas? Dawg you already know a lot of these young boys don't wanna get no gwop . . . . all they wanna do is gangbang."

"We gonna give 'em some good numbers on the yola. And if that don't work we'll just have somebody go through their blocks every day and shoot it up . . . . they'll get the message eventually after we clear shit out. They won't make no more money plain and simple." Jerome rubbed both hands together and gave him that assuring head nod.

Money Bags smiled broadly and shook his head agreeing with what his partner was saying. Jerome's street philosophy was starting to make since to him. But still, Money Bags knew everything had to be done right or it all could back fire.

"My peoples in the projects was telling me that some dude been coming through the bricks in white Maserati talkin' bout he looking for me. So I put two and two together and came up with a conclusion that must've been Smooth's bitch ass!" Money Bags got irritated just thinking about it.

"How you so sure it was ole boy? You might jus' be noided."

"A few months back I saw him out front the Dublin House kicking it wit dis bitch." Money Bags pulled a rolled a Dutchmaster off the dashboard of his M6 and lit it. "Dawg I'm tellin' you, whenever I see ole boy it's on and poppin' on site. I don't give a fuck who he wit! I'ma blow his top off!" Money Bags scanned the block twice up and down staying alert.

Money Bags leaned up against his M6 BMW while Jerome stood there on the sidewalk. It was in the 40's outside and the wind was light. Jerome had on a polo sweat-suit and Air Max's while Money Bags had on a NorthFace with some wheat Timberlands and a 9mm underneath. Ever since hearing about the contract on his head Money Bags been riding with one in the chamber and off safety. Jerome rubbed his goatee with his fingers as he stood there in deep thought. Jerome wanted to know who was involved with Smooth and find out who was considering taking the hit. Either way he looked at the situation he had to be cautious because Smooth was dangerous. Eventually Jerome would have to get rid of Smooth; but right now he wanted things to die down. At the moment Mercedes was going through it after losing her father and she needed Jerome to console her.

"Damn shit is crazy out here in the hood right now. I don't like having my name all out there in the streets like that, Bags. First thing one of those rats will do is try turning me in for a reward or a time reduction. But you know what, what is done is done. Niggas always gonna gossip like bitches do. As long as Mercedes and Homicide don't know what's up then that's all that matters." Jerome took the Dutch from him and continued, "On some real shit, we gotta find out who's tryna take dem fifty stacks to come get at us. We gotta do our homework and get to the bottom of dis . . . ." Jerome blew the smoke out his nostrils. "But in the meantime, get low and try to keep ya face off the streets for a lil while. What they can't see they can't touch my dude . . . ." Jerome gave one of his neighbors a silent hello with a head nod.

They were posted up out front Jerome's house on Gooddale road on an early Saturday morning. It's been two weeks since the death of Crook and people wanted answers. Even though Crook was a slime ball in the streets—he was a good man and father figure at home; his daughter and girl took it the hardest. Jerome didn't feel comfortable inside the house talking to his right-hand man about anything so they stayed out front. The last thing he needed was Mercedes waking up and ease dropping on their conversation. Ever since her father's demise she'd been constantly with her boyfriend. She didn't feel comfortable at home or by herself so she had to be with Jerome or her mother at all times.

"Nah, fuck that Rome, I ain't getting' low and hiding from that fuckboy! Dis nigga know where my momma stay at in the bricks . . . . what am I 'posed to do?! Go into hiding? My dude you got the game fucked up 'cause Money Bags don't hide from nobody! My heart don't pump Kool-Aid . . . ." Money Bags banged his chest for emphasis.

Jerome shook his head in frustration and sighed deeply. He was well aware of Money Bags ill wit temper and wasn't trying to argue with his culprit. Money Bags was being defensive and taking everything the wrong way and wasn't seeing Jerome's point of view. Even though in age difference Money Bags was much older—Jerome was a lot more wiser and dealt with his problems accordingly.

"Listen, listen my nigga hear me out . . . ." Jerome's voice got louder and he looked around to make sure nobody was listening. "I'm well aware of what you are capable of doing Bags, but right now isn't the time for all that wild shit right now. I say we keep serving these niggas the work and stay low 'til we come up wit a game plan." Jerome passed him back the Dutch. "Don't get it twisted I would love to clip that pussy Smooth, but right now I'm tryna get dis paper and my bitch needs me. I'm all she really got besides her mother, I can't leave her out here fucked up." He spoke from the heart about his feelings For Mercedes.

"Yeah I hear ya talkin' loverboy . . . ."

"Do you hear me or are you listening? There's a big difference."

"To keep it one hunnit I'm not even listening to you."

"Why not my, nigga? What I'm sayin' is logic."

"Dawg, you jus' don't get it," Money Bags was shaking his head, "You over here tellin' me 'bout how ya bitch needs you and all dis other bullshit. What we need to be doin' is tryna find ole boy and put him the dirt! If that nigga catch one of us outta bounds he's toning shit down . . . ."

"I love my bitch. Mercedes, is my heart and I'll always be loyal to her. I told you she needs me right now and I'd be damn if I leave her side . . . ." Jerome said every word slowly to make sure he comprehended. "I'm coolin' right now I ain't trippin' over that pussy nigga. I advise you to fall back for a lil bit 'til we come up wit a plan."

"That's the problem now, you think I'm suppose to jus' ler dis shit go . . . ? Dis pussy nigga tryna put money on my head and you think I'm 'pose to chill?!" Money Bags eyes opened wide as he talked. "You fuckin' crazy, Rome! I don't

take threats lightly! I can't speak on ya behalf though."
Money Bags flicked the last of the blunt on the ground.
"Rome, you over here playin' house wit ya bitch and all
concerned 'bout her feelings, what you really need to be
dong is takin' care of dis problem! Ya bitch's father is the
fuckin' reason we in the middle of all dis bullshit now! . . ."

Jerome released fury and grabbed him by the collar of
his jacket choking him on the hood of the car. Jerome had
him beat in size so he over powered Money Bags with ease
while he lied on the hood of the car. Jerome snapped on
him, "Keep her fuckin' name out of it, Bags, she's innocent."
Jerome released his death grip.

Money Bags stood up quick to his feet and started
to reach underneath his jacket. Jerome glared at him and
backed up on the sidewalk. "So what you gonna do pull
out on me? Nigga you pull out a pistol on me ya betta use
it . . . ." Jerome never took his eyes off him.

Money Bags glared back at him with menacing eyes like
he wanted to murder Jerome. He wasn't much of a fighter he
would rather shoot you if it came down to it. The last thing
he needed was conflict with his right-hand man. Money
Bags thought about it and realized he was being emotional
and didn't want to bring it to the next level. He had enough
on his plate alone just dealing with Smooth.

"My fault 'bout that shit bro, you know I ain't gonna
pop you fool, we like brothers . . . ." Money Bags gave him
dap and a hug. "Jus' don't ever put ya hands on me again,
you know I blackout sometime."

"I understand my dude, it's all gravy. You know how I
get over Mercedes, she's my everything Bags, we like Bonnie
and Clyde." Jerome smiled broadly. "But listen here, I'm

starting to get cold out dis muthafucka, you know dis weather is for the crackas. I'm 'bout to go in the crib and kick back. Holla at me bro."

"You already know, I'ma get witcha doggy so be easy. I got dis bitch Candice waitin' on me anyways, she's a dick suckers nightmare! But first I'm 'bout to go see Tony for a cut, my shit is all grizzly." Money Bags rubbed his hand across his face feeling unshaven hair.

"Bags, you stay wit a hoodrat on deck," Jerome grinned slightly, "Dat nigga Tony still working at King Kuts?"

"Yep. Still cutting hair and selling trees on the side."

"Pretty boy ass Tony, he get all the hoes wit dem green eyes."

"That nigga in love with his wifey, jus' like yo ass . . . ."

"Don't knock it 'til you try it."

"I know that's right . . . . if I ever find a real ass bitch I can vibe wit. Seems like all the hoes I come across be scandalous! Low down dirty scoundrels!" Money Bags sighed and shook his head. "Until I find miss right, I'm jus' fuckin' bitches and getting' money." He said defiantly.

"You jus' been lookin' for love in all the wrong places. What you think you gonna find wifey in the club, or one of these backstreets? Fucks no . . . . when and if you do find that right broad for you, you'll know she's the one; you can feel it inside ya gut." Jerome nodded his head.

"I feel you on that one, Rome. Only time will tell." Money Bags hopped in the driver's seat. "If any plays hit me while I'm in the Barbershop I'ma hit you. One of my dudes 'pose to be comin' down from Fall River for a nine piece." Money Bags drooled on himself as a high yellow Spanish girl strutted by. "Damn she got a fuckin; bubble! I need to go's and get that . . . ." Money Bag stuck his head out the window and watched her walk down the street.

"Aight, jus' hit me if you need me. You need to go and get that I see how she looked at you." Jerome said, encouraging him.

"Say no more playboy." Money Bags chuckled. "I'm out my nigga . . . ." He turned the music up and sped off.

The BMW M6 screaming down the street from the way Money Bags was speeding and shifting gears causing the dual exhausts to holler. All the way at the other end of the block Jerome could hear the bass booming from the car. Jerome climbed up two flights of stairs and shook his head laughing at his partner. When Jerome walked into the second floor apartment he smelled the aroma of food in the air. Already in the mood to eat, he walked into the kitchen and saw Mercedes over the stove cooking. Mercedes had on some pink boy shorts, and white Nautica T-shirt, two sizes too big for her that belonged to Jerome. Her olive brown skin glistened off the light on the ceiling. Jerome admired everything about his woman. Mercedes smiled from ear to ear while he held onto her.

"Babe, ya hands are freezing . . . ." He let go of her waist. "Good morning to you my love." Mercedes cooed softly.

"Good morning back to you."

"You up early today I see, where did you go?" Mercedes continued scrambling eggs.

"I ain't go nowhere, I was out front wit Money Bags smoking." Jerome took his sweater off and placed it on the back of the chair. "Baby what you making over there? I hope it ain't no swine . . . ." Jerome started rubbing his stomach.

"I'm making your favorite, Romeo. I got cheesy eggs, grits, toast and some salmon cakes . . . ." Mercedes turned the stove off. "And you should know by now that I wasn't making you any pork, silly. The bacon in the oven is for me." Mercedes turned and gave him a kiss.

"You must've been reading my mind 'cause I sure am hungry."

"Well have a seat 'cause breakfast will be ready in a minute. I'm just waiting for my bacon to finish." Mercedes opened the oven and took out the flat pan with bacon on it. "Looks done to me, I'll make you a plate now, what kind of juice you want?"

"Doesn't really matter babe . . . ." Jerome said, "Can you please put my grits in a separate bowl, I don't like them on my plate."

"Ok. I'll get apple juice then and I will put ya grits in separate bowl, you big baby." Mercedes made plates for both them and sat them on the table. "Babe, I've been doing some serious thinking lately about furthering my career and getting my Bachelor's Degree in Criminal Justice, after I get my Associate's in Medical Assisting, what you think? I know way too much about the judicial system to let it all go to waste." Mercedes poured two glasses of Apple juice and sat it on the table.

"Cedes, you can do anything you want if you put your mind to it." Jerome took a bite of salmon cake mixed with grits. "Criminal Justice is an excellent career to get involved into, but at the same token it's not up to me what "your" choice will be. You have to follow your heart baby." Jerome took a sip of Apple juice. "I sure wouldn't mind seeing you become a DA or lawyer though. Think about it, we'll make a lot of connections with the right people . . . ." Jerome grinned.

"Babe I'm still kind of confused and don't know which one to pursue and make a career out of." Mercedes curled up her bottom lip pouting. "I always did wanted to be a Probation Officer, so eventually I would have to get my Bachelor's in Criminal justice." Mercedes put a piece of bacon in her mouth.

"The way I look at it either career is a good choice; there's always gonna be people getting sick, and there's always gonna be people getting into trouble, plain and simple. But if you do decide to become a Probation Officer—best believe ya gonna be working with juveniles. I don't want none of these thirsty dudes getting out of jail smiling in your face trying to bag you." Jerome looked at her defiantly.

Mercedes began laughing so hard that she almost choked on a piece of toast. Her smile was so innocent and beautiful with her baby teeth on the side. Mercedes picked up her apple juice and took a sip to wash down the food.

"You are so silly, I'm not giving no man the time of day. I'm only concerned about my king; Jerome Jenkins, is all the man I need and want forever." Mercedes beamed.

"And your all the woman I want and need forever, my love."

"Baby I love you so much . . . ." Mercedes looked into his eyes and felt complete. "From the first time I saw you in school I been checking you out." She blushed.

"Is that right baby? I couldn't tell, 'cause the first time I saw you, you were acting shy 'round me." Jerome said, in a matter of fact tone. "I love you more than life itself gurl . . . .

until death do us part and beyond." Jerome meant every word.

"Babe you are so sweet to me . . . ." Mercedes eyes started getting red and teary. "After losing my daddy I've been worried about you crazy, and sometimes I get these messed up dreams that something is gonna happen to you next. Romeo, I don't want to lose you, I already lost my daddy, I'll go crazy if something ever happened to you." The tears fell down her cheeks like rain coming down a windshield.

"Cedes, I ain't goin' no where, I promise you that. And I promise you that as long as I'm alive and breathing I'd never let nothing happen to you. I'd rather die than let something happen to you. I was meant to be with you and you was meant for me, our bond is unbreakable." Jerome got out his seat and held her hand. "I want you to be my wife one day and have my kids . . . . nothin' is goin' to happen to me I promise." Jerome knelt down and kissed her forehead. "Let's go to the bedroom, I need to feel ya insides right now, I want to taste ya first though . . . ." Jerome held her hand as they walked to the bedroom.

"I want to feel you inside me too daddy . . . . every last inch of you." Mercedes pussy was getting wet just thinking about him inside her. They went off to the bedroom and went to do what grown folks do.

Chapter 24

"I'm front ya spot now, X." Money Bags said, "Don't take all day to come downstairs either, I got shit to do and places to be." Money Bags kept his eyes in his rearview.

"What you want me to bring down?"

"Bring me down a seven, and the shit betta not be that bullshit ass dro. Bring me some of that purp down, duke."

"I only got three point fives left, so I'll bring you down two of them. I don't got that dro no more anyways, I got sour and purp left."

"Yeah nigga whatever . . . . jus' bring yo ass downstairs. Got me sittin' on dis hot ass block." Money Bags hung up the phone.

Money Bags sat parked on Middleton street with the car idling while waiting for the weed man to come outside. He grew up with Xavier back in the days and they went to school together. While Money Bags chose to sell coke for a living and put people in the dirt—Xavier branched off to selling weed. Xavier was afraid to crossover to selling coke 'cause of the numbers they gave you were too much. Even though they lived two separate lives and rarely hung out together, Money Bags always put money in his pocket and bought weed off him. Money Bags wanted to kill two birds with one stone, since he was about to get his haircut around the corner at King Kuts, he figured why not get some weed while he was at it. He was all out of weed and needed some for later when he was going to see one of his freaks for the night. She was a hood chick and enjoyed getting her drink and smoke on.

Money Bags watched as Xavier walked down the stairs of the triple decker house and looked around puzzled trying to locate Money Bags. Xavier reached into his pocket and pulled out a cell phone. He tooted the horn twice and Xavier saw him sitting low in the BMW M6 that was parked two houses down from his house. Money Bags clicked the unlock button and let him jump in the passenger seat.

"Damn, nigga, every time I see you, you in a different whip," Xavier gave him three finger dap. "Hoe you been out here though, Bags?"

"You know in the hood niggas identify you by ya car, so I switch up whips to stay off the radar." Money Bags passed him some money. "But besides that I've been maintaining, I can't complain."

"I can dig it . . . . be easy out here and stay safe bro." Xavier passed him the weed. "What's dis you gave me? I ain't even gonna count it, I know ya money is good." Xavier stuffed the twenty dollar bills in his pocket.

"That's a buck twenty, X, you know I don't come short baby. Yo you be safe out here too bro," Money Bags gave him threes. "And tell mom dukes I said hello for me."

"I'll do that Bags, holla if you need me." Xavier said, and stepped out the car.

Money Bags put the weed inside his NorthFace sleeve pocket and dropped the emergency brake and pulled off. He drove down Middleton street and on his right and saw a couple of females he knew and honked the horn at the

Wildwood chicks sitting on the porch. He done slept with half them chicks from that crew and knew they were nothing but trouble. He wouldn't give them the time of day to stop and converse, they were affiliated with too many different dudes in the hood, that was one of the main reasons he never trusted them. They looked on in awe trying to put a face on the car and figure out who's vehicle it was.

He sat low behind the dark tinted windows and kept driving as he took the only turn onto Theodore street which was a left turn. People in the hood called it a death trap 'cause it was only one way in and one way out. The two streets Wildwood and Theodore were one way streets and they ran parallel with each other forming a V-shape. The area was drug infested and was a high crime area due to gangs feuding between each other. Nothing but trouble came from that area and the police stayed on the prowl.

Money Bags banked a left turn and merged onto Morton street and drove up three blocks until he stopped at a red-light at a busy intersection. The P.A. Shaw Elementary School was on his left Walgreens was on his right as he sat behind a two tone purple and white Dodge Charger tinted out. The light turned green and he banked a left turn onto Norfolk street and parked on his right a few houses up.

He hopped out the car with his Red Sox fitted pulled down low almost covering his eyes. He scanned the block twice and walked with his right hand by his waist at all times. He was prepared for anything out the unusual, he wasn't going to be caught slipping. His was trigger finger was itching and he was ready to shoot at anything that looked like Smooth. A couple of non-descript dudes waiting at the bus stop parted way and stepped to the side when they saw Money Bags walking with a sinister look on his face. Money Bags stayed with an attitude and is eyes. He didn't play games with nobody in the hood and a lot of dudes feared him.

When he walked into the Barbershop the first thing he noticed was that it was partially empty. Besides the young kid getting a haircut by heavy set older black woman and the other customer who looked like he was in his early twenties getting his afro cut off by a barber with dreads, the shop had nobody else inside there. Money Bags could see that his barber wasn't busy, so now he could get right into the chair this particular morning it was slow. Money Bags was glad he decided to come in early before business picked up.

"Money Bags what it do my nigga," Tony gave him dap. "Sit down in the chair so I can tighten you up. What you getting done to ya head?" Tony reached into the draw and grabbed the Barber's apron.

Money Bags took off his hat and jacket and placed them on the chair where the chair where the customers sat and wait until it's a Barber chair open.

"Tee jus' give me an all around and don't cut my waves out, please. How ya been through?" Money Bags peered through the window and the busy intersection of cars going up and down Morton street.

"Aight, I got you. I been chillin', same ol shit jus another toilet." Tony tied the apron around him. "Moving a lil bit of trees here and there tryna stay afloat." Tony turned on the clippers and started cutting hair.

"I can dig it, you gotta do what you gotta do out here. Ain't nothing gonna come to a nigga who sit around on his ass all day."

"That's real shit there. A lot of niggas don't see it that way."

"And the niggas that don't are jus' gonna be fucked up in the game."

Money Bags sat there watching the flat screen plasma that sat on the wall in the middle of the shop and was trying to figure out what it was they were watching. It looked like a documentary of somebody's life the way Ice-T was being the narrator and telling the story. Then after watching it for a few minutes it dawned on him once he saw C-Murder walking through the projects talking while the camera was focused on him. C-Murder had three dudes around him while he spoke for the camera with a mouth full of gold.

"What's dis y'all watching, Tee?" Money Bags intrigued by what C-Murder was talking about. "I fucks wit my nigga C-Murder, he a real nigga who jus' happened to become a rapper." Money Bags felt his phone vibrate but left it alone.

"Dis that "Strait from the projects" DVD, did all about C-Murder and his record label, TRU Records. Dis shit is official though, watch dis part." Tony continued cutting his hair. "What you want me to do with dis hair on ya face?"

"You can cut all that off and jus line my mustache up." Money Bags watched the door as three teenagers walked in and sat down. "Damn Tee, y'all don't never close dem blinds, huh? Muthatfuckas can ride by or walk through and see all up in the shop." Money Bags scanned the outside of the shop and then looked back at the TV.

"I got you I'ma jus' line ya mustache up and shave everything else. The shades is open so we can get some sunshine in dis piece. Why you so noided for? Damn . . . . I see how ya watchin' the outside."

"Nah I'm good, I ain't noided not at all. I'm jus' stayin on point 'cause too many niggas got caught slippin' in barbershops in the bean and they ain't here no more." Money Bags voice was calm. "You member what happened to Barhar back in the day, dem niggas ran up in the barbershop and did him dirty . . . ." Money Bags felt sorry for the young boy back in the day when he died.

"Yeah I member that shit was crazy." Tony started doing his outline.

"That's why I don't be bangin no more that shit is for the birds . . . ."

"You damn right it is . . . . you can't bang and get money, gotta be one or the other." Money Bags said, matter-of-factly.

Money Bags watched as they showed C-Murder's apartment that was right in the middle of the calliope projects. The apartment was restored and done completely over with a studio inside. Money Bags couldn't understood how multi-millionaire like C-Murder still wanted to keep an apartment in the projects.

"That nigga C-Murder keep it real, dude still got a spot in his projects where he grew up at. It don't get no hooder then that," Money Bags said, "I hope dat nigga beat his case too, dem crackas tryna smoke dat nigga."

"Man if I ever touched the paper he saw, I'm moving far away from the hood as possible. Don't get me wrong, I love the Bean my nigga, but at the same token the hood is fucked up. There ain't no unity or loyalty amongst each other." Tony finished up his line up and rubbed alcohol over his head. "That will be thirteen dollars my nig."

"It ain't no love in the bean . . . . everybody is jus' forself round dis muthafucka. You gotta keep ya circle small."

251

Money Bags dug in his pocket and pulled out a twenty dollar bill. "Keep the change bro."

"Good looking out baby." Tony pulled the apron off him. "Be safe out here too, Bags." Tony gave him dap.

"I'll be in touch with you soon." Money Bags put his hat and jacket. "Holla at me if any of ya peoples is tryna get some fliggidy, I'm real right, right now." Money Bags reached in his pocket and pulled out his cell phone.

"Aight I got you. As a matter-of-factly I might have a play for you later on who knows, my homeboy Twin had hit me lookin for somethin' earlier." Tony sprayed the clippers down with disinfectant spray.

Money Bags finished scrolling through his missed calls and put the phone back in his pocket after realizing it wasn't anybody impoortant. He zipped up his jacket and said, "Aight hit me if ya homie tryna do somethin, I gotta get goin'." He headed for the door.

"I sure will do," Tony said, "I'll be in touch my nigga."

Money Bags threw up a peace sign and walked out the door. Soon as he walked around the corner of the Barbershop he saw two dudes walking with their hoodies on tied up in the front. That instantly threw up red flags and paranoia sunk in and he was alert. He didn't know if he wanted to shoot first and ask questions later. He really wasn't sure if these dudes were a threat or not. He had a gut feeling that things could get ugly at any moment. Something in the back of mind was telling him that these could be goons who took the contract. Maybe these dudes were just going about their business and kept their hoodies on. But whatever the situation was Money Bags kept his right hand by his waist where the 9mm was concealed at just in case shit popped off. He was ready to pull out and start shooting but needed a reason to do so. If the two dudes in front of him even itched the wrong way he was letting off rounds.

He heard someone behind him humming and turned around to see a little boy on a bike riding up behind him. That broke his whole concentration 'cause he took his eyes off the two dudes. When he turned back around he saw both dudes reaching for their pistols. Everything happened in slow motion and Money Bags had to think quickly 'cause his life counted on it. In the blink of an eye he whipped out his 9mm and released the safety all in one swift motion. Both the goons in front of him was already sizing him up with their guns drawn.

Boom, Boom, Boom, Boom! Bang, Bang, Bang, Bang, Bang! They both let off their pistols at the same time on Money Bags. The little boy on the bike fell to the ground from a bullet wound to the chest. Money Bags took two bullets in his left shoulder knocking him against a parked car. Money Bags shook that off and stood up to return fire.

Blacka, Blacka, Blacka, Blacka, Blacka! Money Bags caught one of them in the leg and he fell to the ground howling behind a parked car. Money Bags squatted behind a Comcast van and stayed out the way of the other shooter. The blood was pouring out of his shoulder profusely as he sat there trying to catch his breath. As he hid behind the van he realized that death was knocking at his front door. He refused to go out dying without a fight. The only thing that mattered at the moment was getting out of there alive. He stood up in position with his gun extended ready to let off more rounds. He looked to his left and saw the two goons hopping into a black Suburban across the street. Both of them was almost inside the truck when Money Bags started shooting.

Blacka, Blacka, Blacka, Blacka!

Money Bags emptied the rest of his clip on them shattering the driver's side window and rearview window barely missing them. They sped off and ran a red-light in the intersection of Norfolk and Morton street. Money Bags looked at the little boy on the floor who was fighting for his life with a gunshot wound to his chest. Police sirens wailing from blocks away could be heard and that was his cue to leave. The police station was a few blocks away and it was only a matter of time before they arrived on the scene. It really wasn't nothing Money Bags could do he had to get away far as possible from the scene. He jogged to his car and got up out of there driving the opposite way.

When he pulled up at Carney's Hospital he parked across the street not wanting to bring any heat to him. Then he put the gun in the glove-box and walked himself into the ER. He lost so much blood that soon as he walked through the door he started getting woozy and his steps were harder to take. Then eventually that's when he saw darkness and passed out on the floor. The paramedics rushed to his aid and they escorted Money Bags to the back room for surgery.

Chapter 25

Jerome sat in the lazyboy watching college football while Mercedes laid there on top with her head on his chest. Boston College was playing one of their great rivalries Notre Dame; the Eagles were up by two touchdowns in the middle of the third quarter and had the ball with good field percentage. Jerome was a diehard Boston fan who rooted for all the teams that played; he even liked the Bruins too, even though majority of the blacks in the hood didn't watch hockey. If he wasn't out and about handling business on the weekends, then usually he'd be right on the couch in the living room watching football on Saturdays and Sundays. Mercedes sat there right along with him watching the games. Before in the past she would never watch football or any sport on TV, but now she'll sit there with her man watching it all. Even on nights that Jerome would be out making runs and the Celtics were on TV, she would sit there and watch the entire game just to keep him updated through text messages. Jerome really liked the fact that she was so caring towards him and did the littlest things like that to make him smile. Mercedes would do anything for her man and Jerome would do the same.

"Ring . . . . Ring . . . . Ring . . . ." Hearing the house phone ringing really surprised them. Not too many people had the number to the crib and the people that did rarely called that line. Everyone that called usually called their cell phones and the house line was there for the internet that Mercedes needed. She had to do plenty of Research papers for Umass college and always had to go online. Mercedes got up off his lap and walked in the kitchen answer the phone. When she picked up the phone off the charger, she looked down at the caller ID and noticed it said wireless caller and underneath it was a number she didn't recognize. So right off top she assumed it had to be somebody for Jerome.

"Hello . . . ." Mercedes spoke into the phone. "He's in the living room hold on." Mercedes brought the cordless phone into the living room.

"Here babe the phone is for you, it sounds like your annoying as cousin, Rell." Mercedes passed him the phone.

"Why wouldn't you ask who's on the phone? You do any other time you answer my cell, you PI." Jerome took the phone from her.

"That's right 'cause I wanna catch one of your lil bitches callin', I know you ain't stupid enough to give them the house number." Mercedes went and sat on the long sofa.

Jerome brushed her off not paying her any attention as he put the phone to his ear and said, "Talk to me."

"Why the fuck you ain't been answering ya jack?! Nigga I been callin' ya cell all day!"

"Who the fuck iz dis?"

"It's Rell . . . . who the fuck you thought it was fool?"

"What's good witcha cuz. Man you sounded different, but my phone I ain't even hear it ringing no bullshit." Jerome thought about it and realized it was in the bedroom on vibrate. "Why whassup wit ya though? You callin' da crib phone like it's an emergency." Jerome watched as BC went in for another touchdown.

"Nigga Bags got hit up earlier today comin' outta King Kuts." Tyrell sounded hoarse over the phone.

"What the fuck! You can't be serious . . . ." Jerome jumped out his seat and began pacing. "When you hear dis Rell? What hospital the nigga at?" Jerome's blood was boiling that's how mad he was.

"He's at Carney Hospital right now, I jus' got word from one of the homies what happened."

"I gotta get down to the hospital ASAP! How's he doin'?" Jerome was worried about his partner he hoped all was well.

"The homies said the nigga good, but he jus' has to stay overnight to monitor him after surgery, it's protocol I guess."

"Aight, I'm 'bout to get up outta here, I'm going to the hospital right now."

"I'll meet you up there, Rome."

"See you up there then Rell." Jerome hung up the phone feeling horrible. "Mercedes throw somthin' on . . . . we goin' to the hospital."

"Baby what happened?" Mercedes stood by his side.

"Money Bags got shot." Jerome said. "Shit is fucked up, ma."

"Oh my god . . . ." Mercedes felt awful and hugged him. "Is he gonna be alright?"

"I hope so, now come on let's get dress and get goin'."

Jerome put back on his polo sweat suit and some Air Max 95'. Mercedes put on some jeans and a pair of pink and white Nikes and then grabbed her jacket out the closet. Jerome grabbed his .40 caliber out the top drawer and put it on his waistline. Mercedes frowned at him when she saw the gun 'cause she didn't like guns at all. He grabbed his car keys and cell phone and was out the door. All he kept thinking about was Smooth and knew deep down inside he had something to do with Money Bags getting shot.

He hit the clicker on the alarm to the Toyota Avalon and they hopped inside. The past week Jerome been in a rental and planned on keeping it that way until every thing died down. He didn't want to take any chances being seen I one of his cars, so he was just going to ride in rentals for a while and switch them up every week at the airport. The rental was under a fiends name so if anything ever happened out of the car Jerome couldn't be held accountable for. Jerome turned the key over bringing the engine to life and pulled off.

Over the years Jerome lost many loved ones and friends due to violence. He couldn't even count how many people he went to school with that were now dead. In the hood you be lucky if you make it to see twenty-one. And the one's that did live to be twenty-one were either in jail or on their way; that's how it was in the hood growing up. He understood the rules to the game and knew that nothing was promised but death. That's why he lived by certain standards and always tried to stay a few moves ahead of his competition and enemies. Dying in vain was something that he dreaded coming up as a kid and even until this day was heavy on his conscience. He wanted to make an impact on peoples' lives. Eventually he would have to make that transition from being illegal to becoming legit. He always had dreams of opening his own Mechanic shop someday. But in all actuality he was knee deep in the coke game and it was no turning back. Jerome was too heavy in the streets to just abandoned them. Even though people lost their lives and went to prison for a long time over drug money—he still couldn't walk away from the life if he tried too. He was born into this cold world without a chance, nothing ever was easy for him. The streets owed him so much right now and he was going to wreck havoc on them until Smooth was dead.

Jerome glanced over at Mercedes sucking on her thumb staring out the window. If something ever happened to his better half 'cause of the things he did in the past he would lose it. He prayed nothing ever would happen to Mercedes. Living the life he was living he knew it all came with the territory. In the streets there isn't any rules and some dudes don't discriminate at all. When the workers come out to play they'll get at your loved ones just to get close to you. A lot of big time hustlers got their kids and girl friends kidnapped and held for ransom. Jerome witnessed that with his own eyes at an early age so he was well aware how treacherous men could be. For years he was shell-shocked and afraid of life. But as he got older he grew out of all that and turned cold. Jerome would kill half the city if anything ever happened to Mercedes.

Every turn he took he stayed in his rearview mirror making sure he wasn't being followed. When he pulled up at red-lights he never stopped directly behind cars, he always gave himself space between a car just in case somebody ran up on the car and started shooting. He always tried to stay prepared for any situation and always tried to have the upper hand. He done seen so much happen in his lifetime that it would make the average person crazy. In the city he lived in it was about getting even and never backing down. So it was no wonder people were getting murdered every other day. At all times he had to be alert and if he wasn't that could cost him his life. Jerome took his life serious and was determined to stay alive in the city where the young boys die.

Jerome pulled into the parking lot at Carney's Hospital and parked near the entrance of the ER. The rain started coming down hard right when they stepped out the car. Mercedes hurried up and ran inside because she didn't want her hair to get wet. He put on his bloody and speed walked until he got to the entrance of the ER. Mercedes waited in the lobby until he walked into the hospital. He walked over to the desk where a black woman was working at. The medical assistant looked no older than twenty as she was sitting behind the desk texting on her sidekick T-mobile. She pointed Jerome and Mercedes in the direction where Money Bags was located and gave them the room number.

When they walked into the room, Money Bags was lying in bed with machines hooked up to him. The Doctor wanted to monitor him after surgery to make sure there wasn't any internal bleeding. Money Bags grinned slightly when he saw them walk through the door. Even laid up in the hospital bed, he still was the same ole Money Bags with his tough guy demeanor. Jerome and Mercedes occupied the seats by the bed. Some untouched food on a tray sat beside his bed with a ginger ale. The last thing on Money Bags mind was some food.

"How you feelin' bro? I'm glad you aight though on some real shit my nigga, I'll lose my mind if you would've died on me . . . ." Jerome said, sincerely.

"Hey knuckle head . . . ." Mercedes added. "I'm glad you're ok though and your recovering fast. Too many people are dying out here in the city and I hate to see you go." Mercedes shook her head.

"Whassup y'all . . . . I'm glad y'all made it down here. I'm good baby, my fingers and toes can move, I'm still breathin', a nigga good. I'll be outta here tomorrow the doctor said." Money Bags grinned. "Y'all don't start gettin' emotional on me, I ain't dead . . . ."

Mercedes just shook her head in disbelief and couldn't understand the way Money Bags was. Here he was laid up in a hospital bed with bullet holes inside him and he's joking about it. Mercedes looked at him with a twisted face and said, "You need church in your life."

"Why you gonna take me . . . ? Matter-of-fact I can't go to church bein' a sinner. G od wouldn't be able to forgive me for my bullshit." Money Bags concluded.

"Don't put yourself down, God forgives everybody and their sins if you talk to the man above. Everybody makes mistakes . . . . I'm taking you and Romeo to church with me. Mercedes said, defiantly.

Jerome looked at her like she was crazy. He felt the same way Money Bags did and knew that with all the dirt he done did he wouldn't feel right sitting in church. Not in this lifetime would either one of them be sitting in church. Jerome kept them thoughts to himself 'cause it was pointless arguing with Mercedes about the situation.

"Shit iz crazy in the 'hood right now, Rome. Member what I was talkin' 'bout dis morning outside the crib?" Money Bags grimacede in pain trying to reach for the ginger ale off the tray. "Can you pass me that Rome, please."

Jerome stood up and passed him the ginger ale. Money Bags shifted the bed up some so he could sit up and sip his soda threw a straw. Jerome sat back down after Money Bags handed him the soda to put back on the tray. Money Bags let a burp out his mouth and clicked the remote by his leg until it was on the news.

"Yeah I member everything we talked 'bout." Jerome nodded his head knowing exactly where he was getting too. "We'll talk 'bout that on another note. Rell posed to be on his way up here too. He called me and tol me you got popped. I wasn't even hipped bro."

"I think ole boy definitely had something to do with it. Dawg when I stepped out the—"

"Let's not talk 'bout all that right now."

"Yeah you right." Money Bags realized he was talking too much around Mercedes. "Sure can't wait 'til I get out dis hospital tomorrow."

"You need to take it easy and worry 'bout getting' some rest." Jerome said, "You'll be out dis place eventually."

Mercedes sat there looking at her nails realizing she was in need of a manicure. She put her hands back on her lap and said, "If y'all got something important to talk about I'll step out the room." She glared at Jerome and sucked her teeth.

"Cedes the less you know the better off you are."

"So now you keeping shit from me? Now you don't trust me?"

"I ain't say all that . . . . certain things you don't need to know. I rather not have you know about what's goin' on in the streets. This life ain't for you and I'm gonna make sure it never becomes a part of you." Jerome wanted her secluded from the streets.

"Romeo I'm gonna give y'all some space to talk. I'm going to the cafeteria, you want anything babe?" Mercedes stood up out her seat headed towards the door.

"You can get me somethin' to drink my love."

"What about me Mercedes?'

"Alright babe I will. What the hell you want, Money Bags?"

"Nah I'm jus' jokin, thank you anyway."

"Yeah punk whatever. Babe I'll be back in a lil bit."

Money Bags and Jerome both watched as she walked out the room. Jerome walked over to the door and closed it shut. The last thing he wanted was somebody walking in on their conversation unannounced. Jerome kept what he did in the streets away from Mercedes. Even though she knew he sold drugs, he rarely brought her around any of it. Jerome planned on keeping it that way.

There was no other roommate inside the room with Money Bags so he felt comfortable talking. Jerome sat there listening intently to everything Money Bags saying. Everything was making since and now it was confirmed that a contract was put out on their life. Jerome gritted his teeth as he sat there hearing about the botched hit. Late breaking news came on the TV and they sat there listening to the reporter. The cops were on a prowl looking for any suspects who were involved in a broad day shooting that injured a nine-year-old boy leaving him in critical condition. The reporter also stated that the shooting was believed to be gang related and as of now there is no motive.

The police had the scene cordoned with yellow tape not letting anybody through. Detectives walked through the crime scene with flashlights in their hands searching for shell casings. A Latino woman stood on the porch with Detectives pointing at her first floor window indicating bullet holes. Neighbors that lived in the area had to detour around the scene if they wanted to go home. Jerome shook his head from side to side not believing what he saw on TV.

"That shit is crazy, right? Them niggas who came for me they shot the lil boy off the bike." Money Bags said. "When I find out who it is, I'm burying both dem bitches. Then I'm murking Smooth." Money Bags voice was cold.

"You gotta be easy when you get out the hospital. Dem peoples gonna be lookin' for anybody to tie to that shootin, specially 'cause a lil boy got hit." Jerome rubbed the top of his head. "Whoever the fuck that was we getting at dem bustas. Smooth got his comin' too, mark my words." Jerome meant every word he said.

"The boys came up here questioning me bout that lil boy getting shot. I played possum and told dem nothing. Them cracka think I got shot in Fields Corner by mistaken identity." Money Bags grinned and hit the clicker changing it from channel 7 news. "It's gonna be a lot of blood shedding when I get out dis bitch. These niggas violated tryna clip me." Money Bags looked at his shoulder and shook his head from side to side. "Them pussy's had their chance and missed, it won't happen again."

"You better believe it we gonna get to the bottom of dis. It's time to turn it up in the streets and send a message to anybody who ever thinks 'bout tryna get at us." Jerome said, with a stoical look on his face.

There was a light knock at the door and they cut the conversation short. Jerome walked over to the door to open it and saw Tyrell and Mercedes standing there. Mercedes had a bag full of junk food and Tyrell had McDonalds in his hands. Jerome greeted his first cousin with three's and Tyrell bypassed him to check on Money Bags.

"Babe, my eyes are getting heavy." Mercedes passed him a cranberry juice. "I'm ready to go home, I have to study for my finals tomorrow."

"I was 'bout ready to go anyways, bay. Lemme go say bye to Money Bags first." Jerome walked over to the bed. "I'm 'bout to make moves op outta here." Jerome gave him a pound. "Get some rest and call me in the am."

"I'll do that fam. Make sure ya up 'cause you might have to come scoop me from here in the am. I had my bitch come grab the beamer lil while ago, you know dat shit on fire. Be safe bro out there, I love you, Rome." Money Bags said. "By miss lady Mercedes . . . ."

"Later punk, bye means forever. I hope you feel better too." Mercedes said. "Later Rell."

"Good seeing you Cedes." Tyrell said, "What you doin' for the night, cuz?"

"Shit . . . . I'm in for the night wit wifey." Jerome gave Tyrell three's. "Jus' call me Bags if you need me to come snatch you. I'll get wit y'all niggas. I love y'all."

"I'ma talk to you cuz. Hit me on the horn if you need me." Tyrell replied. "Love you too my nig."

Jerome and Mercedes walked out the hospital room. The streets were getting out of control. Everything was happening so fast lately. The money been slowing up on the streets ever since Crook died. All the blocks where Jerome had coke on it were getting shut down by police 'cause of all the shootings. When dudes are hungry in the streets they become desperate and will take food off your plate. Jerome wanted to slow things down a bit. But he knew that wasn't possible at the moment until Smooth was put to rest. Crook was an important dude in the streets and his goons wanted retribution. He made a mental note to himself to eliminate all possible threats in his life. Jerome rode home in silence as he planned his next move. Mercedes could see that all the series of events were beginning to take a toll on him. She held his hand and told him it was going to be alright even though she was worried. Jerome hoped it was 'cause lately everything been getting out of control.

Chapter 26

The corridor was extremely long and narrow with no sign of an exit. There was nothing that could be seen but complete darkness. It was so quiet and vacant if he uttered a word it would echo. There was nobody around but himself as he stood there by his lonesome pondering. Where he was virtually was a mystery. He didn't know what would transpire next. For the first time in years he was petrified. His heartbeat was rapid and he could feel it throbbing.

Then out of nowhere he saw the light illuminate the corridor. The brightness caused him to squint his eyes. He put a hand above his eyes to subdue the light. Then came a woman walking out into the darkness. Every step she took the light shined on her. Jerome stood there transfixed by her gaze. The closer her steps came upon him, he could see her smiling at him. The woman had on a white gown and her hair hung loosely to her shoulders. Jerome squinted his eyes and tried his hardest to see who it was. The steps she took were slow and calculated as if she was in no hurry. Jerome smiled broadly once he realized who the woman was before his eyes; it was his mother.

"Look at my baby all grown up now . . . . your father and I miss you so much . . . ."

"Well how come he doesn't come see me like you momma? I wanna see my pops sometime, too."

"Your father feels bad about what happened on that night and feels as though it was his fault. I told him that it wasn't his fault. When God calls your number it's nothing anybody can do. Now we're in a better place."

"Momma sometime feel lost without y'all not being here. Sometimes I wonder what my life would've been like if y'all was here. It bothers me all the time."

"Son, you have to stay strong and keep pushing. We always gonna be here watching over you. You have to let go of the past and move forward. It's nothing you can do to change what happened that night."

"Momma I know that and it still bothers me. Even though I took care of that coward who did that to y'all I'm still going through a lot out here. Every time I turn around it's another problem coming my way."

"I know exactly what you did, Rome. You gotta always remember, what is done in the dark must come to light. Life is full of heartaches and pain, Rome. You have to stay strong. You must find peace within yourself and then maybe you'll feel free."

"What do you mean by all that? Momma, I'm tryna become a better man and one day I'll eventually be, but right now the streets got a hold of me. I can't walk away from them right now. It ain't that easy. The streets is all I know . . . ."

"You remind me of your father with your stubborn ways. Rome, eventually you will have to responsibility for all your actions. Baby I want you to be careful out in the streets. The streets don't love nobody, Rome. It's time for me to go . . . . I love you, son." The light slowly drifted away and Karen left his right.

"No! Momma . . . . don't go please . . . ? I want you to stay wit me! Nooooo . . . . come back to me! . . ."

"Aarrrgh!" Jerome jumped out his sleep grunting. He sat up in his bed looking around in the darkness of his bedroom. After sitting there for a brief moment he realized it was just a dream. Mercedes had awaken and turned on the lamp that was on the nightstand. She looked at him sitting in the bed with just his boxers on, his entire body was drenched in sweat. Mercedes glanced at his tattoos on his body; Jerome had two portraits of his parent on either shoulder with "R.I.P" Underneath and their names; and in the middle of his chest he had two huge Angel's wings with the words "R.I.P. Angel" underneath. Mercedes climbed out of bed with just a bra and panties on and ran to the bathroom. She ran back in the room with a towel in her hand.

"Babe are you alright? Your sweating like crazy . . . ." Mercedes wiped all the swear off his upper body. "Did you have one of those crazy nightmares again, Romeo?" Mercedes rubbed her hand across his clammy back.

"Yeah I'm good, jus' had a fucked up dream that's all."

"Babe you scared the shit outta me screaming like that. I thought something happened to you . . . ." Mercedes kissed him on the neck. "You taste so salty right now." Mercedes giggled showing her dimples.

"Sorry for waking you outta ya sleep. I feel mad sticky right now, I'm sweating like crazy."

"I know, this whole towel is wet from your sweaty ass."

"Don't front like you don't love this sweaty ass." Jerome rubbed on her thick thighs. "Damn that cat looking good right 'bout now . . . ." Jerome looked between her thighs at her pussy print.

"Never said I didn't like you sweaty. Babe this cat is all yours whenever you want it." Mercedes caressed his dick through the boxers. "Mmm-hmmm babe I need some of that before I go to school."

"You sure we gonna have enough time to get it in?"

Mercedes looked over at the clock, "It's only six o'clock, I don't have to be at school 'til eight-thirty." Mercedes kissed him long and hard on the mouth. "I want you to fuck me in the shower . . . ."

Mercedes grabbed his hand and led him into the bathroom. Soon as they got into the bathroom they took off their clothes and went inside the shower. Mercedes turned the hot water on and the steam instantly fogged up the bathroom. They kissed passionately as the hot water cascaded off their bodies and ran down into the drain. He scooped her up into his arms and leaned up against the wall inside the shower. Mercedes guided him inside of her slowly and he pushed until he was all the way in. Jerome penetrated her and she closed her eyes as he worked his magic. Everything felt so good to them as both their bodies gyrated together.

Jerome sucked on her neck while he continued to give her slow strokes underneath the water. Mercedes was moaning out his name and the more she did the harder he would stroke. He fit perfectly inside her tight pussy. Ever since they been together she hasn't been with anybody else. Mercedes was a rare breed and all she knew how to do was be faithful and loyal to her man. She wrapped her legs around him as he stood up in the shower fucking her.

Her hair was getting soaked and wet from the shower, but Mercedes didn't care she was on her way to ecstasy. She dug her nails into his back as she was having an orgasm. Jerome's knees buckled and that's when he came to a halt letting out all his sperm inside of her.

They washed up after making love in the shower. Jerome lathered up her back with soap and placed small kisses on the back of her neck. Mercedes smiled as she out soap all over her body. Jerome lathered up his body thrice and rinsed and he was finished bathing. He got out the shower first, put a towel around him, and went into the bedroom.

Mercedes got out the shower right after him. They took turns putting lotion on each other's body. Jerome always let her lotion hi back, the rest of his body he did on his own. He reached inside his draw and put on some polo boxers with a tank top. Mercedes put on baby phat panties with a matching bra, then she hit the clicker and Channel 7 news came on. Every morning she would watch the weatherman to see how the forecast would be.

A loud noise came from the front of the house and then some more from the back. Jerome knew what the sound of that was all too familiar. The flashbacks came back to him the night his parents were murdered. The front door came crashing down and the back door did too. Jerome ran over to the dresser and grabbed his .40 cal. He wasn't going out without a shootout. Mercedes was paralyzed in fear and didn't know what to do. Jerome ran to the doorway and soon as he stepped foot in the hallway that's when he saw police officers swarm him.

"Freeze! Drop the weapon and lay face down on the floor!" Jerome did as he was told. "Your under arrest for the murder of Christopher Walker . . . ." The Homicide detective walked up to Jerome and kicked the gun away from in front of him.

Homicide Detectives ransacked the house for anything incriminating that could be used against Jerome. They showed Jerome the warrant they had for his arrest. Mercedes came running out the bedroom screaming at the police officers.

"He didn't kill my father! . . . Let him go! Please?!" Mercedes was crying hysterical.

"Miss, calm down, please, for your own sake. He's under arrest and we're taking him down to Boston Headquarters."

"Mercedes . . . . I love you . . . ." Those were the last words Jerome said before they walked him to the squad car.

"I love you too . . . ." Mercedes sat there in the middle of the floor crying.

Chapter 27

Money Bags couldn't believe the devastating news he heard about Jerome being arrested. Mercedes explained everything to Money Bags and told him that Jerome was at Boston Police Headquarters. When he got off the phone with Mercedes he felt awful about the whole situation. Homicide Detectives were no joke and Money Bags knew that without a doubt. Usually whenever they come to arrest somebody on a warrant, they usually have a witness or multiple witnesses. Sometimes they would even indicted a person off of hearsay. Virtually all suspects arraigned on murder charges in the Commonwealth were held without bail. No matter how he looked at it, somebody was cooperating with the law, Money Bags wanted answers pronto.

After sitting there mulling in the lobby, he knew exactly what to do for Jerome; he was going to call Linda Roseberry. When it came to fighting murder cases Roseberry was the lawyer to call, her theatrics inside the courtroom were impeccable. She could persuade just about any judge or jury inside the courtroom during trial; that's why her reputation was superb and everyone around the city spoke highly of her. She had remarkable success in the past years with numerous high profiled cases ending with not guilty verdicts. Anybody who hired her had to have long money, everything came with a price including freedom.

Money Bags got up out the chair inside the lobby and walked to the double sliding doors inside the ER. His arm was in a sling and the Doctor recommended he keep his arm that way until his shoulder healed. Then before giving his papers to leave, the Doctor subscribed him a prescription of Percocet's five milligrams. The doctor also warned him that the pills were highly addictive and should be taken as prescribed. Standing outside the ER was a Caucasian brunette with freckles on her face smoking on a cigarette. She wore green scrubs with white Reeboks, she stood there in the cold with no jacket on tapping her foot on the ground. Even though he wasn't a cigarette smoker, he still opt to smoke one 'cause his nerves were bad.

"Thanks . . . ." He put the cigarette to his mouth and lit it. "Damn these muthafuckas is nasty!" He spit on the ground.

The nurse looked at him and laughed as he tried to smoke the cigarette. She stepped on the cigarette and walked back inside. Money Bags took a couple of more pulls off the Marlboro and flicked it. A maroon Cherokee pulled into the parking lot and Money Bags walked over to the truck. He climbed in the passenger seat and slid his seat back. Tyrell pulled off and drove down Dorchester Ave.

"Dawg shit iz fucked up right now, Bags, I can't believe my cousin iz bagged right now on a body. I can only imagine what he's going through right now. We need to find out who's tellin' on my cousin's case, and once we do that I'm putting the muthafucka to sleep." Tyrll said, with a solemn look on his face.

"Rome gonna be aight you can believe that. It's all a waitin' process and he jsu' have to be patient. He definitely gonna have to sit in Nash for a couple years 'til trial come, but he's gonna be good, trust me. Soon as he get them jury minutes from the lawyer we'll know exactly who's snitching. But 'til then we have to do what we gotta do and get dis money for the lawyer. Let her work her magic and Rome will be aight." Money Bags said, defiantly.

Tyrell nodded his head agreeing with what he said. They knew what the lawyer Linda Roseberry was capable of doing. The price would be hefty but well worth it 'cause Jerome's freedom was on the line. Tyrell drove through Lower Mills down River street. Money Bags reached in the ashtray and grabbed the half of Dutch.

"Nah don't light that while I'm driving, I'm dirty right now. I got the joint on me, Bags."

"Hurry up and get to the spot, I need to smoke . . . . my nerves iz bad doggy."

"Relax, would ya, we almost in Hyde Park." Tyrell bypassed the Mattapan T Station on his left and stopped at the red-light. "Bro you like a junkie for some purp . . . . I can on only imagine how you'd be without it." Tyrell shook his head.

"Muthafuckin right . . . . I likes to get faded, it helps me cope wit all the bullshit I'm goin' through."

"Yeah I know that's right . . . . if it ain't one thing it's another. Always some problems in the hood. I wonder if dis shit will ever change." The light turned green and Tyrell drove straight across down River street.

"The hood iz always gonna be the same dawg. No matter how many projects dem crackas tear down and call themselves rebuilding—shit always gonna be fucked up.

Niggas iz always gonna be gangbanging, and there's always gonna be drugs to be sold."

"You ain't lying 'bout that, it iz what it iz out here."

"Damn right, that's why I'm murking anybody outta pocket."

"That's why I fucks wit ya 'cause ya cooked, Bags."

"Call it how you wanna, I'm jus' keepin' it one hunnit."

Tyrell drove over the bridge and took a sharp right onto Oakcrest street. Then he turned left onto Taunton Ave and then the first left onto Rosemont. Halfway up the street Tyrell pulled over on his left and parked. They got out the truck and walked upstairs to the front door. Money Bags unlocked the door and made their way inside the house.

"I need you to help me count out a hunnit stacks,' Money Bags said, "After that we gonna bring it to the lawyer."

"Aight, go get the money and bring it in the living room."

"Yep, roll up some of that purple too, I'm tryna get high."

"What you think I'm 'bout to do." Tyrell sat down on the sofa. "You got any woods here? I only got Dutch's on me, got a taste for a wood." Tyrell pulled out a sandwich bag full of weed.

"Nah, jus' twirl dem Dutch's up, I need to smoke." Money Bags walked off into the other room.

Tyrell broke up a few lines of weed on the coffee table. The weed was so sticky he had to cut it apart with some scissors. After splitting a Dutch Master down the middle, he filled the inside of it with exotic weed. Tyrell rolled two blunts with finesse. Money Bags came into the living room with a duffle bag in hand.

"Scoot over some nigga." Money Bags sat down on the couch. "It's time to count all dis money again, gotta make sure it's all here." Money Bags unzipped the whole bag.

"Damn y'all niggas was getting' it out here." Tyrell's mouth dropped wide open.

"Jus' help me count dis all up, would ya." Money Bags sat the money counter on the table. "Every ten g's you count slide it to the side, now pass me that blizz hoover . . . ." Money Bags ran the first stack of bills threw the machine.

"I got you, Bags, nigga I know how to count money."

"Well act like it, youngster."

After sitting in the hospital for two days, Money Bags was back in effect. Now it was time to get things done and restore order in the streets. There wasn't any time to play games or go to sleep. All Money Bags wanted to do was get back to the money. The only thing that mattered was making sure the lawyer had the retainer fee, once that was done he would keep giving her vast payments until she was paid in full. Earlier that day Jerome was arraigned at Boston Municipal Court and held without bail. So already realizing that he would not get bail, Money Bags knew majority of the money would go to the lawyer. Money Bags sat there quietly with a blunt dangling from his mouth as he counted money. So much stuff was on his mind.

Money Bags thought about the connect and wondered if he heard Jerome getting pinched. The connect was a low-key dude and would be spooked if he heard about Jerome getting arrested. The connect would sever all ties with both of them just so he wouldn't be affiliated. Money Bags was mulling over the idea and refused to lose his connect. Right now was crucial and he needed to keep coke on the streets and money coming in. Money Bags put ten stacks of hundreds to the left on the table.

"Aight . . . , that's the lawyers gwop right there, now let's count the rest of dis inside the bag. Everything else left over I gotta see the connect wit," Money Bags said. "Rell, go get a brown paper bag out the ktichen.

"I got you, Bags." Tyrell got up and went to the kitchen.

Money Bags sat back smoking and thinking to himself. He flicked ashes on the floor not really caring at the moment. Tyrell walked back in the room with a paper bag in his hand.

"Put that hunnit thou in the paper bag, but first put the rubber bands back around them."

Tyrell nodded his head and did as told. While Tyrell loaded the paper bag with money, Money Bags kept counting money. Money Bags lit up the other blunt and kept putting money through the machine. Tyrell rubber banded all the money for the lawyer and threw it in the paper bag and sat it on the floor; then went back to helping Money Bags count the rest of the money. Every stack that went through the machine, Tyrell put the rubber band back on it. Money Bags sighed relief after counting the last of the bills.

"That's a quarter mill right there, plus the hunnit thou in the paper bag, so it's three-hunnit-fifty-thou all together. Plus, we still got three bricks left, so that's another eighty thou jus' 'bout." Money Bags passed him the blunt. "Help me throw dis money back in the duffle bag. I'm gonna see poppy wit that gwop later dis week."

"Come on let's hurry up and get up outta here before we bump into traffic downtown, you know how rush hour traffic iz, Bags. You know I got road rage like a muthafucka." Tyrell grinned at him.

"Yeah ya right, it's almost two o'clock time iz flying."

They put all the money back inside the duffle bag. Money Bags picked the duffle bag up and put it back in the other room. Tyrell picked up the brown paper bag in hand. Money Bags retrieved a black .380 Lawson automatic form underneath the airbed, cocked it back, put one in the chamber, and they were out the door.

Linda K. Roseberry's office was located on 605 Union Wharf street in the Financial District. Her office was half a mile from downtown Boston and two blocks over from the World Trade Center. The Financial District was cluttered with high end restaurants and Five Star Hotels. The area also had multimillion dollar high-rise condominiums with panoramic views overlooking the Boston Harbor and other parts of the city. This was one of the many parts of the city where the wealthy people dwelled.

Tyrell double parked outside of the high-rise building and put on his hazards. Money Bags departed with a paper bag in his good hand and walked into the building. Soon as he walked through the spinning doors he was accosted by a heavy set Caucasian security guard.

"Excuse me sir, we are closed for today!"

"I don't see no sign on the door saying closed. And the doors are still open, move out my way, buddy!" Money Bags sniped.

"Well we're not actually closed, but the lawyers are not actually seeing anybody else for today." The security guard pulled his pants up over his stomach. "So whatever it is your gonna have to wait."

"Listen, call upstairs and tell Linda Roseberry somebody iz here to see her. I'm not going anywhere 'til I speak wit her." Money Bags glared at him.

The security guard got the picture and realized he wasn't going to leave until he spoke with her. The security guard walked behind his desk and picked up the phone. After a brief moment on the telephone he hung it up and walked back over to Money Bags.

"She said for you to come upstairs and see her, ya lucky day, eh.

"There's no such thing as luck, money talks. Prick!"

Money Bags looked him up and down walked off leaving him there fuming red. Money Bags got on the elevator and pressed number eight and the elevator ascended. When he stopped off the elevator he walked over to the secretary's desk. The secretary buzzed Linda K. Roseberry over the phone. After chatting with the lawyer briefly, the secretary directed him around back to where Roseberry's office was located.

A woman with dark hair sat behind a mahogany desk as he walked into the office. Money Bags walked over to her desk and dropped the paper bag down. Linda Roseberry gave him a quizzical look.

"A friend of mine iz locked up for murder and iz sitting in Nashua Street Jail, he needs ya help and heard ya the lady to see." Money Bags got strait to the point.

"That's all money inside that paper bag?" Linda Roseberry inquired.

"Yes, ma'am, there's a hundred-thousand in the bag."

"Wow! Ok . . . . so tell me about your friend, take a seat sir." She gestured.

"My name iz Money Bags, by the way, pleasure to meet you." He shook her hand firmly.

They sat there having a conversation for about thirty minutes or so about Jerome. Money Bags told her everything he knew about Jerome. Linda K. Roseberry sat there jotting everything down on a yellow legal pad. She wrote down Money Bags cell number and gave her Mercedes house and cell number. She promised him that she would try and make it up to see Jerome within a week to speak with him about the case. She gave Money Bags her business card and also jotted down her cell number also. Linda K. Roseberry was about her money and didn't turn down no cases unless the money was funny.

Money Bags left out the building feeling a lot better. Now that his right-hand man's lawyer got paid, he could execute his other plans. Now it was time to get things into motion. Money Bags had a few tricks up his sleeve.

Chapter 28

"Jenkins! Visit!" the C.O. bellowed.

Jerome got up from the table where he was playing chess at and walked up the stairs. He looked through the first two doors on his right and didn't see nobody, so he walked down to the last door and looked inside, Mercedes was sitting down on the other side of the wall. The only thing separating the two of them was a two inch Plexiglas. He opened the door and stepped inside the small visiting room that only held one inmate at a time. Jerome was clad in a two piece white uniform, he took the shirt off and hung it on the door blocking the window. No other inmates would be walking by peeking through the window looking at his woman, he wanted some privacy. Jerome took a seat on the metal stool.

Mercedes looked at the white v-neck polo t-shirt and wondered how long he had that on, she brought that to him days ago at the Boston Police Headquarters. She looked at his scruffy face and realized he didn't shave in a week. On the streets Jerome stayed well groomed. Mercedes was hurting inside seeing her man like this at his all time low. There was nothing he could do from behind the wall but have faith. Since the day the police took Jerome away she been crying every night. Mercedes was tormented over her man being locked down in Nashua Street jail.

"Whassup babygirl, you look cute in ya scrubs." Jerome said, making small talk. "How was school today? I hope ya learning too, don't be stressin' over me, Mercedes." Jerome spoke through the air holes underneath the Plexiglas.

"Hi babe, school was alright, I guess." Mercedes shrugged her shoulders. "My teacher is driving me crazy! I can't understand shit he says." Mercedes leaned her forehead on the glass. "Babe, I promise you coping with you not being here as best as I could. Romeo, I miss you . . . babe I need you home with me in my arms."

Jerome leaned in closer too and was all the way up close staring into her eyes. He hated the fact that they had to speak through the air holes underneath the Plexiglas. Nashua Street County Jail didn't show no sympathy towards inmates and never bothered installing phones inside the visiting rooms like other county jails.

"I miss you too, 'Cedes . . . . all I think 'bout iz you my love, ya my heart. I'm so in love wit you and it scares me sometime, 'Cedes, I'm scared . . . ." His voice trailed off. "Baby I don't wanna ever lose you. I'll sacrifice my whole life for you. I want you to be strong out there and hold it down." Jerome said, sincerely.

"Romeo, your my king, you mean the world to me. I'm never gonna leave you no matter what. You make me complete and you're the reason why I smile. I'm gonna be strong out here for us, I promise you that babe. I can't imagine life without my king by me side; Romeo, I'm here for you . . . ." Mercedes let out some tears.

Seeing Mercedes like that really touched his heart. The past week being in jail taking toll on him mentally. Mercedes was there for him mentally and made sure he didn't want for nothing. Mercedes was there for him mentally and made sure he didn't want for nothing. Once her name got cleared to come up and visit him, she been up every day since. She also put "Evercom" on her cellphone and wrote him letters.

'Bay, don't cry, I'm gonna be aight and you are too. You heard?"

"Yes, babe, I know. It's in God's hands, I know you'll be home soon."

Jerome smirked at what she said. Mercedes was oblivious of the system and didn't have the slightest idea how things worked. Jerome kept his thoughts to himself and decided to leave it alone. The last couple of days she been saying he'll be home in a few months, but Jerome knew how the system worked, he was preparing himself to sit-down for a few years until trial.

"So two more weeks of school left and then you're starting ya externship. Are you excited bay?" Jerome smiled at her.

"Yes, thank god I'm almost done, babe. After I do all my hours I'll graduate and be certified, I'm that close." Mercedes put her two finger close together. "I want you to be proud of your babygirl, daddy."

"I'm proud of you bay, too bad I ain't gonna be there to see you walk across the stage."

"It's alright babe, you're gonna be there in my heart, I'ma have mommy take plenty of pictures of me." Mercedes smiled at him. "Mommy said hello too, and keep your head up."

"Tell my mother-in-law I said hello."

The C.O opened the door and told Jerome he had five minutes before the visit was over. Jerome looked into her eyes and all he saw was loyalty. He saw his future with her and planned on having kids with her one day. Those were the thoughts in envisioned as he stared at his woman. But the reality of the situation wasn't looking too bleak being locked up in the county jail.

"Guess what, babe?"

"What?"

"I'm getting your name inked on me."

"Don't play games wit me."

"Who's joking? I'm in love with a "G" and I'm tatting his name on me."

"Where you putting it at?"

"Wherever you want me too . . . ."

"Baby, put it right on dis arm." Jerome showed her his right forearm. "Put it right there bay, or ya lower back."

"No, babe, I'm not getting no tramp stamp, I'll put it on my arm where you showed me. I'm getting it done this weekend."

"Aight. When iz my lawyer 'pose to be comin' to see me?"

"She said before the week is over."

The C.O stepped back into the room and held the door open. Jerome looked at the C.O and then back at Mercedes. He didn't want to leave the visiting room and she could sense it.

"Romeo, I love you with all my heart . . . ." She blew him a kiss. "Call me later on, there's money on the phone."

"I love you more. I'll call you tonight, later."

Jerome grabbed his shirt off the door and walked back to his cell for count. He put his Walkman on and put it on

"Hot 97" and kicked back on his bunk. Ten minutes later he was in dreamland.

———◈———

"Yeah . . . . mmm-hmmm mami jus' like that, suck the balls too. Ooohhh deep throat that dick . . . ." Money Bags grunted.

Money Bags was reclined in the driver's seat of a Chevy Tahoe enjoying the sensation. The Spanish chick worked her magic on him and took all him inside her mouth without gagging. She used all lips and tongue muscles while she did her performance. She leaned over from the passenger seat with ass propped up in the air and devoured his shaft. He guided her with his left hand on top of her head and fingered her pussy from the back with the other hand. The juices coming from her pussy dripped down her thighs and soaked the passenger seat. He was on the verge of climaxing, his toes curled and his eyes rolled to the back of his head. The harder he ran his two fingers in and out of her pussy, the more vigorously she sucked and licked his shaft. Money Bags released his fluids inside of her mouth and she swallowed every last drop. She kept going trying to get him back hard again. He was defeated, he pushed her off him and pulled up his pants.

"Whooooo, that mouth of yours iz the truth, Cynthia." Money Bags pulled a rolled Backwood from inside the armrest. "Mami I'ma get witch though, I gotta bust dis move. I'll call you though, sexy." He looked at her shaved vagina and smiled tentatively.

"Papi make sure yu cal me afterwards 'cause I need some of that dick. My pussy is so wet right now papi . . . ." She ran her fingers inside her pussy and then pulled them out and sucked them. "I'm soooo horny right now."

"I'ma call you up later no bullshit, I wanna hit that fat ole pussy from the back . . . . call one of ya homegirls over too, I wanna fuck both y'all." He hit the blunt and inhaled deeply.

"Well you'll just have to wait and see papi . . . . only if yu good boy." She learned over for a kiss but he turned his turned his head. "Papi no kiss?" She pouted and pulled her pants up.

"Come on Cynthia, stop it . . . . you jus' sucked my dick and swallowed my nut." He shook his head and kept smoking.

Cynthia sucked her teeth and sighed deeply, she was hurt. She put her hair in a scrounge and let her long blond hair down her back. She was a bad bitch with a pretty face and nice body, but to Money Bags she was just another bitch. He treated them all the same, once he got his nut he was up and gone. She stormed out the truck and walked down the driveway around back to her apartment. Money Bags started the truck up and pulled off. He drove to the end of Selden street and turned left on Milton Ave. It was time for him to go see the connect.

The entire way there to meet the connect he took all back streets. After getting the rental from the airport he paid somebody to tint the two windows. Now the truck was completely tinted and he felt incognito. The rental had Mass license plates so he blended right in with everybody else. He didn't want to take a chance getting out-of-state plates on a rental car and be driving around the city, he knew the police stay pulling those over so he needed to be inconspicuous.

Now with his arm out the sling, he was ready for combat. Money Bags wasn't showing any remorse for anybody. If you wasn't a part of his circle or not down with his movements, he was cutthroat towards you. Anybody could get it right now that's how he was feeling.

After talking to his connect about Jerome being indicted for murder, the connect was acting shaky. Initially he wanted to cut all ties with Money Bags. But after persistently telling the connect that he was their only plug, and that he had nothing to worry about, the connect agreed to keep doing business with Money Bags. The only term was that the prices would go up and he wasn't fronting Money Bags nothing on top of what he usually bought. That right there alone made him furious with the connect. Every time him and Jerome spent money with the connect it was always big money. They always paid back any money owed to the connect. Now all of sudden things were changing for the worse.

This would be Money Bags last time dealing with the connect. The connect wasn't budging on the prices. Money Bags refused to get taxed an extra three-thousand on top of each kilo. Especially not after all the money they brought the connect. Now it was time to get even. Since the connect didn't want to show love anymore, he was going to take some bricks from him. The connect knew that Jerome's lawyer was Linda K. Roseberry, and that Money Bags needed to keep the streets flooded, in order to stay in the game and pay the lawyer. But the connect still wasn't trying to give him no good deals. So Money Bags had enough of the back and forth debating. He was just going to take what he wanted and call it a day. Eventually he would need to find a new connect, but right now he wasn't concerned with all that at the moment. All he wanted to do was get the bricks and keep it moving.

In the backseat of the Chevy Tahoe was duffle bag with money inside. The top layer was lined with money, and underneath all of it was stacks of paper. So when the connect would look inside the bag, it would look like it'd be full of money. They been doing business for so long that Money Bags didn't worry about him counting it on the spot. This would be an easy lick and knew it. But he was still prepared and fully equipped just in case it back fired. Either way he looked at it, he was taking those bricks from the connect; the easy way, or the hard way.

Money Bags pulled over and parked across the street from a used car lot on Centre street. The traffic was heavy in Jamaica Plain during this time of day. This was usually when everyone commuted home from work and kids got out of school. Majority of the people on this side of town were Spanish descendants. Half of them migrated here for a better life and had no green card. Some of them came to America to work and then the other half just sold drugs. On this side of town if you know the right people you could go places. The Dominicans dominated this side of town with the best coke and heroin in the city.

Before stepping out the truck, Money Bags surveyed the area with a keen eye. Everything looked good at the moment, he took a deep breath to relax himself. If this didn't go as planned, he knew it would be a shootout on the scene. He released the safeties on both .380 automatics and placed them on his waist; he grabbed the duffle bag off the backseat, and departed from the truck. The bulletproof vest underneath his champ added some more pounds on him. After getting shot he kept his vest on everyday and two guns on him.

Cars zoomed up and down Centre street with reggae tone blasting. He stood next to the truck waiting for the cars to come to a halt and let him crossover. Directly across the street from him was the connects used car lot. Inside the lot held a couple foreign cars and a few American cars, this was a cover up to wash dirty money. Down the street the connect also owned a bodega and an auto body shop. A neon green Honda Civic squatting low to the ground came to a halt, the Spanish kid beeped the horn to signal him to walk across.

When he walked into the car lot three men stood there having a conversation with smiles on their face. Money Bags saw that the connect was the main in the middle doing the talking. The connect noticed him walk into the yard and stopped talking. The connect was clean shaved with long cornrolls to the back. The fitted jeans he wore gave him the pretty boy look. But he was far from a pretty boy, the connect was all business and would have you hit in a heartbeat.

"Whassup, Primo." Money Bags shook his hand. "Talk to me, papi, everything all good."

"Of course everything is all good, my friend. How's my buddy Jerome doing?" Primo was all smiles.

Money Bags wanted to brush that question 'cause deep down inside he knew Primo didn't care about his right-hand man. Primo was strictly business; there was no genuine friendship, he only cared about the money they spent.

Money Bags decided to answer him anyways just for good measures.

"Yeah Rome iz doing alright, I tell him you said hello." Money Bags fake smiled. "It's two-hunnit-fifty-thou in the bag, here ya go Primo." Money Bags tossed the bag in front of Primo's feet.

"Primo gave a head nod to one of his partners and they walked around back. Less than a minute the man returned with an army duffle bag in his hand and dropped off in front of Money Bags. "That's twenty-five bricks in there amigo . . . ." Primo smiled showing two gold teeth.

"Good doin' business with you, Primo, I'll be in touch soon as I get rid of all these bricks." Money Bags picked up the army duffle bag.

"No problem my friend, anytime . . . ." Primo shook hands with him.

Money Bags looked at the three goons beside Primo one last time and walked off heading towards his car. He was nervous as he was walking out the car lot. Money Bags didn't know if Primo was going to count the money right away or what, so he put a little pep in his step. Soon as Money Bags stepped foot on the sidewalk he heard Primo call his name. he gripped his hand on his waist and contemplated if he should pull out his pistol. Then he decided not to do it and turned around to see what he wanted.

"Yeah whassup Primo?"

"It's nothing personal my friend . . . . it's just business . . . ." Primo said, and smiled before walking off to his office with duffle bag full of money.

Money Bags felt relieved once he heard Primo say that to him. He just shook his head and turned his back and kept walking until he got his truck. Money Bags just came up twenty-five kilos and was feeling good about himself.

"Dis shit iz personal you bitch ass nigga! . . ." Money Bags said, to himself and pulled off.

Chapter 29

After getting the twenty five kilos the connect Money Bags hit the streets hard flooding all his traps with work. The streets were a little dry due to the loss of Crook and then Jerome being incarcerated didn't make anything better. Due to the drought Money Bags was able to add a little street tax and bumping the prices to thirty-thousand a kilo. Few people tried complaining about the numbers on the work, but in the end they still ended up copping weight. The work was gone in a flash once Money Bags put the word out that he was back rolling. He got rid all twenty-five kilos in less than two weeks and found him a new connect.

It's been about three months since the day Jerome got taken off the streets. Money Bags kept the money coming in and Jerome's lawyer kept getting monthly installments of ten grand until the lawyer was paid in full. The lawyer let Jerome know that it was one witness that was willing to testify against him. Money Bags got word sent to him in code from the county jail and was now well aware of who was the witness. Money Bags was now ready to eliminate the witness on Jerome's case; Money Bags was aware of that and had to solve the problem promptly.

Jerome's life was on the line and he couldn't afford to let his homeboy take a chance going to trial against a witness who claims to seen everything. Money Bags refused to let that happen to his homeboy, he was going to fix the problem, he needed his raoddawg home with him getting money and enjoying life. Nothing was the same anymore ever since they took his partner away. He wasn't even hitting the clubs no more and balling out. Now he was much more reserved and keeping a low profile, he couldn't afford to be caught slipping somewhere the heat was on with the law and the wolves were onto him. There were some people out there aiming for his head. So that's why he tried staying two steps ahead of his opposition.

The heat was on Money Bags and he was more alert than ever. Every week he switched up his rental just to stay under the radar. He would never give someone the chance to say they saw him in a certain car, he like to switch up and not be consistent with the same car. He never wanted to be comfortable with any rental. Nothing was ever put in his name and state. Money Bags wasn't trying to be caught slipping and having shit come back to his name, he wasn't going to let any little slip ups cause him to catch a case.

Money Bags sat at the edge of the bed wiping down his bullets with a red bandana and then loading them into the clip. He just finished cleaning both his .380's and then oiling them down. He wanted to make sure that his guns worked, plus whenever he cleaned his guns they worked better. He loaded up the last clip and then cocked both guns back, inserting a bullet in the chamber, then he threw both guns on his waist and walked out the door. The only thing on his mind was killing.

The pastor stood at the podium preaching his eulogy for the Sunday morning church-goers at Morning Star Baptist Church. It was a standing ovation inside the church as the pastor spoke. Everyone inside the church were brushing shoulder's that's how packed it was. The pastor spoke on gang issues and drugs being sold in the urban communities. There was too many senseless shootings all throughout the city in the past year. So many church-goers clapped their hands and bellowed "Hallelujah" in unison as the pastor continued on with the speech. Some parents and loved ones search for solace and serenity after losing a loved one and find church. So hearing the pastor speak on the urban community about stopping the violence, they could feel the pain and hurt, it was like opening a new wound.

The pastor brought the church to a closure. Keisha said goodbye to few people at the church she knew and departed from the church before everyone else started leaving. Keisha hated to be the last person leaving church, to many church-goers would have the hallways congested, she didn't like to stay and mingle. Keisha hastily sashayed down the corridors until she found the front entrance and departed from the building. Soon as she stepped outside Keisha felt the grating frigid weather. She buttoned up her pea-coat and took slow strides until she got to her car. The parking lot had ice on the ground and was slippery to walk across. Walking in a pair of heels just made matters worse trying to walk in through the parking lot. Keisha put the key inside the door to unlock her '89 Taurus.

"Come on . . . . what the hell, please start, don't do this to me now . . . ." Keisha thought to herself as she tried starting her car. The car wouldn't turn over for her. She kept toying

with the car trying to get her jalopy to start. She turned the key again, this time slightly giving it some gas too, desperately trying to get the car running.

Nothing!

The car was not trying to start at all. Keisha sighed deeply and then banged on the steering wheel. These were the times when she missed Crook the most. If he was still alive she would never have to worry about her car starting, Crook would've had her in something plush or a rental; either way it would've never been something so old like her Taurus. She just sat there in a daze for the moment just thinking. Granted she wasn't rolling in the life no more or making the good money she became accustomed too, but now she found God in her life and was a peace with herself.

Keisha turned the key over this time while tapping on the gas and the car started. She smiled feeling relieved after being able to start her car. The car was fairly old so she had to let the car warm up a lot longer than any other car. Keisha tapped on the gas revving the engine up some to let the car warm up faster. She adjusted her heat to defrost and turned it up high to get the ice off the windshield.

She scrolled through her phone and noticed there was no missed calls or any texts messages and then she put her phone back in her purse. She adjusted her radio to the oldies station before throwing her car in reverse and then pulling out of the church parking lot. Keisha sang along to the lyrics of the Isley Brothers.

"Perry, slow dis muthafucka down a lil bit and pull up to the driver's side window . . . ." Money Bags sat in the passenger seat of the black-on-black Dodge Charger tinted out with both guns on his lap. The Charger pulled up right beside a white Taurus on Blue Hill Ave at the red-light. Money Bags rolled down his window and hung both arms out. Money Bags emptied both clips out on the car.

Keisha never had a chance to get away. Before she even saw the guns it was too late. Money Bags put holes in her head, and torso area causing her brains to go on the dashboard. Keisha's head fell on the steering wheel and she drifted through the intersection and her car ran into a telephone pole on the corner of Fessenden street. The black Charger peeled off flying up Wellington Hill.

"Drive, drive, drive dis muthafucka, Perry!" Money Bags commanded. "Hurry up and get to the low spot, I gotta change clothes and get rid of the joints."

"Aight, I got you, Bags!" Perry put the pedal to the metal and they were long gone.

Chapter 30

"2 Years Later"

Jerome sat stoically inside courtroom 808 in Suffolk Superior next to his lawyer as the district attorney litigated in front of the jurors and judge. The courtroom was clustered with people from all walks of life. In the far right corner there were the new reporters, and journalists and interns, and on the other side were people there to show support for Jerome. There were a few people there for Crook also to show support. The district attorney was out to destroy Jerome's image in front of the jurors by portraying him as some monster. The D.A. even went as far to try and bring up the mysterious death of "Keisha Valentine" in front of the jurors. Jerome's lawyer intervened and objected to the attempt of desperately trying to bring up some circumstantial evidence.

Mercedes and Gina sat directly behind the defense's table where Jerome was seated at. It hurt like hell hearing the D.A. bring up everything that happened on the night of her father's death. Gina wiped a tear away as she tried not to let it fall out. Hearing the D.A. rant on about Jerome being a killer was like opening new wounds on Gina and Mercedes. The D.A even went as far as to bring up what happened fifteen years ago on Christmas Eve, when both of Jerome's parents were murdered, but Jerome's lawyer, Linda

K. Roseberry objected once again, and D.A. had to move on to the next theatric.

The D.A lacked any credible witnesses at the time of trial. Without his star witness Keisha Valentine, there wasn't really a case the Commonwealth had against Jerome Jenkins. Everything being said during trial by the Commonwealth was more so hearsay, and without a witness it would be nearly impossible to convict Jerome. Now it was Jerome's lawyer turn to lay down her closing arguments against the D.A. Linda K. Roseberry wasted no time getting out her seat and standing firmly in front of the jurors box, as she litigated in the courtroom, all eyes were on her as she chose her words carefully, and delivered analogy after analogy, making the District Attorney David Connor, look like an imbecile.

The entire week during trial Jerome was clad in different three piece and donned a pair of glasses to appear more modest. He was clean shaven and his hair cut in a Caesar, looking more of a college kid than a gangster on trial for murder. Jerome kept his hands folded in front of him on the table as his lawyer swayed back and forth from the jurors box to the judge and then to the audience in the courtroom. Linda K. Roseberry exuded confidence as she laid it on thick for all spectators. Jerome sipped some water at the defense table and tried his hardest to remain calm. Jerome's mind was rambling a thousand miles per minute, and his heart beat was erratically.

Linda K. Roseberry took her seat next to her client after stating everything she needed to say. The judge addressed the court and announced to jurors that it was now time for them to go deliberate. The courtroom was now in recess and everyone departed from room 808 as the jurors stepped out the back door behind the judge's table. The bailiff's brought Jerome back downstairs to the holding cells. Jerome said nothing to anybody as he sat down on the bench inside the holding cell. A few people tried asking him how his case was looking in the cell, but Jerome just ignored them and sat with his head down thinking. Too much was at stake right now and his life was now on the line. Jerome said a silent prayer to God and hoped that he would be answered.

The bailiff came back downstairs with sandwich's for all the inmates in holding. Jerome refused to eat the ham and cheese, he was sick to the stomach and could not eat. He sipped from the Pepsi thrice before he sat it on the floor next to his foot. Jerome couldn't think rational right then at the moment, he didn't want to talk to anyone. Only thing he wanted to hear was what his fate was going to be. This was the longest two hours of his life sitting in holding.

The Bailiff's came back downstairs to get Jerome and bring back to the courtroom. Jerome was seated in the courtroom and unshackled before anybody else was back into the courtroom. Linda K. Roseberry walked back into the courtroom and sat next to her client and made small talk with him. The judge came back into courtroom 808 before the jurors walked back inside. All the spectators sat quietly and patiently until they heard the verdict.

"Court all rise . . . ." The judge bellowed. "Now everyone may take a seat." Everyone in the courtroom sat down. "Jurors, do we have a verdict, yet?" the judge inquired.

"Yes, your honor, we reached a verdict." The sole Caucasian female juror said.

"Well, you may proceed, ma'am with verdict." The judge commanded.

Jerome sat there with his eyes closed waiting patiently for the juror to read off the verdict. The Caucasian lady juror looked down at the paper in her hand and then glanced to her right at the other eleven jurors before reading off the verdict from the paper, "We find the defendant, Jerome Jenkins, not guilty on all counts!"

Tears fell freely down Jerome's face as he stood there with a smile over his face after beating the murder charge. He embraced his lawyer hugging her tightly after hearing the not guilty verdict. The bailiff unshackled Jerome and released him right from the courtroom. Jerome hugged Mercedes and kissed her right inside the courtroom. Then he went and hugged all the rest of his loved ones. Next he hugged Mercedes mother Gina and then he went to hug and chat with Carolina and Gloria.

"I'm so glad your home now, Rome." Carolina said, sincerely.

"I am too, thanks for all the love and support, big sis." Jerome hugged and kissed her on the cheek.

"No problem, bro, that's what family suppose to do. When one person takes a fall, the others should be there to support."

Carolina stood there next to Gloria smiling and happy to see Jerome a free man again. Jerome stood there in the hallway around his loyal supporters from friends to family chatting with all of them. Jerome stood there taking it all in and enjoying the moment as he was once again a free man. More than anything Jerome wanted to get home and be with his lover, Mercedes. Before saying goodbye to all his friends and family, Jerome went and said thanks one more time to his lawyer before leaving the courthouse with Mercedes.

Jerome looked around amazed as he enjoyed the freedom again. He looked on as court personnel's traversed from work to home. The duck tour boat-cars drove thru the city with tourist looking on in awe. A UPS driver pulled up and parked dropping off a package. A waiter delivered a pushcart of catered food to a business in the area. Everyone was going on with their everyday normal life. When you're in jail everyday is the same day sort like groundhogs day, these were the little trivial things Jerome missed a lot. Just the simple everyday things people in the world take for granted; but to man who's incarcerated he'd appreciate the simplest things like a walk in the park. Being away either can make you or break you, Jerome was a whole other person now after having a reality check.

The streets downtown by Government Center were congested with pedestrians' walking along the sidewalk and others loitering around conversing and smoking cigarettes. Jerome walked aimlessly with Mercedes by his side. Mercedes parked inside a parking garage on Chauncy street downtown. As they walked, Mercedes held onto his hands tightly, savoring the moment and not wanting to let go. It felt perfect having Jerome by her side again. Jerome's gut feeling was telling him that something wasn't right. It was like he had a sixth-sense or something of that matter. Jerome turned around just in time to see Smooth closing in on him with a pistol in his hand.

Jerome had to think quickly and in the spurt of the moment he pushed Mercedes out the way to safety. The last thing Jerome wanted was the love of his life getting harmed. Smooth closed in on him and aimed his pistol at Jerome. The pedestrians on the streets took off running

causing pandemonium all throughout downtown. Jerome
braced himself as best as he could before Smooth squeezed
the trigger. Everything happened in a flash; Jerome saw his
whole life flash before his eyes. Smooth shot him five times
from .357 magnum close range.

Smooth tucked his pistol away and took off running,
blending in with the crowd. Mercedes ran to Jerome's side
holding onto him as blood got all over her clothes and
hands. Mercedes held onto his body as he lied there the
street bleeding. Jerome was losing a lot blood as he watched
it come out his body. Seeing all the blood come out his
body, Jerome went into shock and started choking on his
own blood.

"Somebody pleas help! . . ." Mercedes screamed out the
top of her lungs. "God please don't let him die! Please! . . ."
Mercedes kissed him on the lips and told Jerome she loved
him.

The ambulance arrived on the scene with a stretcher and
defibulator on hand. They got Jerome up off the ground and
onto the stretcher as fast as they could. They rushed him to
back of the ambulance and then they cut his shirt off. The
paramedics hooked the defibulator to Jerome's chest and hit
him with the volts.

"We're losing him . . . . come on hit him with the
defibulator! One, two, three, clear! . . . ."

TO BE CONTINUED . . . .

My name is Jaron O'Bannon. The last five years have been a lot to take in. In the process of writing, I lost friends and family to the street life. Being incarcerated helped me find my craft; I say it was a blessing in disguise. There have been times when I had writer's block and was stressed out that I didn't think I would ever finish the novel. If it wasn't for my persistence and ambition, I would never have finished the novel that I worked diligently on. I've put blood, sweat, and tears into my novel. I enjoy writing about my environment. My life has been a bumpy ride and is something like a roller coaster; one minute I'm up, and the next I'm down. I've delved deep down inside my soul and realized that this is everything to me. But most importantly, I'm thankful to be alive today. I wake up and thank God.

I'm thankful to tell my story to the world. Because coming from where I come from, there's no such thing as dreams. In the hood, it's easy to get sidetracked and lose your focus. I'm doing this to show the youth and people where I'm from that it's never too late to dream. Lord knows I seen just about it all. I'm not writing this story to try and glorifying anything. And most importantly, I'm doing this for my son. Family means everything to me. And of course, I can't forget about you—my love, my heart, my confidant, Teasia Montgomery. I miss you with all my heart and soul. I will always love you forever . . . till my demise. I'll see you again one day, baby, when it's my time. But until then I'm gonna hold it down for our son and make sure he don't want for nothing! Rest in paradise, TA, I miss you . . .

My name is Shongi Fernandes. Where I come from, guys in the neighborhood have no hopes and dreams. At one point in my life, I was thinking the same way; all I wanted to do was hustle and gangbang for my hood. I'm from Boston, Massachusetts, born and raised. I've been shot and stabbed in the same streets that I write vividly about in an eighteen-month time span. The one night I was stabbed, I almost lost my life in the process of trying to complete the novel. My partner, Jaron, was sitting in the county jail, fighting a case while putting the final touches on the book. I was once a young and reckless teen running through the hood with nothing to live for. At that moment, I really didn't know any better. But going to jail slowed me down a lot, and that is where I started writing our book with my partner. Thinking back on everything I've been through, I feel proud of myself and my partner for completing this series of novels. I'm just trying to make an honest living out here now and will hopefully be able to bring my work to life and life to novels. There wouldn't be anything in this world I would love to see than to see Ain't No Love in the Bean being sold out in stores; it would be like a dream come true . . . I hope y'all enjoy our book. You can contact me through shongif@gmail.com.